Stalking Around the Christmas Tree

Also available by Jacqueline Frost

Christmas Tree Farm Mysteries

Slashing Through the Snow
'Twas the Knife Before Christmas
Twelve Slays of Christmas

Kitty Couture Mysteries
(writing as Julie Chase)

Cat Got Your Secrets
Cat Got Your Cash
Cat Got Your Diamonds

Stalking Around the Christmas Tree

A CHRISTMAS TREE FARM MYSTERY

Jacqueline Frost

CROOKED
LANE

NEW YORK

Copyright © 2023 by The Quick Brown Fox & Company LLC

Published in the United States by Crooked Lane Books, an imprint of The Quick Brown Fox & Company LLC.

Crooked Lane Books and its logo are trademarks of The Quick Brown Fox & Company LLC.

Library of Congress Catalog-in-Publication data available upon request.

ISBN (hardcover): 978-1-63910-451-2
ISBN (ebook): 978-1-63910-452-9

Cover illustration by Rich Grote

Printed in the United States.

www.crookedlanebooks.com

Crooked Lane Books
34 West 27th St., 10th Floor
New York, NY 10001

First Edition: October 2023

10 9 8 7 6 5 4 3 2 1

To Tiffany, it's been lovely killing you

Chapter One

"Hold that pose, Mrs. White," my best friend, Caroline, called. She rose onto her tiptoes, phone poised before her, sizing up my mother for another photo. Caroline's long blond hair hung over her shoulders in loose waves, and her pale brows furrowed over bright blue eyes as she snapped the dozenth picture since her arrival.

Mom paused, frosting bag frozen above a tray of cutout reindeer cookies, where she'd been piping patterns onto the little blankets over the reindeers' backs. "Cheers," she said, beaming for the camera.

"Got it!" Caroline lowered her phone, and Mom's bright smile fell into a more natural one.

"I still can't believe you asked me to be on your show this week." She set the frosting aside and rubbed her hands into the folds of her apron. "I hope you won't regret it."

"I won't," Caroline assured.

"You'll be there, right Holly?" Mom asked me.

"Try to stop me," I said, stealing a cookie from her tray. "You'll knock them dead for sure."

Mom tucked a swath of thick brown hair behind one ear and grinned. I looked like my mom. She was twenty years older than me,

1

a few inches shorter, and a couple dozen pounds heavier, but that didn't diminish the effect. Our dark hair and eyes, fair skin, and pointy noses left no room for mistaking our relationship. I imagined looking at her was a lot like looking into a mirror that showed my future, and I was okay with what I saw. Mom was beautiful, happy, and kind. As in love with Dad as the day she'd married him, and over the moon about her life in historic Mistletoe, Maine.

I hoped all that joy and contentment came with the looks, because our personalities were quite different. I'd inherited Dad's big mouth, for example, and much to Mom's eternal dismay. I'd also recently come to realize I was a bit of a busybody. I suspected I should work on the latter, but that particular personality trait often helped me get things done. I usually knew who to ask for what, and where to quickly find anyone or thing I needed. With little more than a week left before Christmas in a holiday-themed town, and my wedding scheduled for Christmas Eve night, I needed all the help I could get.

I sipped my cinnamon-flavored coffee, then slipped another stick of ammo into my hot glue gun. The morning was getting away, and Caroline would soon have to leave and open her cupcake shop on Main Street. Then Mom would flip the sign on the large wooden doors behind us, opening the Hearth, our family's tree farm café.

Reindeer Games was the only tree farm in Mistletoe, which made it, by default, the most frequented. My family and I made it the most fun by intent. Mom was the baker. Dad was the lumberjack. I was the innkeeper. Collectively, we were living our best lives.

The Hearth was Mom's domain, essentially a life-sized gingerbread house where she baked and sold her cookies and cakes, along with a variety of hot drinks and occasionally soups, to guests. Red and white candy-striped booths lined the dining area under gumdrop-shaped chandeliers. Eyelet curtains adorned the windows, and hand-carved chocolate-bar tables with licorice-legged chairs sprinkled the floor. The furniture had all been made from trees grown on our property. Scents of warm vanilla and spun sugar had long ago permeated everything in sight. It would've been the perfect venue for Caroline's feature on Mom, but this was the busiest week for Reindeer Games, and Caroline had likely sold more seats than the fire code would permit inside our little café.

"I still can't believe I'm going to be on television," Mom said, setting a hand against her throat, mystified.

"It's not television," Caroline said, returning to her lollipop-shaped stool at the counter. "It's a web show on my YouTube channel."

I grinned as Mom frowned, trying to make sense of the answer.

Caroline had opened her shop a couple of years back with a little help from our friend Cookie, and Caroline's Cupcakes had become an instant hit. They rarely made it to closing time without selling out, even at five bucks a pop! Earlier this year, she'd started a weekly livestream, called *Merry in Mistletoe*, as a favor to her father, the mayor. He'd hoped to generate positive press for our little holiday hamlet following a string of annual Christmas murders. Three in as many years, to be exact.

The most recent murder had earned us some negative national attention, and a lot of locals had feared tourism would suffer this season as a result. So Caroline had been doing her part to showcase the merrier aspects of Mistletoe by featuring locals and their lives. This month had been all about the shops, trades, and destinations. Mom was the featured baker, ready to talk about a day in the life at Reindeer Games and more specifically, the Hearth Café. Like most things Caroline touched, *Merry in Mistletoe* had grown into yet another wonderful success.

"I don't understand," Mom said, wide brow furrowed. "It's a show on your channel."

"Right, and folks can watch live or replay it later. We'll also have a studio audience for the recording."

"But your channel isn't on television," Mom said.

"Correct."

I went back to hot-gluing twisty metal spirals into the tops of pine cones with flat bases. I didn't have the vocabulary or wherewithal to help Mom make sense of livestreams or online channels. Honestly, I had no idea how it all worked. I was just glad it did.

Mom looked to me for help, then caught sight of my craft. "What are you working on, hon?"

I lifted a finished product for her inspection. "Do you like it?"

"Adorable," Mom cooed, ever supportive.

"What is it?" Caroline asked.

"I thought we could set these on the reception tables. If we slip a place card into the spiral, the pine cone becomes a seating marker."

The results would double as a cute nod to our location. Not to mention, Evan and I were on a budget, and there were few things more abundant on a tree farm than pine cones.

Caroline took the finished product from my hand. "I love it. We can spray them with faux snow and a little silver glitter. They'll sparkle under the twinkle lights and mirror ball."

Mom gave a dramatic sigh. "My little girl's getting married."

Her little girl was twenty-nine, but I was, in fact, getting married. A smile spread over my face.

I'd met my fiancé, Sheriff Evan Gray three years ago, after finding a dead body on the farm. Evan had thought my dad was a reasonable suspect, and I'd worked hard to help the new sheriff see my father for what he really was, a six-foot teddy bear in a lumberjack's clothing.

Time was a funny thing, because our first meeting felt both as if it had happened yesterday and as if it had occurred a millennium ago. And though we'd been planning for a year, it was hard to believe the big day was only a week away. We'd be married on Christmas Eve in the big barn on our property. Mom and her ladies had decorated the cavernous space for the annual Christmas Tree Ball last weekend, and it was still decked out in twinkle lights and set up for a party. What better, prettier, more perfect place for our ceremony and reception?

Pulling together a wedding at this time of year hadn't been easy, but it'd been a group effort, with Caroline at the helm. After months of to-do lists, endless choices, decisions and dress fittings, Evan and I were in the home stretch.

"One week to go," Caroline said with a dreamy sigh. "Are you ready?"

Physically? Emotionally? "One hundred percent."

Did I understand how a zillion last-minute things were going to get done while we all simultaneously performed our full-time jobs in Mistletoe the week of Christmas? Not at all.

Mom stroked the backs of her fingertips across my cheek, sentimentality carving lines around her eyes and mouth.

I pressed her hand to my face, then kissed it before setting her free.

Caroline set the pine cone down. "Your big day will be perfect. I'm making sure of it. Just like your mom's internet debut. Your dad has your ticket for the live recording, by the way. We sold out for this one, which is doubly great because all the proceeds from ticket sales will go directly to the Mistletoe foodbank."

Mom looked ready to burst with pride. "That's wonderful news."

"I only wish we could've held the show here," Caroline said. "You'd have been able to actually bake a batch of your whoopie pies, instead of just talking us through the steps and recipe. And look at this place." She waved an arm around her in explanation. "Nothing says Merry in Mistletoe like this café."

I added another finished pine cone to the basket and evaluated the number of place markers remaining. Then I performed some mental gymnastics in an attempt to determine if there was enough time to finish the entire project this morning. I hoped the correct answer was yes, if I worked fast enough.

Caroline sipped her cooling cocoa and sighed with contentment. "Thanks for being so patient while I got enough shots. I'll add this morning's pictures to the collage I'm using as promotional material on the website and social media."

Mom waved her off and pulled a chocolate cake from the refrigerator. "I'm right here doing this every morning. Today I was just lucky enough to visit with you ladies while I worked. Tell me what you think of this," she said, sliding the cake onto the counter. "The icing is a ganache with peppermint chips."

Caroline widened her eyes, then swiped a fork from across the counter. "That sounds amazing."

Mom grabbed a knife and a plate, then glanced at me. "Holly?"

"No, thank you," I said, distracted by my craft.

"You're making great time on those," Mom said. "How's Evan doing with his list?"

"He's nearly finished."

I tried not to sound as jealous as I felt. I was too easily distracted. Evan, on the other hand, was single-minded where anything of importance was concerned.

He'd been involved with the wedding planning since the day he'd asked for my hand. Some grooms might not care about the details, but I hadn't gotten one of these. Evan considered things like registering for gifts, tasting cakes, and selecting caterers fun little adventures and new life experiences. Not to mention excellent opportunities for two busy people to have a few extra dates. He held my hand, listened to my opinions, and made me laugh when

I wanted to scream. He kept me grounded when I couldn't decide between two nearly identical shades of white for tablecloths, and he insisted every DJ we interviewed play our song so we could dance. He'd also assigned himself a set of things to accomplish this week so I wouldn't have to. He knew I had my hands full with tasks only I could perform, like a final gown fitting, a bridal luncheon, and an inn full of VIP guests for the next few days.

"He's a good one," Mom said. "A partner."

I nodded. It was true.

Caroline grabbed a metal spiral from my stack and took the pine cone from my hands, assembling the product after I'd administered the dollop of glue.

"Thanks."

She smiled, set the cone aside, and opened her hand for the next. "How's it going at the inn?"

Caroline's dad had spent a large portion of the town's annual tourism budget on bringing the state conservatory of ballet to Mistletoe. The group would perform *The Nutcracker*, a holiday staple and emblem of Christmas since 1892, for several nights before returning to the capital for a final Christmas Eve performance. Mayor West and the local business owners thought the added ballet would secure this year's seasonal success.

The mayor had made special arrangements for the choreographer and several key dancers to stay at the inn. The dancers weren't my typical guests, but if it helped Mistletoe, and they cleared out on Christmas Eve morning, I was happy to help.

"It's been good so far," I said. "They arrived after dinner last night and went to their rooms pretty quickly." The bulk of my communication had been with their choreographer, George, and most of our exchanges were in the form of emails before their arrival. His messages mainly were lists of demands: specific foods and drinks to have on hand; the necessary number of blenders for post-workout protein shakes; and a transport vehicle large enough to accommodate the guests and their equipment to and from the theater.

Thankfully, he hadn't requested a driver, because that would've been me, and I was already buried under an avalanche of tasks.

"I saw them this morning," Mom said. "Not long before you both got here."

"You did?" Caroline and I asked in near unison.

I'd taken a long shower after waking and setting out the fruit and blenders. Then I'd headed to the Hearth before the dancers got up. Or so I'd thought.

"Sure did," Mom said. "They rolled in here just after six, looking so cute in their pink silk coats."

"They were here at six AM?" I asked, still processing.

The inn had been still when I'd tiptoed around setting up the blenders. I'd assumed they were all asleep.

"Yep." Mom covered the cake and slipped it back into the fridge. "They filed in here; collected their coffees, yogurts, granola, and fruit to go; then loaded up in the transport van and headed out. The coach said that will be the daily routine."

Inn guests received complimentary breakfast and dinner at the Hearth. I kept a hearty assortment of drinks and snacks on hand for the moments in between.

"Ballet master," Caroline said, leaning in Mom's direction. "The one who teaches the dancers the choreography is the *master*, not a coach."

Mom nodded. "That's interesting, and . . ."

"Pretentious?" I guessed.

Mom pressed her lips together, fighting a smile.

"It's what they're called," Caroline said on a dreamy sigh. "I love the ballet."

I tented my brows. "Yeah?"

"Oh, yeah. Since I was small," she said. "My parents took me to see *The Nutcracker* every Christmas, then to other shows as I got older. I always wanted to be a dancer."

"Really." I let the unexpected announcement settle, and I could see it. Not only did Caroline have the grace and work ethic for something as grueling as professional dance, but she also had an abundance of artistic flair.

Mom refreshed her hot chocolate. "He said they'll practice at the theater every day, before and after the show begins."

"Rehearse," Caroline said. "Sorry." She cringed.

"Rehearse," Mom corrected. "Apparently they'll be gone until after dinner every night. I asked about their preferences for tea and meal service, but they're going to eat elsewhere, so I don't have to worry about those, I guess." She deflated a bit. "I was looking forward to feeding ballerinas."

Caroline tucked a bite of cake into her mouth and let her eyelids flutter. "This is killer. Please tell me I can have the recipe."

Mom produced a note card from her apron pocket and passed it to Caroline with a grin. "I hoped you'd say that."

"Ah! Bless." Caroline took it reverently, then checked her watch. "Are you guys going to the parade this morning?"

Mom shook her head. "I can't. I have too much to do before I open. But I wish I could. I'd love to see the dancers perform."

Caroline sucked chocolate ganache off her thumb. "It's only the lead ballerina in the parade. We set her up in a snow globe with some promo. Dad gave me his ticket for opening night. And extras for my friends, if you're interested."

Mom waved her off. "I'll be here from opening to closing all week, aside from taping your show."

"Well, count me in," I said. I loved outings with Caroline, and seeing her so excited about this particular show only made me look forward to it more. "But don't envy the dancers too much," I said. "From what I saw last night, they're treated like children. One woman had to sneak out to ice skate. The choreographer shut her down, saying she could get hurt, and he couldn't allow that. And they had a time for 'lights out.'" I formed air quotes around the final two words.

Caroline didn't seem offended enough, so I continued.

"They had a bedtime," I clarified, hoping to make the words register. "Can you imagine that? Or being told you couldn't do something you loved, like skating? Another dancer snuck out for a walk at midnight just to get a few minutes alone. I saw her leaving, and she reacted as if she'd been caught committing murder."

Caroline finally frowned. "Do you think they're all friends? Spending so much time together must make them close. Maybe there's a deep camaraderie that overshadows all the rules. I follow the conservatory on social media, and I've always wondered about the interpersonal dynamics outside training and performing."

Mom gave a humorless chuckle. "If their usual schedule is anything like the one they're maintaining here, I can't imagine they get much time outside training and performing."

Caroline rested her chin in waiting hands, elbows planted on the countertop. "What do they talk about?"

I added dollops of hot glue to two more pine cones and passed one to Caroline, continuing our speedy little assembly line. We each pressed a wire spiral into place. "In the few minutes I saw them, they seemed fixated on the big Christmas Eve performance at the capitol after they leave here. Apparently there's a one-night-only, sold-out event at the State Theater on Christmas Eve, and some scouts will be there. All the dancers want to be chosen for something bigger. They talked about possibly heading out after the matinee performance the day before, but they aren't scheduled to leave until the next morning."

"There are ballet scouts?" Mom asked, checking the time. "Like the ones who recruit for sports?"

I shrugged and followed her lead with a peek at the clock.

The Hearth and tree farm would open soon, and the twelve days of reindeer games were in full swing, so tour buses were likely already en route. Tourists who weren't starting their days with my family were probably looking for a good spot to watch the parade along Main Street.

"Apparently an offer from a larger ballet company would come with lots of press and pressure, but they all want both," I said, summarizing what I'd heard the dancers say. "Honestly, their performances here seem a little like obstacles in the way of the big show."

"Costly obstacles," Caroline mused. "But at least people are excited about *The Nutcracker*. I'm interviewing the lead ballerina at the start of this week's show. Dad thought it would be another good way to keep the enthusiasm going. And great cross promotion. Hopefully, fans of the ballet will tune in for the interview, and viewers of my show will buy tickets for the ballet."

I tried to picture the dancers I'd checked in last night. "Which one is the lead?"

"Tiffany Krieg. She plays Clara."

I squinted my eyes, still unsure.

Caroline tried again. "She has all that great thick hair like Libby."

Mom looked up, and the three of us stilled.

Libby was Evan's little sister and a waitress at the Hearth. She lived in the on-site guesthouse where I'd stayed before moving to the inn. More importantly, she was our friend. Recently, she'd become withdrawn, but so far no one was talking about it.

Mom sighed. "Something's going on with her. I don't mean to pry, and I know it's none of my business. If she wanted me to know, she would've told me. But I'm officially concerned. Do either of you have any idea what's wrong?"

Caroline and I shook our heads.

"No," I said.

Libby had pulled away unexpectedly several weeks back, talking less and less at first, then only coming out in public for her shifts. Most recently, she'd begun to dramatically change her hair and makeup. It would've been evident from outer space that there was a problem, but so far, she hadn't opened up to anyone. Not us and not Evan. Not even her boyfriend, Ray.

I slid off my stool and set the final finished pine cone into a basket with the others, then moved the hot-glue gun to the business side of the counter, to cool. "I'll be back for these," I said. "Since the inn is empty, I'm going to meet Evan at the pie shop. Maybe we can watch the parade together."

I probably should've spent the day addressing the stack of Christmas cards on my desk or wrapping toy donations for the holiday gift drive, but I really enjoyed a parade, and any excuse to see Evan was a good one.

"That sounds lovely," Mom said. "Do you need any help wrapping gifts later?"

"Not yet," I said, knowing she had enough of her own chores to worry about. I'd do my best, then ask for help if I truly needed it.

"Well, let me know if you run low on paper." Mom tipped her head to a row of gift wrap tubes leaned against the wall near the café's tree. "Christopher dropped more off this morning. I must've missed him, because one minute the paper wasn't there, and the next minute it was. He left a card to say he has more if you need it."

Christopher was a family friend who'd begun as a contractor building the inn. He was heading up the annual toy drive for the second year in a row and apparently providing the wrapping paper.

Caroline made a deep humming sound. She turned her palms up when I looked at her.

I fought a smile. "Christopher isn't Santa Claus."

"He looks a lot like him," she said. "White hair and a beard, rosy-red cheeks, and twinkling eyes."

I shook my head.

"Holly, he heads the annual toy drive, knows everyone by name, and comes and goes without being seen. I'm just saying. It all checks out."

Christopher certainly had some Santa-esque qualities, but that didn't make him St. Nick.

I redirected my thoughts downtown and put on my coat.

Caroline followed suit, stretching black leather gloves over her elegant hands, and threading thin arms into a designer wool swing coat. "I'd better go too. It's time to open my shop if I want to get all the extra pre-parade sales. Cookie took the morning off to watch from the sidewalk. I'll take the pine cones and get them sprayed with faux snow and glitter."

We said our goodbyes to Mom, then split up in the parking lot.

Caroline got into her smart black sedan, and I headed for my truck, a big red pickup with a red nose tied to the grill, all-weather antlers protruding from the windows, and a "Reindeer Games" logo painted along both sides.

I did a double take as I noticed Libby's SUV rolling down the drive, away from the farm, the transport vehicle used by the ballerinas following closely on its bumper.

Chapter Two

I motored away from the farm, enjoying the view. Libby's SUV and the ballet transport had disappeared while I'd scraped ice from my windshield and let the defrosters work their magic. The roads were clear and dry, the sky a seasonal, cloudless blue. A perfect morning for a parade. Excellent news, because the town, and our farm, needed the business and traffic that would come with the lovely day. We'd had a couple recent weather scares that could've put us behind on commerce for the year, but Mistletoe had prevailed. The two major snowstorms predicted to bury us had missed our town completely. Hope was thick in our collective hearts that the pattern of good fortune would continue until Christmas. For now, the couple feet of snow already on the ground and occasional flurries in the air were enough to continually set the mood for holiday shopping.

Rolling hills and pristine white valleys stretched out on either side of me as I trundled across the miles between Reindeer Games and town. Farms popped onto the horizon with big red barns and livestock out for a little exercise. Houses came next, few and far between at first, then closer and more plentiful as the square drew near. Each home had a unique and peppy display of holiday lights and decor. Inflatable Grinches perched on rooftops. Snowman families guarded the yards. A winter wonderland of chasing bulbs cast rainbows across the snow.

The twisty iron "Welcome to Mistletoe" sign arched into view above the road a few miles later. A thousand visitors filled the sidewalks beyond. I slowed to merge as extra-large tour buses struggled around the corners of our historic square, the streets, designed long ago for people on horseback and cars the size of sleighs.

I checked the massive clock near the center of town, then took a left past families seated on Santa-red benches and couples kissing beneath mistletoe hung from lampposts.

Shoppers with rosy cheeks and wide smiles moved merrily in and out of stores as I headed down Main Street toward the pie shop.

Evan's cruiser was already there.

Every parking spot I passed was full, for three blocks. Eventually I took what I could get and hopped out. The beginning beats of a drum solo reached my ears as I hurried back the way I'd come, on foot.

Food vendors lined the streets, and the air smelled of warm kettle corn and candied pecans. A burst of energy punched through me, invigorating me as I strode. Officials had erected wooden barriers to clear a path for the parade. A banner hung between lampposts, announcing the arrival of the state ballet.

I thought of Caroline's interest in the dancers and what she'd said about the way they were treated by their choreographer, and frowned. Then I turned the corner and ran into a nutcracker.

"Pardon," I said, jumping back with a little shiver. Humans in full costume of any kind freaked me out. The big dead-eyed masks were the worst. I shook off the willies and raised my eyes to see a dozen more just like the first. A kaleidoscope of people in toy soldier costumes with giant macrame heads mixed with Mistletoe's usual array of Santas. "Good grief," I muttered, picking up my pace.

Cookie came into view a moment later. "Holly!" She waved a hand overhead, and I changed direction. Cookie was Caroline's business partner and a lifelong friend of my family. She'd taught me everything I knew about crafting, which was to say—a lot. She had bright, mischievous blue eyes and a cloud of white hair. No one really knew how old she was, but my best guess was somewhere between sixty-five and eighty. The exact number varied depending on the story she was telling. And Cookie had a lifetime of amazing stories. She lived large, despite her diminutive size, and loved every minute of her daily adventures. I was glad to be part of at least a few.

"Hey, Cookie!" I called, meeting her halfway. Her real name was Delores Cutter, but her late husband, Theodore, had nicknamed her Cookie because she liked to bake. I'd called her Cookie Cutter for years before realizing the adorable joke. She'd since adopted a pygmy goat named Theodore in homage to her husband. Cookie thought the two males were strikingly similar, with their stoic natures and handsome salt-and-pepper beards. These days, Theodore the second was the center of her somewhat quirky world.

"What are you wearing?" I asked, eyeballing her flashy pink spandex-clad legs beneath a shiny silver coat.

She looked down at her outfit and smiled. "I was in the middle of dance practice. We wrapped up early so we could come down here and save our seats for the parade. Some folks have been here since last night!"

"Really?" I couldn't imagine, and I wasn't sure how they'd survived the cold. My teeth began to chatter just thinking about it. The other thing she said drew a smile across my face. "I didn't know you'd joined a dance group."

"Sure did," she said. "We're a swing dancing team. Everyone's over sixty and loves the music of my youth. We call ourselves Swingers."

I bit my lip against a smile. "That might not be the best name," I said. "Do you have a backup?"

She frowned. "Why? It's right on the nose. We're all swingers."

A few passing shoppers cast sideways looks in our direction.

A bubble of laughter escaped my lips.

"Why don't you sit with us?" she suggested. "We're right over there." She pointed, and a collection of other white-haired women in hot-pink spandex waved back.

"I'm meeting Evan at the pie shop," I said. "I can't stay long, but I'd love to say hello."

Cookie's phone dinged, and she lifted it into view, then frowned at the screen.

"Everything okay?" I asked. "I haven't seen you at the farm much lately." In fact, she'd been uncharacteristically absent from Reindeer Games all month. I'd supposed she was covering the counter at the cupcake shop more often ever since Caroline had started her web show, but the way she looked at her phone made me wonder if something more was going on.

Her eyes returned to mine. "Sorry." She shook her head and tucked the phone away. "I'm calling Holiday Bingo for your folks in a couple of days, and I plan to stick around for Carol Karaoke. So I'll definitely see you that night. I've even collected some great new pieces for the karaoke costume trunk. What do you think? Will you be singing this year?"

"Probably not." I chuckled. "I wasn't built for the spotlight, and I definitely shouldn't be singing anything into a microphone." In a group of carolers, I made what my folks lovingly called a joyful noise. Singing on my own was another story. And no amount of costuming would help. "You've been extra busy with dancing?" I asked, changing the subject. "Spending more time at the shop?"

"Yes, but that's not all," she said. "I'm working on a big project with Theodore."

"Oh yeah?" My mind struggled for ideas on what she could've partnered with a goat to accomplish. I came up empty, but for Cookie, the possibilities were probably endless. "What's the project?"

"Well," she said brightly, "did I tell you I'm an ordained minister now?"

I blinked and barked a laugh. "No. When did that happen?"

"About a week ago. It's for the project."

"For Theodore? Is he getting married?" I teased.

"Maybe." Cookie squinted pensively against the sunlight. "He's been getting a lot of attention from his calendars. Folks started reaching out to me about stud service." She paused to purse her lips. "This year's calendar will be geared toward finding him the right woman. Once he's paired off, we can put a stop to all the indecent proposals."

I bit the insides of my cheeks.

Cookie had partnered with our friend, Ray, for the past two years to create a Goat for All Seasons calendar with images of Theodore on every page. She dressed him as everything from the Easter Bunny to a sunflower, and the finished product sold like hotcakes. All the money went to charity, and it wasn't a big surprise that Theodore had gained some fans. Not every goat has his own calendar.

"Are you interested in breeding him?" I asked, carefully, unsure how a goat marriage would work.

Her expression turned affronted. "Holly! Theodore's not that kind of goat."

"Of course not," I said, waving my gloved hands apologetically. "I meant after he's married. Sorry, Cookie. I'm still processing."

"It's a lot to take in," she allowed. "I want to find him a nice wife, but when I learned no one in local ministry would marry them, I had to take matters into my own hands. "

"Ah." I nodded. "Marriage is a big step," I said, going along with the prospect and imagining a goat bride in my wedding veil. "Is Theodore ready for a family?"

"He's open to the possibility," she said, "but he wants to do things right. He's not the sort to father a bunch of kids and not raise them."

I nodded solemnly, delighting in her perfect use of the word kids. "Totally."

"Instead of taking appointments for stud service, we're doing interviews for matrimony, and I have high hopes. I don't want him to be alone when I'm gone."

"Reasonable," I said. Though I was sure Cookie would outlive us all.

"I thought so." She turned toward her friends and tipped her head in their direction. "Let's go see the girls. I want to introduce you before you have to leave."

Libby appeared and cut across our path several yards away, barely visible before being swallowed by the crowd.

"Was that Evan's sister?" Cookie asked, rising onto her tiptoes for a better look.

"Yeah."

"Did she change her hair again?"

"She did." Today's look was more likely a wig than a new style for her own locks. Platinum blond and dramatically straight, angled along her chin. I was sure she'd hate the look, if I hadn't just seen her in it.

"Huh," Cookie said. "I wonder what she's up to?"

"You and me both."

My best guess was that Libby had been trying to find herself after testifying at a trial against a man with criminal ties in Boston. Her words were at least partially responsible for convicting him in the death of her best friend and college roommate, Heather. The experience had to have been hard on her. Scary for obvious reasons, and heartbreaking, drudging up all the details of a life she'd tried hard to save. I understood why it had taken a toll. But it'd been nearly a year, and she'd been fine at first, even relieved to have the ordeal behind her. It wasn't until recently that she'd started pulling away.

A sharp whistle cut through the day, and Cookie waved a hand at her friends.

"We're coming!" She clasped my wrist and pulled me in the group's direction.

A woman with a red purse and spikey white hair smiled. "We saved you a spot. Come on!"

We landed on the sidewalk beside the ladies in matching shiny silver coats.

"Everyone," Cookie said, "this is Holly White. Holly, these are the Swingers."

"I'm Marianne," the woman with the red purse said. "Don't you love the theme of this parade? And all these costumes? Especially the nutcrackers. I love a man in uniform."

"It's nice to meet you." I waved at each of the smiling women, then turned my eyes to the street, where the first signs of our town's high school marching band had appeared in the distance. "It seems like bringing the ballet to Mistletoe was a good choice. Did you know Caroline loves ballerinas?" I asked Cookie.

"Everyone loves ballerinas," Cookie said.

Someone in a Mouse King costume pushed through the crowd in my direction, and I ducked out of the way.

Stalking Around the Christmas Tree

My toes curled inside my boots. It was time for me to get away from all the costumes. "I should probably get going," I said to Cookie and her Swingers. "It was very nice to meet you." My eyes caught on a figure I recognized, several yards away, stalling my retreat.

The ballet master, George, strode along the sidewalk's edge, watching the parade march nearer. He must've been the one driving the transport away from the farm when I was leaving. I watched for a long moment as he stepped into the street, then hurried across, his breaths coming in hearty puffs. His usual scowl was in place above a charcoal-gray scarf and black wool coat. His hands were buried deep in his pockets.

I thought of the dancer who'd snuck out the night before, and hoped she hadn't been caught. Everyone deserved a little peace, and it'd been a beautiful star-filled night. A great one for enjoying some time alone.

"You should give this to Caroline," Marianne said. She outstretched her arm, passing me a magazine.

Cookie's eyebrows rose. "I can take it to her. I'm going to the cupcake shop after the parade."

Marianne shrugged, then handed the periodical to Cookie instead.

I craned my neck for a look at the cover. I recognized the featured ballerina. "Hey, I know her," I said. "She's staying at the inn."

"That's Tiffany Krieg," Marianne said. "She's the star. She'll be in the snow globe when it gets here."

The young woman on the cover looked completely different in her costume and makeup than she had at the inn, with her curls around her shoulders. The caption above her image called her a shooting star.

"Is she famous?"

"She will be," Marianne said. "She's been on the rise all year. She came onto the scene out of nowhere and became an immediate fan favorite. She was struggling to maintain her spot in the conservatory last year—then bam! She's playing Clara."

I considered all the ways she could've launched her career so suddenly and was glad things had worked out.

My phone rang, and Evan's number graced the screen beneath the time. "I've got to go," I said again, smiling at Cookie and her friends. I kissed Cookie's cheek. "Merry Christmas! Enjoy the parade!"

I hurried to the pie shop, thankful for a place to warm up and time to spend with my fiancé. I gave the crowd one last look as I pushed through the door, hoping to catch another glimpse of Libby. But she was long gone.

Chapter Three

The pie shop had a retro theme, with red vinyl booths and black and white checkered flooring. The seats were packed with happy, chatting patrons, and everything smelled of black coffee and fresh-baked crusts. I searched the crowd for Evan as ovens opened and closed in the kitchen, sending waves of other delectable scents, like warm and savory spices or candied nuts, into the air.

Evan spent most of his mornings at the pie shop. He'd discovered soon after his move that the bulk of our citizens visited here regularly, got jazzed up on caffeine and sugar, then spilled their secrets. It was a teenager's worst nightmare, but a small-town sheriff's dream come true. The mouth-watering pies and coffee were the icing on top.

My heart rate picked up at the sight of him seated in his favorite booth. He was in his sheriff's gear, sans hat, and I could suddenly relate with Marianne. I too loved a man in uniform. This was my fourth Christmas with Evan, our second as a couple, and he meant the world to me. I said regular prayers for a smooth week ahead, because anything could happen and throw us for a loop so close to the big day.

I slid onto the bench across from him, and his expression lit. "Howdy, Sheriff."

"Hey," he said, reaching across the table for my hands. "I just tried to call you. How's your morning?" His green eyes and faint Boston accent made me smile.

He and Libby had been born and raised in the city. He'd been a homicide detective there until Mistletoe's low crime rate and his need for a break had motivated him to relocate. It'd taken some time for him to adjust to our little town, but I'd always suspected he secretly loved it. Now I knew he did.

A young waitress with big brown eyes and lashes that nearly reached her brows popped into view. Her retro pink uniform and white apron made me smile. Plenty of my high school friends had worn that uniform at one time or another. Nostalgia pulled me instantly back in time.

"I'm Casey," she said. "What can I get you?"

"Just coffee," I said.

"No pie?" She cocked her head, confused. "We're celebrating the twelve pies of Christmas this week, and today's feature is bowlful-of-cherries tart."

I grinned. "Just the coffee, but thank you."

Casey shrugged and dragged her gaze to Evan's steamless cup. "I'll grab her a mug and be right back to refresh your drink for you."

He nodded, and our waitress zipped away.

"Sorry I didn't answer your call. I was right outside, and I wanted to surprise you. It's been a good day so far," I said, turning my attention back to him. "How about yours?"

"Better now. And I'm glad I made room in the budget for added security this month. I get to breathe a little. Tourism is running strong. The streets, stores, and inns are all at max capacity, but crime is nearly nonexistent. I'm not sure how we aren't dealing with more problems than we are, but at least I know that if the tides turn, we're ready."

"What kind of problems are we having?" I asked, glancing through the window at a happy crowd enjoying the parade.

"Fender benders mostly," he said. "A couple shoplifters, and last night we had a flasher."

My eyes widened, and he nodded slowly.

"Scouts honor," he said. "A sixty-seven-year-old retired science teacher from Pennsylvania. We booked him for indecent exposure and sent him home on bail this morning."

I sat back in my seat with a chuckle. "Wait until Cookie hears that story."

"I'm surprised she hasn't," he said. "Are you sure you don't want pie?"

I wasn't. I'd skipped breakfast in favor of completing the pine-cone place markers. I took a moment to eyeball the menu, scripted on a big white board behind the counter. If it wasn't mid-morning, and if I'd been sure my wedding dress wouldn't need to be let out, I'd have ordered a slice of Santa's apple cinnamon to enjoy immediately and another slice or two to go.

"You were smart to hire the added security," I said. "Even if you don't wind up needing them, having the extra muscle around is sure to make potential criminals think twice."

"The extra eyes and ears are nice," he agreed. "They aren't official law enforcement officers, so they can only advise and instruct the public, but it's been good so far. I think their presence has helped things remain so orderly, considering the town has more than doubled its population for the week. The only downside is that they can't officially detain or arrest anyone, which means I have to keep tabs on them as well as my deputies. Even with the extra hands, we've been a bunch of spinning tops today thanks to all this hoopla." He motioned to the approaching parade and masses of people outside.

I knew what he meant. Tourism was the town's bread and butter, but it could be a crowded nightmare this time of year. "The parade probably made the already complicated logistics even worse," I guessed.

"Definitely." He groaned. "We had to close roads, and we can barely handle all the holiday traffic with every road open. Monitoring the revised traffic patterns has been tough, and handling the increased number of complaints about overcrowding is exhausting. The good news is that we're in the homestretch for Christmas, and we haven't had a major issue. I just have to stay vigilant and available."

I completely understood. "Do you need to get back out there?"

His lips tipped into a casual smile. "I have a few more minutes."

Casey returned with an empty mug for me and a carafe. She filled my mug before topping off Evan's cooled cup, then left the rest, with a wink. "Let me know if you change your mind about that pie."

She certainly wasn't making it easy.

I redirected my thoughts to my wedding dress and the honeymoon that would follow. I had the rest of my life to load up on sweets—after all the photos were taken and I donned a swimsuit for the first time in far too long.

"Debating the pie?" Evan asked.

Boy did he know me. "I was mostly thinking it seems surreal that we'll be on the beach next week."

"Agreed. Are you getting nervous?"

"No, I love the beach."

Half of his mouth turned up in a crooked grin.

We'd secured a rental in a small southern seaside town for our honeymoon. Images of the ocean and suntanned people had been creeping into my daydreams for weeks, though part of me hated to leave Mistletoe while Libby was so clearly in crisis.

"Not what I meant," Evan said. "Everything else okay?"

I nodded, but my expression must've failed to back me up, because he frowned.

"It's all the people in nutcracker costumes, isn't it? Did you see the ones with the rat heads?"

"They're supposed to be the Mouse King from the ballet," I said. "And yes. I saw enough of them to last a lifetime."

"I don't think it will last much longer. As soon as the ballet begins their nightly performances, the costumed people, aside from the Santas, will likely relocate somewhere nearer the theater. You'll have your downtown back to enjoy."

I felt his stare on my cheek as I looked at the crowd outside the window. "That will be nice."

"Is there something else?" he asked.

I glanced his way and found deep concern in his caring eyes.

"Talk to me. Maybe I can help."

I searched my mind and realized he was right. I was worried about everything that needed to be done. "I'm not sure how I'm going to accomplish all the things I'm supposed to do this week, and I don't want to let anyone down. I promised Christopher I'd wrap the toy drive donations left at the inn. I promised Mom I'd send this year's holiday cards for the farm. My inn's full of ballerinas and their cranky choreographer. There's a bridal luncheon this week, and I'm helping with some of the reindeer games. Plus I have a stack of jewelry orders to fill and mail out."

Cookie had taught me to craft and sew when I was small, and I could probably thank her for my growing business making jewelry from recycled bottles. I'd discovered the process while I'd lived in Portland, Maine, after college, and it involved melting down broken pieces of glass to create tiny replica Christmas cookies and candies. I attached those as charms to bracelets, necklaces, and earrings. The finished products sold out regularly at shops around town, and I had a seemingly endless amount of orders online. I'd had to add a banner to my website at Thanksgiving, announcing I couldn't guarantee delivery in time for Christmas anymore, but I was still trying. Somedays I wasn't sure I could get my current orders finished and delivered before next year's holiday season.

"It's all beginning to feel . . . heavy," I admitted.

Evan stretched back in his booth, bumping my feet under the table with his. "That's a lot on your plate and mind, Holly White. Lucky for you, you have a partner to help sort it all."

"Yeah?"

"Of course. I can help wrap gifts and address cards after work. There's not much I can do about the ballerinas, but we can be a united front while I'm there. And I can make trips to the post office with your finished jewelry. We'll get it all done. Trust me. I'm your guy."

"You are. Thank you," I said, meaning it in my bones.

"What else?" he asked, not missing a beat as another thing flickered through my mind.

"I'm a little worried about Libby," I admitted. "Have you spoken to her lately?"

He straightened and shook his head, all pretenses of a carefree disposition vanished at the sound of his sister's name. "I'm worried about her too. Mom thinks we should have an intervention when the family arrives for the wedding, but I don't want that to put a damper on our memories of the weekend."

My heart lightened, and I rose to kiss him across the booth. "I will gladly accept all that help. And I'm with your mom. I think we need to get to the bottom of what's going on with Libby before it gets any worse. She's clearly in crisis, and she needs us, whether she wants us right now or not. I'm not worried about the wedding. I get to marry you: everything else is just details."

Stalking Around the Christmas Tree

Evan rose with me, pressing his palms to the table and his lips to mine.

The moment was lovely, and I knew everything would get better soon.

Outside the window, someone screamed.

Our kiss broke, and we turned in unison to survey the scene. The parade had stopped, and people spilled into the street. Muffled shouting and chaos stirred the crowd like agitated bees. The float carrying the snow globe seemed to be at the center of it all.

Evan dopped some cash on the table for our coffees and grabbed my hand as we dashed outside.

Cookie met us near the pie shop door. "I was coming for you," she said. "Hurry!" She turned away, and Evan cut a path through the crowd, on Cookie's heels. I trailed behind like a duckling.

"What happened?" he demanded.

"I don't know," she said. "I got pushed back from the curb. I couldn't see a thing—then someone screamed, and everything stopped for a beat. Next thing I know, the crowd's moving and people are shouting about the snow globe and ballerina."

Cookie stopped short, and Evan swung his arms wide as we arrived on the street.

"Get back," he bellowed. "I'm the sheriff. Stand down."

Slowly, onlookers backed up several paces.

Evan squeezed the radio device on his shoulder and ordered emergency responders to the square, along with additional law enforcement.

I peeked around his side and gasped. A ballerina lay motionless inside the batting-lined snow globe. A creepy Mouse King mask lay at her side.

A little curse fell from my lips as my eyes jerked to Evan's.

Beside me, Cookie clutched my coat sleeve. "Ah, rats."

Chapter Four

An hour later, the crowd had significantly dispersed. All remaining lookie-loos had been pushed back by Evan's deputies and added security. Wooden barricades blocked the street at each corner, and emergency response vehicles clogged the space in between, circling like wagons to provide a measure of privacy for officials to do their jobs.

The extra muscle Evan had hired for the month wore matching gray wool coats with black leather sleeves, with "Security" written in reflective white letters across the back of each. The team, composed solely of men, appeared to be in their late twenties and early thirties. All were built like bouncers, and they had flat expressions and no-nonsense stares. They didn't look like people I'd want to mess with, which I supposed was the point.

One man in particular seemed exceptionally focused on Evan, and I couldn't decide if he was interested in the job, the crime, or something else.

Evan was in work mode, surveying and monitoring the big picture while the crime scene team scoured the float up close and personal. The coroner had extracted Tiffany's body from the snow globe after his initial exam. I didn't see any evidence of injury or foul play, but officials were treating the area like a crime scene.

"I can't believe this is happening again," Cookie said, rubbing gloved hands up and down the sleeves of her shiny coat. "How do you think she died?"

"I don't know," I said, dragging my gaze over Evan and his men. Whatever they saw, it wasn't good.

Cookie shook her head, baffled and heartbroken. "She was so young. It doesn't make sense. Her poor family. They probably don't even know yet. It doesn't seem right that all of Mistletoe knows, and her mother doesn't."

"I'm sure someone from Evan's team has called."

"What a way to hear," she said, small hands wringing. "It's just awful."

"It is," I said, hooking an arm around her narrow shoulders and appreciating her big heart. "Did you notice anything unusual before the crowd realized she'd collapsed? Did your friends say anything?"

"No." Her eyes went wide. "Everything was fine. Then suddenly it wasn't."

The Swingers had left with the crowd, inviting Cookie to come along, but she'd volunteered to stay with me. She was the second mother I didn't deserve but appreciated more all the time.

The wind was incredibly cold, and there wasn't anything useful for Cookie or me to do, so I considered taking her inside somewhere to get warm. Maybe to the cupcake shop, where we could fill Caroline in on the few details we had.

A glint of light off glass redirected my thought before I could make my suggestion. Our friend, Ray Griggs, Libby's boyfriend and a photographer for the local paper, snapped shots of the action from a storefront across the street. I'd gone to high school with Ray, though I didn't remember him. He'd been a freshman when I was a senior. He remembered me from those days, but I didn't notice underclassmen back then—or any man whose name wasn't Van Gogh or Rembrandt.

I waved a hand overhead to get his attention. "There's Ray," I told Cookie. "Maybe he knows more than we do."

"Oh!" Cookie perked up, and she shot both arms into the air. At five eight, I had several inches of height on her. If Ray didn't notice me, he'd never see her at my side, but it was nice she put out the effort.

"Hey." A quiet voice turned Cookie and me in our places. Libby stood a few inches away, having approached us as we tried to flag down her boyfriend.

We lowered our arms.

"Hey," I said, a ripple of hope coursing through me. It'd been too long since she'd approached me to chat. "How are you?"

She hugged her middle, gaze darting around the scene. "I've been better," she said. "Hi, Cookie."

"Hello to you," Cookie said. "I love the hair. I never would've recognized you if you hadn't spoken."

"That's the idea," Libby muttered. She shook her head and pressed on before I could question her response. "What do you know about this?" She tipped her platinum head toward the crime scene.

"Not much," I said. "Evan and I were inside the pie shop when someone screamed."

"And I'm too short to see anything," Cookie added. "How about you? Did you see anything?"

"No." Libby looked in the direction of the float. "I was picking up some last-minute gifts before my shift at the Hearth. With my family coming in from Boston for the wedding, I thought we could have a normal Christmas this year. Exchange presents in front of the tree instead of shipping them across the state."

"Sounds like a nice plan," I said.

Libby wet her lips and leaned closer. "I saw the body when they removed it from the snow globe. Do you think that ballerina looked like me?"

"Not now," Cookie said. "Your hair is too different."

Libby's fingers rose to tug the locks dusting her jaw. "It's a wig."

"She looked a little like you," I said. "When you wear your hair naturally. Caroline and I were just saying so this morning. We admire your thick waves."

Libby inhaled audibly. "I'd better get going. I don't want to be late for my shift."

"Wait!" I stepped in the same direction she did, blocking her path. "Don't you want to say hello to Evan? Or Ray?"

She glanced briefly in each man's direction. "No. They're both working, and I don't want to be late." This time, she turned on her heel and walked back the way she'd come, leaving me to stare after her.

"Was that Libby?" a deep tenor asked.

I spun to find Ray crossing the street to meet us. He was tall and lean, a few years younger than me, and head over heels for Libby Gray. His press badge hung on a lanyard around his neck and bounced against his ski coat with every hurried step. He carried his professional camera in one big hand.

"It was," Cookie said, "and she looked fabulous. I've always wanted to try my hair in a dramatic style like that one. Do you think I could pull it off?" She smoothed a mitten-clad hand over her curls.

Ray cast me a look. His cheeks were rosy from the wind, and he'd tugged a blue knit cap over his sandy hair.

"Absolutely," I said. "You'd be beautiful in any hairstyle. But I have to admit, I really like it the way you wear it now."

She beamed. "Thanks!"

Ray's eyes traveled above our heads, presumably in the direction Libby had gone.

"She said she was in a hurry to get to work," I told him. "Or she would've gone to talk to you."

"I doubt that." He pulled his attention back to me, lips turned down in a brokenhearted frown. "She dumped me."

"What?" Cookie and I yipped.

"When?" I asked.

"Why?" Cookie demanded.

Ray shrugged. "She said she was going through something, and she had to figure it out on her own. I can't help her, apparently, so she thought it was better for us to stop seeing each other."

I hated her vague, indirect explanation, and I wasn't sure I believed it.

"Sounds like a load of hooey to me," Cookie said, apparently reading my mind. "She knows she has friends here who'll do anything to help her. Listen. Encourage. Make her laugh. Execute revenge on her enemies."

"Well, she didn't want any of that from me," Ray said, batting his eyes against the frigid wind. "So there isn't much I can do about it."

Cookie sucked her teeth, and I suspected she was plotting to get to the bottom of Libby's problems, with or without Libby's blessing.

It was a project I could get behind. If Libby wanted to become a voluntary recluse all of a sudden, that was one thing. Hurting Ray in the process was another. He loved her, and he deserved the whole truth, not a set of excuses.

He was looking at me when my eyes cut back to him. Probably seeing straight into my head and hating the pity he found there. "I'm going to see if anyone wants to give me a quote to go with these photos for the paper," he said. "I'll see you guys around."

My heart was heavy as I watched him leave. Ray was too sweet and kind to be so sad. I hated it for him.

And I abhorred the much more gruesome problem a few yards away. Tiffany Krieg had died on a parade float. Her lifeless body lay curled on a pile of cotton batting and iridescent glitter, for thousands of people to see.

Worse? Based on the way Evan and his men were handling the scene, and the tension weaving through their ranks, every instinct I had said this was murder.

I was certain Mayor West was somewhere losing his mind, as well as a bunch of votes. He'd petitioned hard for the right to overspend on bringing the ballet to Mistletoe. Residents and shop owners had been slow to sway but eventually agreed the cost was worth it to save our collective reputation. We'd willingly foregone several annual community events throughout the year, and shop owners had agreed to a short-term tax increase as a means to raise funds for the ballet bid. And now there'd been another death. A ballerina no less, and the lead.

It wouldn't matter that Mayor West couldn't have predicted or prevented what had happened. People would want somewhere to point the finger at if tourism plummeted during the busiest week of the year. And the man who'd spent the money was the obvious target.

I cringed, feeling guilty for thinking about the mayor or his approval ratings when a young woman's life had ended. And I wondered when I had become so casual in the face of death? As if it was merely par for the course.

As if a Christmas killing was to be expected.

I hoped uselessly that Tiffany hadn't really been murdered. Maybe she'd simply had high cholesterol. An undiagnosed heart problem or an aneurysm. But reading the scene around me made that impossible to believe. None of those things would explain the Mouse King mask at her side. Or the fact her body hadn't been swept quickly away in an ambulance.

Emotion stung my eyes, and I took several full, deep breaths to recenter myself.

Through the blur of tears, George, the ballet master came into view.

Cookie rubbed her mittens together. "Maybe we should visit the cupcake shop," she said. "It's cold, and I don't have my special tea."

Cookie's special tea was one part Earl Grey and ten parts schnapps. She shared it generously and used it frequently to stay warm. I was sure that with a single match the contents of her thermos would burn for hours.

"I'll meet you there," I said. "I see someone I want to talk to first."

"I'll save you a cup!"

I waved goodbye to Cookie, then darted in George's direction before he vanished into the waning crowd. He wasn't supposed to be downtown this morning, and I wanted to know why he was. He might not play the role of Mouse King, but he surely had access to all the costumes and props associated with the show. More importantly, he had access to Tiffany.

I steadied myself as I approached, hating to confront a presumably grieving stranger so brazenly. His twisted expression was one of outrage, effectively slowing my steps until I remembered Evan was nearby. I didn't have to worry about the grouch lashing out. There were too many members of security and law enforcement around. He couldn't afford to lose his temper.

I felt Evan's eyes on me as I closed the distance to the ballet master. "Excuse me, George," I called, drawing his attention a moment before arriving at his side. "I'm so sorry about what's happened."

His dark brows furrowed, but recognition didn't seem to land.

"I'm Holly," I said. "From the inn."

His frown deepened. "What are you doing here?"

"I came to watch the parade." I didn't like his general look of confusion. His thick brown hair was mussed, as if he'd been running a hand through it, and he wasn't wearing a hat or gloves. Were they in his pocket? Dropped onto the street as the reality of Tiffany's death settled home? Was he lost in shock and grief? Or perhaps something more sinister? Like guilt. "I thought you went to the theater to rehearse with the dancers."

His brown eyes snapped to mine, and his expression cleared. "I came to encourage Tiffany. She wasn't feeling well, but the promotion was too important to miss."

I perked up at the new information. "She was sick? What was wrong with her?"

He shook his head, mystified. "At first it was just a headache, but by the time she got in the float, she was feeling weak and nauseous. I told her we'd see a doctor when the parade ended. All she had to do was sit still and wave."

I caught Evan's eyes in the crowd and lifted my chin. "I understand," I said. "I actually have someone I'd like you to meet."

"I can't," George said. "I'm going to the inn to collect myself before I have to tell the dancers." He scraped a hand through his mussed hair before stuffing it back into his pocket. "How is this happening? How is something like this even possible?"

I weighed his tone and words against the disheveled appearance, trying to gauge the authenticity of any of it and hating myself a little for my cynicism. "Did you know she snuck out last night?" I asked. The words were out of my mouth before I'd thought better of them. And suddenly I couldn't help wondering if she'd fought with someone while she was out. If so, had that person still been angry this morning?

Maybe mad enough to kill.

George's eyes widened. "What?"

I pictured her leaving again. Her startled expression when she'd noticed me in my office, wrapping up jewelry orders for the night. She'd nearly jumped out of her skin, and she'd begged me not to mention her little excursion. "She said she needed some alone time."

I watched as my words sank in, my mind racing with possibilities. "She wanted a quick walk to clear her head. I wondered if she might've been meeting someone."

His eyes darkened. "Like who?"

I rocked back on my heels, having clearly hit a sore spot.

A large hand landed on my back as Evan swooped in. He steadied me, then stepped forward, shoulders square and frame taut. "I'm Sheriff Gray." He extended his hand to George. "You are?"

"George Ashton." The choreographer looked smaller in Evan's presence. Beside the dancers last night and at breakfast, even talking alone to me, he'd seemed more than a little intimidating. But with Evan for contrast, George wasn't particularly large or frightening. A few inches shorter than the sheriff and narrower at the hips and shoulders. Not to mention his perpetual scowl had fully faded.

I moved to Evan's side. "George is the ballet master traveling with the group that's here to perform *The Nutcracker*. He's staying at the inn with several lead ballerinas and Tiffany."

George's angry expression returned, and Evan lifted a brow.

"I see. Then I have a few questions for you, George. If you have some time to talk now, that would be best."

A chill skittered down my spine. Evan hadn't used the voice of someone planning to comfort a grieving friend. He'd employed his sheriff's voice, deep and low, rife with authority.

Stalking Around the Christmas Tree

I fought a little nonsensical smile. I loved his business voice when it wasn't pointed at me. Also, clearly I was right. Tiffany Krieg hadn't died of natural causes.

Around us, a large number of lingering bystanders quieted and stared, as if they could somehow sense something important was going down. Among those faces were rows and rows of costumed nutcrackers and Mouse Kings. Tiny ballerinas and sugar plum fairies.

"Any idea who would want to hurt Tiffany?" Evan asked.

I leaned closer to hear George's reply. Something inside me suspected he knew the answer.

Chapter Five

I was distracted the next morning, discontent to rattle around the empty inn after George and the ballerinas left for the theater. I packed up a few jewelry orders and stacked them on my desk, mind wandering out the window at my side. It didn't take long for me to give up hope of any real productivity. I bundled up in my shapeless puffy coat, hat, scarf, boots, and gloves, and then headed to the Hearth, knowing Mom was there and made of warm hugs.

I needed something familiar and comfortable to set my nerves at ease, unlike the long evening spent with silent, grieving ballerinas. Evan had arrived shortly after their return from the theater, to break the news I'd seen coming. The coroner's initial evaluation found evidence suggesting Tiffany had been poisoned, possibly with cyanide, delivered via her daily protein shake. He'd know more after a full workup and official toxicology report.

George had turned green as Evan spoke.

Afterward I'd peppered Evan with questions, but he couldn't stay to entertain them. Mistletoe had its fourth murder in four years, and if the killer was with the ballet, whether as a guest or someone part of the show, he needed to work fast. The production and their fans would be leaving town in less than a week. Any free time Evan might've had before Tiffany's death was long gone now.

I slipped into the cold day and marched down the path to the narrow road cutting through the property. The walk was beautiful and bright as the brilliant morning sun reflected off fields of snow. I burrowed deeper into my coat and watched my breath rise in crystal clouds before me as I traveled the lane. Cardinals pecked food from feeders erected on poles throughout the grounds, and squirrels played chase across powerlines, sharpening their long jump skills on distant limbs.

It was an unbelievably beautiful world and so hard to believe there'd been another murder. I'd locked the door to my private quarters for the first time in a long while before bed, unsettled by the possibility a killer slept upstairs.

Twinkle lights glowed beneath piles of snow on the Hearth windows as I approached. I let myself inside, reveling in the warm air blowing down from above.

Mom chatted with Libby at the counter, and I stilled for a moment, reminding myself to remain calm. I wanted to bound over and give them both hugs, but I didn't want to scare Libby away, or cause her to clam up, if she was finally rejoining the land of communication with friends and family.

I bumped the toes of my boots against the floor instead, buying time and announcing my arrival. Tufts of snow fell into little piles on the mat, soon to be dried by the overhead vent.

The women looked up as I squeaked across the dining area to the counter, a smile on my face. "Morning."

Libby nodded and glanced away.

"Good morning, sweetie," Mom said. She came around to my side of the counter and wrapped me in a hug. "I was just going over the details of the day with Libby before I head out." Mom was dressed in a crimson blouse and black dress pants with red jingle bell earrings and a pearl necklace. She didn't often forgo her usual uber casual attire, so I took a moment to whistle.

She blushed and gave my hands a squeeze.

"You look amazing," I said. "Far too fancy for a tree farm."

She'd pulled her bobbed hair back on each side with delicate silver pins, and I was sure I detected rouge on her cheeks.

"Thank you," she said, releasing me to return to the business side of her counter. "Caroline wants to begin recording her show in a few hours, and I need to be there early. I'm bringing whoopie pies in various stages of completion, so I can walk through the steps, from bags and bowls of ingredients, to batter and filling, and then a finished product. Libby's in charge here while I'm gone. We're serving a limited menu of ready foods to keep traffic flowing. I've already made extra batches of our most popular sweets and prepared vats of hot chocolate and cinnamon apple cider. Soups are cooking now if anyone needs a little sustenance to go with their treats." She turned back to Libby. "My friends are fully capable and coming soon to help serve and run the register so you won't be bombarded. They know what they're doing, so you can trust them. They've filled in dozens of times over the years when Holly or I was ill, or I was out of town for whatever reason."

I smiled. Calling mom's friends capable was like calling the tornado that took Dorothy to Oz a little wind. Mom's friends were a force of nature, which was fitting because she was too. I supposed it was natural for people to surround themselves with others who understood them and matched their energy. I had a formidable crew of my own these days. I looked in Libby's direction, missing her so much I could scream and hating that she was right there but a million miles away. And I wanted to know why.

"Holly," Mom said, swinging her attention to me once more. "You're in charge of today's reindeer game, so don't be late, and make sure you give all the participants a voucher for something warm to drink. Winners get a half-dozen sweets of their choice and an applesauce ornament." She pointed to a basket with gingerbread-people-shaped ornaments in plastic sleeves tied with red ribbon.

I smiled serenely, hoping she couldn't tell I'd completely forgotten I'd promised to help at the event. "No problem."

"How are the holiday cards coming along?" she asked. "If you can get them all in the mail in the next day or two, most will still have a chance of arriving on time."

"Almost done," I said. Thankfully the word *almost* was subjective, so I hadn't completely lied to my mother.

"And the toys?" she asked. "Do you need more wrapping paper?"

"Not yet," I said. Mostly because I hadn't wrapped any toys in days. "Evan and I are going to work on those together."

Mom stilled and set a hand on her hip. "I don't see how that can be true. Not after what happened during the parade. Won't he have his hands full until Christmas now?"

"I can help," Libby said.

I imagined myself collapsing, one hand over my heart, then told myself not to be dramatic and smiled. "Really? I'd love that. Thank you."

She offered a small smile. "Of course. Don't mention it."

I watched as she crossed and uncrossed her legs on the lollipop barstool. The sleeves of her deep green sweater were pulled over her palms, thin fingers curled to hold the material in place. Today her hair was jet black and hanging in loose waves around her shoulders. Her eye makeup was heavier than she typically wore it, and false lashes curled up in thick fans.

What is going on with you? I asked mentally, willing her to answer. *Tell me. Tell me. Tell me.*

"I just can't get over that poor ballerina," Mom said. "Four murders in a row. What are the odds?"

"Getting better every year," I said dryly. The first murder victim was found in a sleigh on Reindeer Games property, the second in a giant candy bowl filled with mints on the square. Last year the victim's body was left in the toy drive donation box on my porch. Tiffany Krieg made four.

"What happens if the case isn't solved before your wedding?" Mom asked. "Will you have to postpone your honeymoon?"

I sighed, turning my focus to her very reasonable questions.

The Mistletoe Sheriff's Department was small, but the size wasn't usually a problem. I wasn't sure what happened when the sheriff was getting married and planning a couple of weeks out of town while a murder investigation was underway. Not to mention the town was currently overrun with tourists, and the wedding was zooming up to meet us fast. Only six days to go.

Evan's added security team was nice, and they looked tough, but he said they had no authority. So, they wouldn't be helpful where the investigation was concerned. And I wasn't sure who Evan could hand a case of this size off to while he left for the beach. Or if he'd be comfortable leaving it unfinished. "I don't know," I said finally. "I guess we just hope this is sorted before then."

I'd been noodling on ways I could help speed the whole thing along, but falling short of decent ideas.

Mom stared. "Will he need help with the wedding tasks on his list?"

I refreshed my smile, sensing Mom was about to start a downward spiral. Likely brought on by jitters from the pending livestream. "All I know for sure is that you're going to be late if you hang around here talking to us any longer. The rest will work itself out."

She relaxed her stance and returned my smile. "I'm nervous, and I'm making mountains out of molehills, aren't I?"

"A few," I said. "But don't worry. Caroline is really good at everything she does, and viewers love her. She'll put you at ease. I'm sure of it. And you're going to be terrific," I promised. "I'll go to the studio as soon as I finish leading the reindeer game. The ballerinas plan to be at the theater all day, so they won't need me at the inn. I'll leave a note with my cell number and a tray with plenty of low-fat, high-protein snacks on the counter, then head into town."

Mom clutched my hands. "Thank you. You're the perfect daughter."

"I know," I said solemnly. "I love you. Now, get going and drive safely. I'll be there as soon as I can."

Mom kissed my cheek, then hurried into the day, letting a gust of icy wind and puff of snow in behind her.

Libby took Mom's place at the counter and busied herself, probably hoping I'd leave too.

I took her vacated seat. "How've you been?"

She glanced up and shrugged. "How was last night with the ballerinas?"

"Not great," I said. "Evan and his deputies came over. They told us Tiffany was definitely murdered, then they combed through her room while I kept everyone else in the dining area, so nothing could be tampered with. The dancers were shaken. Evan and his men stuck around to speak to each of them. I heard the choreographer ordering black armbands by phone last night. Evan spoke to him at the parade scene."

Libby's eyes were saucer sized as she listened, pupils blown out and cheeks pink.

I was glad to have her attention again, to be part of a conversation with her. Until I realized she wasn't trying to connect with me after our strange break. She was keeping me talking so the topic stayed away from her.

"What happens to the stuff left in her room?" Libby asked, looking almost genuinely curious.

I frowned. "Deputies boxed up everything," I said. "Her folks are coming into town to collect her things and take her home."

Libby nodded, hazel eyes scanning the empty dining area behind me. "Are you planning to get involved in this investigation? Or will your pending nuptials keep you too busy?" Her lips curved into a teasing smile, and my frustration with her fizzled by a fraction.

She might've been trying to control the topic, or maybe she wasn't. Either way, it felt really good to talk to her again. About anything. Even if her interest was marginal or inauthentic. Maybe she was just being cautious and guarded, but still trying. "You know a wedding won't stop me from meddling," I said, playing along. "Not even if I'm the bride."

She made a strangled sound, and her expression went flat. "I wish that wasn't true. I don't see a reason for you to mess with this. No one you love was accused or injured. Why not let it go so we don't have to worry about you this time?"

I shrugged. "Don't worry about me."

Libby rolled her eyes. "Unlike you, I learn from experience, and every time you start asking questions about a murder in this town, you get threatened, hurt, and abducted. It's a real bummer, and it stresses out my brother."

"She was staying at the inn," I said. "I didn't know her, and no one's being accused yet, but it bugs me that the ballet master was at the parade when he should've been at the theater. He said he was there to support her, but from what I'd seen up to that point, he wasn't very nice to the dancers. Let alone supportive."

Libby's eyes narrowed, and her lips parted, ready to tell me curiosity alone wasn't enough reason to do this again. Not now. Not less than a week before my wedding.

Something else popped into my mind before she spoke, so I pressed on. Something that had bothered me as the guests made coffee and selected fruits to take with them this morning. "I overheard one of the ballerinas say Tiffany's death was going to really upset Courtney, but I don't know which one is Courtney."

Libby's expression cleared. "Have you checked the website or playbill?"

"No." But those were good ideas, and regardless of her complaints about my unnecessary meddling, she liked answers as much as I did. "I can't believe I didn't think of that. Usually internet searching is my number-one tool."

She performed a little shrug, and I could practically feel her retreating for no obvious reason.

I didn't know how to keep her with me, and it made me want to scream.

"Everyone's worried about you," I said, gracelessly changing topics. Desperate to grab ahold of her before she disappeared again. "I know you don't want to hear that. You want space, and you're probably going to pretend you have to leave now and do something else because I brought it up. But, Libby . . . please know, Evan, my folks, Cookie, Caroline, Ray, and I would do anything to see you happy again. We're all a lot tougher than we look, so if you think we can't handle hearing the truth about whatever it is that you're going through, you're wrong. And there's no need to shoulder a burden alone when sharing it with us will make it lighter."

Libby looked away and began rolling napkins around sets of silverware.

"If you don't want all of us to know what's going on with you, at least talk to Evan. He's worried sick. If you're struggling with whatever happened in Boston and you need help processing it, get a counselor. Mistletoe has multiple fantastic people you can talk to."

Libby's troubled eyes met mine. "Nothing's wrong, and I'm fig-uring it out on my own."

My skin tingled, and goose bumps chased across my skin. "So there is something wrong," I said.

Her gaze slid away. She'd said more than she'd intended, and she knew it.

"Otherwise, what are you figuring out on your own?"

Libby locked her jaw and set her lips into a thin line.

"This mystery is far more interesting to me than yesterday's murder," I said. "Maybe that's sounds awful, but I don't care. I love you, you're hurting, and I think I can help."

She shook her head, and I raised a finger to stop her from shut-ting me down before I finished.

"You think whatever this is only affects you," I said. "But you're wrong. It hurts me to see you like this, and a lot of other people I love are hurting for the same reason. So, if you're trying to power through something alone in an effort to spare us, you're failing mis-erably. We're all wrecked over this, and we don't even know what's wrong."

Libby made a throaty, disgusted noise. She looked at the ceiling and waved her hands uselessly before dropping them to her sides. "This is why I've been avoiding you."

I cocked a brow. "Go on."

"I knew if I tried to be even the slightest bit social, you'd take that as some kind of crack in the door, then try to break it down." She lowered her eyes to mine and frowned.

I didn't like her tone or the increasing volume. So I leveled her with my best no-nonsense stare. "What's wrong, Libby?" I asked, biting off each word.

She worked her jaw and glared.

I raised my brows in challenge.

A moment later, she reached into her back pocket and liberated her phone. She tapped the screen several times, then set the device on the counter before me. An image of a teal sedan was centered on the screen.

"What's that?" I asked. "Are you buying a car?"

She huffed and used her fingers to zoom in on the back bumper.

"A Suffolk County Theater sticker?" I asked. Did this have something to do with the ballet?

"Boston is in Suffolk County," she said.

"Aren't a lot of places?"

"I don't think this is a coincidence. I've been seeing this car everywhere all year long. Every time I think I've imagined it or the person was just visiting coincidentally, the car turns up again. And that can't be good."

"Why not?" I asked. "What do you think it means?" I kept my voice steady, not wanting to make her regret opening up to me. If that was what she was doing.

"I don't know."

I gave the image another look, then considered her anxious expression. "It's a pretty common-looking vehicle. Is it familiar to you, other than seeing it in town? Is there a reason to care if this car visits Mistletoe?"

"Look." She swiped the screen, each time revealing another image of the same car. The license plate was never quite legible, but the time stamps on the photos began two months ago.

"They visit a lot," I said.

She nodded.

"I'm sure a lot of people visit from Boston, even more from Suffolk County. What is it about this one that's bothering you?" I pressed, silently willing her to be specific.

I didn't know if she was concerned about a nosy reporter following up after the trial, or something infinitely worse. And I needed that information. Especially if it was the latter.

"I'm not sure," she said. "But I haven't seen the car at the farm yet, so I don't think you or your family are in danger."

"Danger?" I squeaked, my fear confirmed. "You think you're in danger?"

She dipped her chin, and an avalanche of details suddenly made a lot more sense.

My heartbeat stuttered, then took off at a sprint. "That's why you broke up with Ray," I said. "You think you're protecting him. Well I've got bad news, because you broke his heart. And you're hurting your brother too. You need to talk to them. And you need to get Boston PD involved if this has anything to do with the trial where you testified."

Emotion flickered in her eyes, and it seemed as if my words were finally settling in.

I rubbed my forehead, got off my stool, and paced. "Is this car the reason you keep changing your appearance?"

She didn't answer, but she didn't have to. I knew I was right. She thought a member of a crime family was looking for her in Mistletoe, and she was trying not to be found.

She was disappearing right in front of us.

"Libby," I said, stopping to look her in the eye. "You have to tell me the rest of this story."

"The dead ballerina looked like me," she said, bottom lip quivering. "You said it yourself. You said Caroline noticed it too."

I closed my mouth against a wave of nausea. Was she suggesting someone had mistaken Tiffany Krieg for her? And committed murder?

She thought someone wanted her to die?

"Do they know what killed her yet?" Libby asked.

"The coroner suspects cyanide poisoning. Evan's waiting on the official report."

She gave up fidgeting behind the counter and slumped onto a barstool.

I reached out to squeeze her hand. "This is going to be okay."

She gave me a very mocking look, which I ignored.

"Is there anything else besides the car that's bothering you?" I asked. "Because you might be reading too far into this. But either way, I will help you find out."

Libby raised her phone and swiped the screen a few more times. "I also get these." She passed me the device.

I scanned the image, then took a seat at her side. A collection of cards—birthday, missing you, thinking of you, and anniversary—filled the screen. "Greeting cards?"

"Scroll through them," she said, and I quickly obeyed.

There were more than half a dozen. "Someone sends you cards?" I raised confused eyes to hers.

"Someone," she said. "I don't know who. They arrive randomly, never on a date that makes any sense to me. And the return address only says 'Boston.'"

I inhaled sharply, suddenly getting a much better picture of what had spooked her so thoroughly.

"They come addressed to me in Mistletoe, Maine. No house number and no street. I don't know how they even reach me, and I don't like it. It feels as if I'm being toyed with and a little like I'm losing my mind."

"You're not losing your mind," I said.

Though she was definitely being toyed with. Luckily, her big brother was the current sheriff and a former Boston detective. "You need to talk to Evan," I said firmly. There wasn't any room for negotiation this time. "He still has friends on the force back home, and he's the boss here. He can help. He wants to help. Let. Him. Help."

"I don't even know if there's something to worry about," she said. Her hands flew up between us again. "It's maddening. And I don't want to take up any more of Evan's bandwidth unless there's definitely a problem." She launched to her feet and moved away in a hurry. "Until there's a reason to add more to his plate, I'm not telling Evan about this, and neither are you. Understand me?"

I crossed my arms and jutted my chin forward. I was without a doubt telling Evan immediately. I pulled my phone from my pocket.

The threat in her eyes and tone was nearly enough to make me laugh.

"I'm absolutely delivering this news to your brother if you won't." Even if it meant she never spoke to me again. Making sure she got the help she needed would be worth the sacrifice. And I'd much prefer her alive, unharmed, and angry than the alternative.

"Tell me what?" Evan asked.

Libby and I jerked around to find him entering the café, a swirl of icy air reaching us a moment later.

His expression hardened as he took in the scene, and he strode swiftly across the space in our direction. Snow had gathered on his sheriff's hat and the shoulders of his dark coat. His cheeks were rosy from the biting wind and darkening by the second as he read the room. "What don't you want Holly to tell me, Lib?"

I smirked and cocked a brow at Libby. Now I wouldn't have to sacrifice her friendship for tattling. "Well, I'd love to stay and help with this, but it feels like a brother–sister conversation, and I have a reindeer game to lead."

Evan dropped a kiss on my lips as he took my seat at the counter. "Have fun out there."

"I always do. Good luck in here."

"Thanks," he said, dusting the snow off his big hat before setting it on the counter. "I suspect I'm going to need it."

I glanced to Libby, who looked less determined than she had before her big brother walked in. "Talk to Ray when you're done," I told her. "He deserves the truth too."

I strode into the day, feeling lighter than I had in weeks.

Chapter Six

I turned the corner and nearly ran into a ballerina wearing one of the cute pink coats Mom liked. I didn't recognize her, but the name "Sophia" was embroidered above her pocket. "Oops!" I said. "I'm so sorry. I need to slow down."

She frowned and flicked a wrist. "What's going on over there?"

I followed her gaze to a crowd I presumed were hopeful players for my game. "That's the game field," I said. "Everyone's waiting for a chance to play or watch the next reindeer game."

"Oh." She glanced from me to the field and back. "What's a reindeer game?"

My smile bloomed instantly. It wasn't often I ran into folks who hadn't heard about our most popular offerings. "My family named the tree farm Reindeer Games after the line in the "Rudolph the Red-Nosed Reindeer" song. And every December we hold twelve days of reindeer games leading up to Christmas. Some are indoors. Others are outside. Some are ongoing, and others are a one-shot deal, like this one." I turned to the field. "It's called Holiday Hat Toss. Farm staff members spent all morning making those snowmen in different shapes and sizes. Now contestants will try to toss hats onto them to win a prize. Prizes always come from the Hearth." I turned back and hooked a thumb at the café beside us.

She wrinkled her nose before I could ask her if she wanted to play. "Weird."

My eyes narrowed on their own, and I pretended to squint against the sun. "Well, a lot of folks think they're fun, and all the contestants will get a free hot drink for playing."

What was there to lose? Did she not like fun?

Sophia didn't seem any more interested than she was impressed, so I didn't push.

She had recently lost a friend, or at least a coworker, I reminded myself. The fact she was a ballerina still hanging around the farm led me to another question.

"What are you doing here?" I asked.

Her eyes flicked back to mine, and she tensed. "What do you mean?"

"Just that the rest of the dancers are at the theater."

She looked away, and the tension became visible in her jaw and posture.

I offered a sad smile, though she took her time meeting my eyes again. "Were you and Tiffany close?" The query felt instantly ridiculous. They'd worked together full time. Even if they weren't the best of friends, people who spend that many hours together develop bonds. There must've been some level of camaraderie among the entire cast and crew of *The Nutcracker* and at the conservatory. Probably more than a few secrets as well.

Her stare drifted again, seeking the horizon. "I didn't really know her."

Well, that blew my theory out of the water, but it felt wrong, nonetheless. Mistletoe was a small town—not an exact comparison to a ballet troupe, but still. Locals didn't spend long days together like the dancers did, and we managed to know everyone else's business anyway. I supposed Tiffany might've been a private person. Or maybe Sophia was intentionally hiding something.

Or perhaps the residents of my town were nosier than the average ballerina.

"Do you have any idea who might've wanted to hurt her?" I asked, a little too bluntly. I cringed inwardly but worked to maintain a gentle expression. "Everything I've heard indicated Tiffany was a rising star and a fan favorite. It just seems so unbelievable to think anyone would want to do this."

Sophia looked at me, and a flicker of something I couldn't name passed in her eyes. "Maybe that was the problem," she said. "Nobody gets to the top without gaining a few haters along with the admirers. Maybe she stepped on a head or two to get there, and someone didn't like that."

I struggled to keep my jaw from dropping. "You think one of the dancers who was passed over for her part could've done this?"

"Maybe. Or maybe it was someone who loved them."

I rocked back on my heels, realizing for the first time how truly cutthroat their industry must be for Sophia to speak so casually about something so heinous. I couldn't help wondering if there was a limit to the lengths some folks would go to see their loved one succeed. How many parents or significant others had sacrificed everything for their dancer's success? Would those folks view Tiffany as a villain? Her sudden rise as unfair or unjust?

Then I recalled what I'd heard at breakfast. "Do you know who Courtney is?"

Sophia considered me for a long beat. "She's the skinny blond one."

The thrill of possibility shot through me, and I worked my stunned expression into something I hoped was encouraging. "You know," I said, "the sheriff is here. He's right inside the café, and I know he'd like to talk to you if you have a minute. Anything you say could help find justice for Tiffany."

She dragged her attention to the building at our side while I sent up silent prayers that she'd agree.

A crowd of tree farm guests rushed past us, headed for the Holiday Hat Toss. "Hurry!" someone called. "It's about to start!"

I bit my lip. I needed to get going, but I also needed Sophia to accept my suggestion to speak with Evan now. I had a feeling she might know something useful, and since she wasn't rehearsing with the rest of her fellow ballerinas, she might as well try to help the sheriff. "It will only take a few minutes," I pressed. "I'd offer to go with you, but I really need to start this game."

Her eyes lifted to the crowd gathered at the game field. "Sure."

"Thank you," I said, smiling despite her utter lack of enthusiasm. "Merry Christmas!"

Sophia headed for the Hearth's door, and I hurried to the table positioned near the rows of snowmen.

My childhood karaoke machine was positioned on top of the white plastic table cover and plugged into an orange outdoor extension cord. I powered on the machine and raised the little pink microphone to my lips.

"Good morning, reindeer gamers!"

The chattering group turned to face me, and applause rose into the air.

"My name is Holly White, and I will be your host for this event. Before we get started, you'll need to pair up into teams of two. While you find a partner, I'll take a moment to encourage you to come back each day from now until Christmas Eve for additional games and prizes. We'll hold rounds of Holiday Bingo, Carol Karaoke, Bling That Gingerbread, and a series of quick play games inside the Hearth in the evenings. And for those of you who prefer the great outdoors, you can participate in our annual Build a Big Frosty competition, hunt for pickles in the pine trees, or join us for the grand finale on Christmas Eve morning, the Snowball Roll!" I raised my hands in a dramatic overhead "V."

The crowd whooped and hooted.

I lowered my hands and tried to stop smiling before my lips froze to my teeth.

The contestants had selected teammates and stepped forward in pairs, creating a clear delineation between players and their audience.

"All right," I said, grabbing the rope handle of a sled stowed under the table and previously hidden by the cloth. "Let's talk about the game."

The shiny red sled slid into view, and everyone began to titter.

"Each team will get five identical hats to toss, that's why it's called the Holiday Hat Toss. But here's the catch. There are only ten snowmen." I began to pass out the hats in bundles according to their style. Pirate hats for the first group. Santa hats for the next. Straw hats. Elf hats. Fancy Sunday hats. Pillbox hats. And so on until each group had a set. "You can toss one of your hats at a snowman already wearing a hat if you need to. If your hat lands on top of another hat, your team claims the snowman. If your hat knocks the first hat off, but doesn't stick, both teams have to grab their fallen hats and try again. In the instance of stacked hats, only the hat on top remains in play. Fallen hats need to be collected and rethrown. The first team to get all five of their hats on snowmen, and not covered by anyone else's hat, wins. Only one member of your team can toss hats. The other person is there to hand the thrower hats and retrieve fallen ones so the thrower can try again. Throwers must stay behind the big blue square painted on the snow around the snowmen at all times. Everyone understand?"

Stalking Around the Christmas Tree

"Yeah!" contestants and onlookers cheered.

"Audience," I said, turning my smile to them, "keep your eyes on these guys. I want to know if anyone tries anything funny." I grabbed an old CD of holiday music from my supply box beside the karaoke machine and popped it into the deck. "All contestants should see me when this ends, because everyone gets a free hot-drink voucher for playing. The winning team gets a certificate for a half-dozen sweets of their choice and a festive, homemade, gingerbread-applesauce ornament. Are you ready?"

The cheering began in full force as I yelled, "Go!"

The scene was chaos. A raging sea of brightly colored ski coats and knit caps bounced on the sidelines. On the field, throwers threw. Hats flew. And a dozen projectiles were airborne over the snowmen, colliding and crashing back to earth. Retrieving partners scrabbled to reclaim their ammo, and the process began anew.

Ten smiling snowmen quickly became cowboys, dunces, elves and pirates.

Energy surged in the air.

Someone tugged my arm, and I turned to find an older woman with wide brown eyes and a broad smile. "I love this game," she declared in a thick New York accent.

"You've seen it before?" I asked. It wasn't a game we played every year, but it was one I always enjoyed.

"Sure! I've been coming to this place every year since I was a young woman. Some of the games have changed over time, but I've loved them all. I was here for the inaugural round, you know? We tossed oranges into oversized stockings that time. Boy, that was a hoot."

"I'm glad you're here," I said, warmed by her fond memories of my family legacy, and meaning it to my core. "Support like yours makes all this possible. I hope you'll continue to come back." *Even if our town gets some bad press this year.*

"Of course I'll come back." She quirked a brow. "Oh, you mean because of what happened at the parade." Her tone was solemn. "I heard all about that. I wasn't there, but I bet it was awful. It's too bad things like that keep happening around here at Christmas. I guess it makes sense things go a little pear-shaped this time of year. You get so many visitors. If anything was going to go wrong, I suppose it would be while you have so many people coming into town from all over the place.

"Anyway, I don't think you have to worry," she said. "People rarely listen to the news anymore. It's all so biased now. As if the stories are designed to work us up. They want viewers and readers like everyone else. I prefer to be calm, and I like having fun. That's why I come here. Later, I'm going to see a live taping of a web show with the cupcake lady."

"That's my friend's show," I said proudly. "I hope to be there too."

"Cupcake Caroline is your friend?" she asked. "No kidding? This really is a small town."

I nodded. "Caroline's fantastic. My mom's her guest on the show today, so you'll see her too. She's making whoopie pies."

The woman pressed a hand to her heart and leaned back as if she might collapse. "I *love* whoopie pies. Maybe I should get out of here early and line up at the studio in case they pass out samples."

I laughed, knowing how she felt. We fell silent as we watched the game unfold.

It warmed my heart to think about how happy Mom was to be on Caroline's show and how much they both loved our town. It didn't take long for that to remind me I had at least one hundred holiday cards left to address and mail on behalf of my family and our farm. Mom had signed the cards, but writing the names and addresses neatly on the envelopes was taking forever. I'd briefly considered printing labels for efficiency, but that wasn't what Mistletoe or Reindeer Games was about. Everything in my world was about personal touches and making others feel seen, heard, and appreciated. No one got any of that from a printed label.

The cards were beautiful. A professional photographer had visited Reindeer Games at the beginning of the year, when our Christmas lights were still up from the previous season, and the property was dressed in its holiday finest. With fresh January snow on the ground, miles of swooping red ribbons on fence posts, and pine wreaths on buildings, the photographer had sent a pair of drones into the air for big-picture views. Mom, Dad, and I had bundled up in color-coordinated outfits and stood in the field that centered it all. We'd waved and peered skyward at the buzzing little robots.

The photographer had pulled still shots from the video footage captured by the drones, then doctored the images into the perfect image for greeting cards. He'd even erased all three sets of footprints we'd made in the snow, leaving us at the center of a pristine field, as if we'd been airdropped or risen from some lower level like an orchestra pre-performance. They were easily our best farm photos to date.

Libby's strange greeting cards returned to mind, and I wondered if there was a reasonable explanation I was missing. I couldn't think of one, and I was immeasurably thankful for Evan's timing.

She was wise to finally open up about what was going on, and even smarter to tell her brother. He'd figure out whether the teal sedan was something to worry about.

As for the cards, I'd already worked up a plan to catch the farm's usual mailman and ask him about the strange deliveries with missing addresses. Surely those were unusual enough that he would remember.

A series of wild squeals erupted, pulling me back to the moment, and I turned my eyes to the game field. A pair of jumping ladies in matching pink ski coats hugged and screeched in front of the snowmen.

I raised my microphone, quickly tallying the numbers. "It looks like we have a winning team! It was a close one this year, but Pirates win!"

The older woman at my side gave my arm a pat. "Another good time," she said. "Now, I'd better see about those whoopie pies. Merry Christmas."

"Merry Christmas," I echoed, waving my goodbye.

I distributed the drink and prize vouchers to my contestants and winners, then looked to the inn, where my truck and jewelry orders waited.

I had a mailman to find.

Chapter Seven

I hurried to the inn, eager to grab my truck and a small stack of finished jewelry orders waiting on my desk. Adding an inn to the farm had been a dream of my parents for as long as I could remember. So much so, it still felt strange to know it was real. And thanks to Christopher, it'd turned out beautifully. A large white Victorian, complete with turrets, a rooftop widow's walk, and a rear patio that doubled as an ice rink, seasonally. Inside, every inch was decked for the holidays year-round. Christmas trees and pine garlands dressed the rooms. Stockings hung from the fireplace with care, an orange tucked inside each for good fortune, and the names of our guests embroidered across the tops. Keepsakes to remember their time here.

It really was a magical place, full of love and beauty. As was our farm and our town.

Which made it all the more difficult to comprehend how murders kept happening here.

My calico rescue cat, Cindy Lou Who, met me at the back door with a long, desperate complaint. She rubbed against my calves and feet when I kicked off my boots and tried to walk. Then she bit me when I paused to pet her.

"Hey!" I pulled my hand back and frowned. "Be nice, Cindy," I scolded. "I know you've been alone all morning, but things are busy right now. I'm only here to grab a few things, then I have to leave again, but when I get back, we can hang out in my office all evening, okay?" She'd likely prefer to curl on my bed, but I had work to do. "Excuse me."

I straightened and hustled down the hallway toward my office and the completed, packaged jewelry orders.

Cindy trotted along behind me making exaggerated Chewbacca sounds.

"You aren't hungry." I grabbed the stack of padded manila envelopes and turned on my toes. "There was food in your bowl. I saw it."

Cindy led me back to the kitchen, stopping every few feet to look over her shoulder. I bent to scratch behind her chipped ear, then straightened to listen more closely to the quiet home.

The house was oddly still and inexplicably unsettling, as if it held its breath. The fine hairs on my arms rose to attention, stirred by an undercurrent of tension hanging thick in the air.

Likely my own.

"Meow!"

I jolted, gaze snapping back to Cindy. "I'm still coming," I told her. "Don't yell at me."

She stopped at her little meal station, where I'd set up a kitty water fountain and placed a personalized, porcelain food bowl in a wrought iron stand so she wouldn't have to bend all the way to the floor to enjoy her meals. Also so she couldn't dump the bowl when she was irritated with me, which had been her favorite pastime for years.

I'd sent her photo to a place online that had used it to create an eight-by-ten canvas with Cindy in a crown and royal renaissance garb. I'd hung the portrait over her fountain and bowl, then slid a pretty pink rubber mat beneath. The bowl was not empty.

I pushed my feet back into frozen boots, trying not to drop anything in the process.

She looked at me and moaned.

"There's food in your bowl," I repeated.

I shifted the packages into the crook of one arm and reached for her treat container. "Here's a little something to tide you over until you give up and eat your kibble." I shook a kitty snack from the jar and set it on the floor. "I'll be back soon. Protect the inn while I'm gone." *Don't retaliate on me by doing something unladylike on my bed.*

I gave the rooms beyond the kitchen another long look before heading into the blustery day and pulling the door shut behind me.

I wondered again what Sophia had been doing on the farm when the group was rehearsing, and if she'd possibly returned to the inn. I pushed the thought aside, nonsensically preferring not to believe someone else had been inside with me and Cindy. Sophia's whereabouts weren't any of my business unless she needed something from me as her innkeeper. If anyone had been at the inn and had a request, I was sure they would have made themself known.

Since no one had, I was free to run my errands.

The drive into town was beautiful as always, and I was thankful for the reprieve. I cranked the heater for warmth and cracked my window by an inch, inhaling the clean oxygen-drenched air. My head cleared quickly, and I sorted through everything on my agenda, searching for what mattered most and making a plan to finish the list.

Helping Libby took first place, hands down, so I was glad to be on the right mission. If I hurried, I might catch the postal workers on their midday break. This time of year it was common for them to return to the post office to restock their trucks, which could only carry so much. I'd seen them pulling up during my other trips to mail packages around this time, so I had a good idea of when to expect them, and I'd seen our mailman, Mr. Peters, among the workers during those trips. After I finished at the post office, I'd drive to the old dance studio in time to see Caroline interview Mom on her web show.

I avoided the main roads and related chaos as I made my way through town. Then I slid the pickup into a space near the back of the post office parking lot.

I climbed down from the cab and piled my packages into my arms, then tugged my purse onto my shoulder and headed for the door. Cars cruised in and out of the packed lot, some dropping letters into drive-up mailboxes, others parking to run inside. I stepped carefully over fully salted asphalt sidewalks toward the front entrance.

The pale brick structure was a squat, single-story building with a green metal roof and windows lined in chasing lights. Wreaths made of red and silver envelopes addressed to the North Pole hung on the double glass doors. Sleigh bells jingled as I opened one of the barriers and stepped inside.

A burst of cinnamon scent washed over me, and "Frosty the Snowman" played through hidden speakers. I moved to the back of a very long line, organized with ropes and stanchions. A mass of locals toting packages shifted and murmured in front of me. We inched forward at a snail's pace, understandably given the date.

My mind defaulted to Tiffany's death, and I ran mentally over the few facts I had on the topic, but there wasn't much to work with, so I let my thoughts drift to Mom. I hoped she wasn't too nervous as she prepared to discuss her famous whoopie pies on Caroline's livestream. And I hoped being at the back of this monstrous line wouldn't make me late for the show.

Stalking Around the Christmas Tree

When it was finally my turn, I set the jewelry packages down with relief, shaking out my stiff arms. "Hello, Hannah," I said. "Happy holidays!"

The pretty brunette grinned. "Right back at ya," she said. "What can I do for you today?"

"I just need to get these in the mail," I said.

"Sure thing. More jewelry orders?"

I nodded.

"Lucky recipients," she mused. "Do you need any stamps? We just got a new box from the holiday collection, and it's going fast."

"I'll take a roll," I said. I could never have enough themed stamps. "Something extra Christmassy."

She punched in the address on my first package. "How about antique Santas? Or cartoon nutcrackers?"

"Santas, please," I said. "Thank you."

She finished adding postage to the packages and tallied it with my stamps.

I paid in cash and smiled when I saw the man I'd been looking for drop an empty mail basket behind the counter. "Mr. Peters?"

Reindeer Games's usual mailman turned to look at me. His bushy brows and handlebar mustache made me smile, as always. "Holly! I didn't see you there. Merry Christmas."

"Merry Christmas," I said, collecting my change and stepping out of the way so Hannah could help the next person in line. "Do you have a minute?"

"Sure. I was just getting ready for a snack. Are you hungry?" His slow, southern drawl never stopped sounding completely strange to my ears.

"No, thank you. I'm on my way to see Caroline West interview my mom on her live stream."

"'Merry in Mistletoe,'" he said. "My wife loves that show."

"It's good," I agreed. "I just have a couple of quick questions for you, if you don't mind."

He met me at the end of the counter and smiled. "Shoot."

"Okay. Someone at our farm has been getting cards delivered with only her name and the town's on the address, no street or number. Do you know how something like that could happen?"

He frowned slightly. "Sure. I take Miss Libby's cards to her because I know she's there."

I considered that a moment. Mistletoe was small, but it was still a full, busy place, and Libby was fairly new. So was Mr. Peters. "Do you know her?"

He scooped his hat off his head and finger-combed his hair, looking slightly pensive. "Not personally, but I recognized her last name as matching the sheriff's, and everyone knows his sister moved to town not long ago. Someone said she worked on the farm, so I put the first card in the Reindeer Games mailbox. When it didn't come back marked as the wrong address or return to sender, I did the same thing for the next card. It's not protocol. Just me taking a chance. Was that okay?"

"Sure," I said. "You found her. I just wasn't clear how you'd managed it, but I understand now. That was smart of you."

He smiled. "Thanks. You sure you don't want a bite?" He turned to pull an insulated bag from a cubby behind the desk. "I've got fruit, cheese chunks, and some roasted almonds."

"I'm okay, but can I ask one more question?"

"Go for it." He opened the bag and withdrew an apple, then shined it on his sleeve.

"Has anyone asked about Libby? Anyone here in person looking for her that you know of?"

Mr. Peters shook his head. "Not that I've heard. Why? Is something going on?"

"I hope not." I forced a tight smile. "Thank you for your time. Enjoy your break." I stepped away from the counter, intuition tingling. The sensation of being watched crept over me as I moved into the day. I scanned the area, but no one was paying any attention to me.

I stepped to the far edge of the sidewalk and sent a series of quick texts to Evan, outlining the conversation I'd had with Mr. Peters. Then I hurried onward, squinting against the sunlight. I beeped the truck's doors unlocked and slowed as something dark came into view on my hood.

A large rubber rat stared back from my windshield.

Chapter Eight

I sent a picture of the rat to Evan, then locked myself inside the truck and hurried across town to the converted dance studio Caroline rented for her livestreams. I turned the rubber threat to face away from me and forced my mind to ignore it for now. Each year after I began to ask people about the local murder, I started receiving threats. I couldn't help thinking that was the purpose behind the rat, but I refused to let it keep me from seeing Mom on her big livestream debut.

I sat tall and concentrated on what I could control: driving safely and arriving on time.

The studio soon came into view, and I breathed a little easier. The building was brown, with a black roof and door. The parking lot formed a ring around it, and vehicles filled the spaces on every side.

I parked across the street, left the rat on the seat, and jogged to the door, hoping I wasn't late.

The welcome area inside was narrow and lined with a service desk. A television monitor mounted in the corner played a live feed of the audience seated on risers somewhere beyond the dramatic black rear wall. Posters from other shows and events utilizing the space were positioned in rows according to the dates they were filming: *The Quilter's Q. Cat Café Live. Fit Over Fifty. Paint Your Way to Peace.* Who knew so many shows were being recorded in Mistletoe?

I made a mental note about that last one before I approached the desk. I loved to paint.

A woman with cotton candy–pink hair and flawless brown skin lifted a finger as I approached. Then she pointed to the phone tucked against one ear.

I nodded and tried not to listen while she helped the person on the other end of the line purchase tickets for an upcoming show.

I hadn't been inside the studio since I was five and took a few dance lessons. As it turned out, dance was not my special talent. Nor was wearing tights, hair buns, or leotards of any kind. I'd always been more of a hiking, tree-climbing, jeans-and-sneakers human. And I'd preferred being alone with a book to pirouetting in a group.

The place had changed in appearance nearly as much as I had since then. What was now dramatically black and decorated in theater posters, for example, had previously been bathed in every shade of pink, with punches of assorted pastels for fun. Lesson schedules and images from Mommy and Me dance classes had hung beside mirrors, tutus for sale, and inspirational posters about taking big leaps.

The woman disconnected the call and smiled. "Sorry about that. This place has been hopping today."

I gave my name, and she beamed.

"Got it," she said, passing a red and white ticket in my direction. "A silver fox left this for you a few minutes ago." She formed a small circle with her lips and gave a sharp whistle.

"Thanks," I said, accepting the ticket and making a mental note to tell my mom folks thought she was married to a hottie.

I took my seat at Dad's side with a grin. "Sorry I'm so late."

"What's with that face?" he asked, fixing me with a curious stare. His hair and beard were neatly combed, and his eyes were flecked with mischief.

"Nothing," I said. "Just glad to be here."

He curved an arm around my back and squeezed me against his side before releasing me. He smelled like the outdoors, fresh pine, and Old Spice, a cologne he'd worn so long it came back en vogue before he'd given up on it. His usual red flannel shirt and broad build gave him a look reminiscent of the man on the paper towel ads. Except Dad's hair and beard were streaked with gray. The skin around his eyes had far more laugh lines, and his skin in general was weathered from a life spent outdoors. "That makes two of us."

I took a minute to admire the scene and relax. The presence of the rat in my truck itched at the back of my mind, but I resolved to think about it later, after I'd fully supported Mom on her big day.

The dance studio conversion included risers for the audience to sit on and a thick coat of black paint on the walls and floor. Spotlights pointed to a stage across from us. A counter with the Merry in Mistletoe logo was centered on the platform, and a set of heavy velvet curtains hung floor to ceiling on the left and right. The set was thoroughly decked out for Christmas, lined in twinkle lights, and flanked by a fully decorated tree and faux fireplace.

Dad hunched forward, probably trying to make himself smaller for the benefit of folks behind him. He rested his elbows on jean-clad thighs, clasping and unclasping his hands where they hung between his knees. "How were things at the farm when you left?"

"Good. Everyone loved the Holiday Hat Toss."

Dad nodded, and I leaned against his side for an extended beat, glad for the quiet moments with him. The busyness of December had a way of keeping us apart despite the fact we spent most of our time on the same plot of land. "Your mom was so jazzed up over this she barely slept all week," he said. "She's terrified of doing or saying something wrong."

"I told her she'd be great," I said.

"Me too."

A round of peppy music began, and the lights dimmed as sleigh bells and a distant voice calling, "Ho ho ho," echoed through the room.

Caroline strode from backstage, stopping in the space before her audience. The lights went up once more, and someone wearing a headset near the curtain lifted a sign overhead. Thick dark letters spelled the word "Applause."

She bowed and smiled, looking like a million bucks in her wide-legged black trousers and well-fitting ice-blue blouse. Her long blond hair hung over her shoulders in elegant waves, and her bright blue eyes seemed to glow with the enhancement of stage lighting.

Slowly the music and cheers softened, and she raised a mic to her glossy lips. "Welcome to Merry in Mistletoe with Caroline West," she said. "I am your host, Caroline West." She laughed delicately and waited for the audience to quiet.

Behind her, images of cartwheeling snowflakes, in a perpetual fall, were projected against the dark curtains.

"As you all know," Caroline said brightly, "it's Christmas in Mistletoe, and we go all out around here to celebrate the holiday anyway we can. This year, we have the honor of hosting the Maine Ballet for several nights as they present *The Nutcracker*."

The audience clapped, and my mind jumped to something she'd told me the morning Tiffany had died.

Caroline planned to interview Tiffany Krieg before introducing Mom, but Tiffany was gone. Who would appear in her place?

Would George? Sophia? Was that why she hadn't been at the theater with the other dancers?

I sat forward, suddenly rapt. Thankfully, my wait for answers wasn't long.

"I'm happy to introduce to you," Caroline continued, "to Ava Monroe, this year's Clara in the state conservatory performance of *The Nutcracker!*"

I sat taller, glancing at Dad and wondering if he was thinking what I was thinking.

He looked bored and a little disappointed. Probably because he'd hoped to see Mom, didn't care about ballet, and definitely wasn't thinking the same thing I was.

The ballerina taking Tiffany's place at this critical juncture, only days before the big show on their home stage, where scouts would be present, made an excellent murder suspect.

"Dance of the Sugar Plum Fairy" played as a small blonde with a petite frame and tightly wound bun moved gracefully into the spotlight with Caroline. She wore a simple but elegant black sheath dress with flats. She paused, curtsied, and waved.

Caroline motioned the crowd to settle down, then turned to Ava with an open and welcoming smile. "Hello, Ava. It's lovely of you to make time for us today."

"Thank you for having me," the dancer answered, causing the audience to applaud once more.

Caroline cast a patient smile in our direction while the clapping stilled. "You were originally cast as the understudy in this role," she said, redirecting her attention to the petite blonde. "How are you feeling about the upcoming performances after such a sudden and major shift?"

Ava nodded somberly, keeping her inevitable enthusiasm for the sudden, massive promotion tamped tight. "I'm sorry the change came under these circumstances," she began. "Tiffany Krieg was a kind and compassionate soul as well as an incredibly talented dancer. I'm not convinced I can truly fill her shoes, but I'm certainly going to try. She will be deeply missed by all who knew her and all who'd ever seen her in action." Ava turned her attention to the crowd, humble and sweet. "In our business, we train under the motto *'The show must go on,'* and we take that to heart. Sick, hurt, happy, sad, grieving." She paused again, and I could practically hear the hearts of the audience swell with respect for her.

Her gaze returned to Caroline. "I'll do my very best to honor Tiffany's memory every time I take the stage this week."

A collective murmur of sympathy rolled through the room.

I was caught up in the significant career leap from understudy to star. It seemed like something a professional dancer would kill for. Possibly literally. And it made me wonder how long Ava had been at the studio this morning. Had she had time to leave a rubber rat on my truck before her arrival here? I'd been inside the post office, waiting in line, then chatting with Hannah and Mr. Peters, for about thirty minutes. Anyone could've left the rat and crossed town in that length of time. And while I appreciated the professionalism of her current performance, I couldn't help asking myself how someone who'd allegedly cared so much for a woman who was murdered yesterday remained so poised and calm today.

Was this a result of her training? Perhaps years of holding herself together, regardless of personal circumstance, for the sake of the show? Or was Caroline's audience witnessing something more nefarious? A cold-blooded killer speaking casually of the life she'd taken and dancer she'd replaced.

I pulled my phone from my pocket, prepared to text my thoughts to Evan, but found a bevy of messages from him instead. He'd sent responses and instructions about what to do with the rat, and then he'd begun to panic when I left his messages unread.

I sent a note to let him know I was okay and that I'd silenced my phone before entering the studio. Then I reread his texts.

Evan: *Without a note, we can't assume it was a threat.*
Evan: *Someone might've set the rat down while they tied their shoe, and then walked off without it.*
Evan: *Thinking of the costumed Mouse Kings.*
Evan: *Just in case, don't touch it more than necessary.*
Evan: *I'll get it when I see you later.*
Evan: *Most importantly, be vigilant and do not ask anyone about Tiffany Krieg's murder.*

I rolled my eyes.

Dad gave me a sideways look, and I put my phone away.

"Sorry," I whispered.

"Dance of the Sugar Plum Fairy" began again, accompanied by another round of applause, and Ava waved.

Caroline raised the mic to her mouth as the dancer performed a deep curtsy. "Let's give another hand to Ava Monroe."

The ballerina straightened, turned, and exited the stage.

My limbs twitched to go after her.

"And now," Caroline said. "I'd like to introduce you to someone very near and dear to my heart. She and her husband own the local tree farm, Reindeer Games, where you can select a Christmas tree, buy ornaments or holiday crafts, play games, and win prizes. She runs the Hearth, an adorable on-site café, and makes the very best sweets and treats. If that's not enough, she is the mother of my dearest friend, Holly White."

I stood, unable to be cool, listen to Evan's advice, or ignore my instincts any longer.

"What are you doing?" Dad whispered.

"I have to go," I said. "I need to talk to Ava before she leaves. I'll be right back."

I stepped over and around adults and children on the risers, then jumped down to the floor. I couldn't run onstage to follow Ava through the back, so I headed along the side of the stage instead.

Behind me, Mom's name was announced, and the audience cheered. Before me, light bled through a glass rear door, and a figure moved quickly in that direction.

I broke into a run. "Ava! Wait!"

The dancer stopped and turned, eyes wide. "Yes?"

"I'm Holly, the innkeeper," I said.

I recognized her as one of my guests, but George was their spokesperson. I hadn't spoken with her directly before now.

She looked me over without apparent recognition or comment, so I pressed on.

"I wondered if you'd be willing to answer a question or two about Tiffany Krieg," I said.

She narrowed her eyes. "Why? What's this about?"

I pressed my lips together, deciding how to proceed. "I just hate what's happened to her," I said, starting with the less-is-more approach.

Ava didn't appear convinced. "Aren't you, like, dating the sheriff?"

I nodded slowly, rethinking my plan to be coy. She clearly saw through my concerned-citizen routine. "We're getting married on Christmas Eve, and I'm hoping to help local authorities get to the bottom of things as quickly as possible."

She looked me over, seemingly unsure what to say next.

"I saw her sneak out the night before she died," I said. "Do you have any idea who she might've been meeting?"

"No. We weren't close. I wish I could help you, but I can't." Ava took a step away, and I hurried in front of her, a polite smile on my lips.

She straightened, shoulders square and a look of irritation on her face.

"Sorry—one more question. Can you think of anyone who'd want to hurt her?"

"No."

I swallowed the urge to beg her for input. "George is awfully tough on you all," I said instead.

"That's a heavy understatement."

"Could he have hurt her?" I asked.

Ava's gaze darted as she seemed to consider the question. "I don't know," she said finally, folding her arms. "George is tough, but it's his job to push us to do our best. Tiffany was at the top of her game, and I'm sure that made people jealous, but I have no idea who'd want to hurt her."

"Was she seeing anyone?"

"Some of the dancers thought so, but no one knew who it was. And I didn't get involved in their gossip." She stared into my eyes, silently begging me to let her pass. "I'm late for rehearsal, and I've got to be ready for this role."

I stepped aside, processing as my thoughts took a new direction. "Could Tiffany have been seeing George?"

Was that the real reason he'd gone downtown to support her?

Ava lifted a hand, then dropped it. "I guess that would help explain how she got the role of Clara this year, but does that really matter now?"

"You don't think she deserved her role?"

"I think she was too old," Ava said, visibly exasperated.

My lips pulled into a frown. Tiffany had been several years younger than me, and I wasn't old. But I supposed we were all ancient compared to Clara, a character who was only twelve. "Right."

Ava moved around me, and something new popped into mind.

"Who is Courtney?" I asked, stalling her progress once more.

"I seriously have to go."

"Last question. I promise." I drew an X over my heart, and she frowned. "I heard one of the dancers say Courtney would be very upset about Tiffany's death, but I'm not sure who she is. If she was close to Tiffany, I'd like to speak to her."

"Good luck. Courtney isn't a dancer. She's a fan."

I stared at Ava for a long beat, attempting and failing to process her words. "A fan?"

"Yeah. She blogs about ballet online and has a big social media following. She decided Tiffany was everything ballet needed, and the whole world seemed to fall in line. If you ask me, I think Courtney's level of interest in a single dancer is creepy."

I added searching online for Courtney to my growing mental to-do list.

Ava took another step toward the door. "They're rehearsing without me, and I have to perform in a ballet I wasn't planning to star in until twenty-four hours ago."

"Of course." I followed after her. "One more."

She opened the door with a low groan.

"I'll walk with you," I said, scurrying along at her side. "What do you know about the dancer who portrays the Mouse King?"

Ava rolled her eyes. "Ian Camp. Talented. Gorgeous. And well chosen for the role. He's an obnoxious, self-obsessed womanizer. And I'm pretty sure he's proud of it."

"Does he have access to rubber rats?"

The big white transport vehicle appeared before us, and the passenger door opened. George glared down at me from the driver's seat.

"I don't know," Ava said. "I have to go, but Ian definitely is a rat."

Chapter Nine

I returned to watch the rest of Mom's interview with Caroline, but my mind replayed the conversation with Ava on a loop. Mom beamed as she spoke, invigorated by the topic of our family farm and her beloved café. She gushed over her life with Dad and bragged about me, then begged everyone to visit Reindeer Games at least once.

Much to the delight of absolutely everyone, she'd brought enough whoopie pies for each audience member to take one home. Each treat was sealed in a clear plastic sleeve tied with a thin red ribbon. She must've been up all night baking to have accomplished such a feat. And she'd somehow still managed to prepare extra items for the café, in an attempt to make things easier for her ladies and Libby while she was away.

Emotion swelled in my chest. The women in my life really were powerhouses. And they truly cared for the people around them. Somewhere in the audience, the older woman I'd met this morning at the reindeer game would be thrilled by Mom's generous offering.

Beside me, there were tears of pride in Dad's eyes as the show ended. I rubbed his back, and he stood to lead a standing ovation. When the rest of the audience made their way outside, he swiped a bouquet of flowers I hadn't seen sitting on the riser beside him, and charged the stage.

I followed on a gleeful laugh. I hugged my Mom and told Caroline she was terrific, then made my excuses to slip away.

"Take a whoopie pie for Evan!" Mom called, turning me back for the chocolaty treat.

"Thanks," I said, trading her for one more hug.

I dialed Evan on my way through the parking lot, headed for my pickup across the street.

"Your phone was off," he accused the moment the call connected.

I frowned at his tone. "I was watching Mom's interview with Caroline. I hoped you'd make it, but since you weren't able, she sent a whoopie pie with me for you."

He sighed, and the sound shuddered across the line. "That was nice. I tried to make it," he said as my eyes caught on his cruiser.

"You're here?" I asked, making eye contact with him through his driver's side window.

He disconnected the call and climbed out, then met me in the street with a hug. "I was only going to catch the last ten or fifteen minutes, but I was trying."

We moved out of the way of traffic together and stopped at his cruiser's side.

I couldn't understand anything about his mood or tone. "What happened?" I hoped he hadn't gotten bad news from Boston about Libby's potential stalker.

He opened the door to his car and reached inside. He returned with what looked like a giant freezer bag with another rubber rat inside. "I found this on your windshield when I got here." He passed the bag into my hands and I gasped.

This time, the rat's neck had been clearly sliced, the head barely attached.

* * *

The following evening, Caroline took Libby and me to opening night at the ballet. She'd secured complimentary tickets from her dad, a perk for having spent a sleigh load of taxpayer dollars to bring the show to Mistletoe. He had no intentions of attending, likely afraid he'd be bombarded by people upset about the recent murder, because in a weird twist of fate, he'd unintentionally brought the next victim to town. Regardless, it didn't seem right for the seats to go to waste, so we took advantage of the opportunity and got dressed up. The outing was a long-overdue girls' night.

I'd gone home and laid low after the mutilated rubber rat was discovered on my truck the day before. Evan had visited after his shift and brought breakfast this morning. His worry was a physical thing traveling with him everywhere, a palpable energy gathered on his shoulders. I did what I could to comfort him, but the truth was that he wouldn't relax again until the killer was caught, his sister was confirmed safe, and all the extra people left town.

I'd spent the day at the farm, mostly inside the inn, and I was glad for Caroline's offer to go out. Even if it meant putting on a dress. I'd struggled deciding what to wear, but my friends looked as if they were red-carpet regulars.

Libby wore a simple black dress, her long, naturally red hair twisted elegantly into a chignon. And though she was obviously nervous about going out in the open sans disguise, she was a total head turner.

Caroline looked like a movie star. Her hair and makeup appeared to have been professionally done. She'd donned extra-long lashes, stilettos, and a silver gown ripped straight out of *Vogue*. The long, slinky skirt shimmered with dramatic flair, and the gown's fitted waist emphasized a perfect figure often hidden behind bulky holiday sweaters and an apron.

I'd found a comfortably navy dress in crushed velvet that I could wear my usual underthings with, and paired it with flats. The wide belt and scooped neckline were flattering, and the long sleeves kept me warm. I'd curled my thick brown hair with a wide-barreled iron that made the locks seem wavy. I reminded myself constantly not to fidget.

"All right ladies," Caroline whispered as we approached the box office. She tucked her silver clutch beneath one bent arm and lifted her chin. "Don't forget to smile."

"Smile?" I asked.

A small knot of people with cameras on straps around their necks broke apart as we entered the venue's grand foyer, and flashes erupted. Caroline paused to pose.

I barely avoided knocking into her.

She tipped her head over each shoulder for a long beat, a patient smile on her shiny lips, while Libby and I stared. A moment later, she was striding onward, with us chasing after her.

"Ms. West! Ms. West!" local reporters called as we beetled along in her wake.

"Was it your idea or your father's to bring *The Nutcracker* to town?"

"Is it true you love the ballet?"

"Did you really dance for the conservatory when you were away for college?"

"Was Tiffany Krieg your childhood friend?"

I gaped, open-mouthed, over my shoulder at the way the questions had spiraled from pleasant to deviously speculative.

Libby wrinkled her nose. "Did you know that was going to happen?" she asked Caroline.

"I assumed."

"Do you have to do that a lot?"

Caroline's smile fell slightly as she answered. "Only for about the last twenty-five years. Before that my nanny shielded me from the paparazzi."

"Paparazzi," Libby echoed. "Every time I think I know all there is to know about this town, it surprises me."

I longed to hug or otherwise comfort Caroline. She'd always been used as a crutch to her father's platform. I'd even gone as far as to wonder if her parents conceived her for that express purpose. Family people were more relatable in the voters' eyes. "Using the tickets probably makes us representatives of the mayor's office tonight," I said, hoping to take some of the weight away from Caroline's pressure to respond. She knew her life was different from most people's and that others were usually quick to judge what they didn't understand. Libby wouldn't be intentionally harsh, but whatever she said next had the potential to hurt Caroline, so I threw myself in the middle.

"It's an opportunity for good press," Caroline added softly as we passed the winding, carpeted stairs. "Given what's happened this week, and the last three years, we need it."

Libby's lips parted in awe. "You handled it like a pro. I wouldn't have had the first clue what to do when I saw all the cameras, and the photos they took would've made me look unhinged in the morning paper. You're going to look like the picture of grace and elegance."

I smiled. "True."

"I promised Dad I'd be prepared in case reporters covered this," Caroline said, pausing to open the door to the theater for us. "As for the rest, I've been training for it all my life."

Caroline was poised and polished, always prepared for an interview or photo, never off guard or out of sorts. She'd been raised for moments like these and groomed to follow in her father's footsteps. A career in politics was first choice; marrying well was second. It was no wonder her parents nearly lost their stuffing when she'd chosen to bake cupcakes for the hoi polloi instead. As for the marriage portion of the Wests' hopes and dreams, no one had yet measured up to Caroline's standards for values and character, but I had faith her happily ever after was on the way. She was too wonderful not to get everything she wanted.

Libby frowned slightly at Caroline's final words, and my heart warmed impossibly further to her. The people who cared about my friends were my favorite kinds of people. "Wow," she muttered as we crossed into the theater. "This is gorgeous."

"Yeah," Caroline said dreamily.

They weren't wrong.

The Mistletoe Grand was a beautiful historic building with high gilded ceilings, a plush inviting carpet runner, and thick velour curtains. We moved in single file down the long aisle toward the stage, stopping at the third row behind the orchestra where we took our seats.

"Seriously," Libby said, "this view is amazing. Even better than in the boxes. I've never sat this close to anything. Not even college productions."

Caroline smiled. "I can't wait for the lights to dim and the music to swell. That moment of anticipation before the dancers appear is such a rush."

We got comfortable and stowed our phones away, then talked about boys until the lights dimmed. Caroline and I insisted Libby talk to Ray, which she hadn't done yet. She claimed to be waiting for the right time. For fun, Caroline described her dream man to us. He'd be smart, tall, and dangerous. I wasn't sure what that last part meant, but it made me smile, because her dad would hate that guy. And as a diehard member of Team Caroline, I shamelessly enjoyed the rare occasions when her dad didn't get his way.

When the topic shifted to my upcoming nuptials, Caroline gave me a rundown on the finalized details, using an app she'd downloaded on her phone. She kept a large whiteboard at her home and a half-sized version at the cupcake shop. But for her on-the-go wed-ding-planning needs, she used the app to track deadlines for final payments, deliveries like the cake and flowers, and more. There was even a complete seating chart for the reception.

"Look how perfect," she said, turning the screen to me once more. "I mocked up a sample table with graphic design software to show you the completed look with your pine-cone place markers at each seat. I've already sprayed them with the faux snow and glitter."

"Thank you," I whispered, completely blown away at her orga-nizational skills.

My head spun a little at the number of things she managed on a regular basis. The busier she was, the more satisfied and unstoppable she became. I was whatever the opposite of that might be.

And at the moment, I was looking forward to a week or two on the beach with Evan more than the wedding itself. No murder to solve or potential stalkers to identify. No posing for pictures, hoping I remembered not to slouch and didn't have food in my teeth— photos that would be in my family and on display until I died. Just sun, sand, sea, and Evan.

A hush rolled over the theater, silencing us and turning our eyes forward. The curtains slowly parted, and the lights dimmed. The orchestra rose from the pit before us, and the conductor raised his arms.

Caroline was at the edge of her seat, as if she might not be able to resist going onstage with the dancers. I loved knowing this about her. She was usually so subdued. Aside from baking, she didn't get worked up about things good or bad.

On my other side, Libby was restless. She squirmed occasionally but smiled when I made eye contact. She'd been reluctant to attend the show with us, but I was glad she'd given in to our pressure. Evan had only asked that she stick close to me and Caroline at all times. Safety in numbers and all that. The fact he didn't have her on house arrest and guarded by his entire staff, town safety be darned, gave me incredible peace. If he believed his sister was in danger, she wouldn't be out in public at all.

On stage, the dancers were magical, and Ava, the new star, was marvelous in her role. The fact she was initially named as understudy either spoke volumes about the skills of her predecessor or the power of social media influencers. I wasn't sure which, and I'd never seen Tiffany dance, so I couldn't compare the two.

The potential for jealousy as a motive made a reappearance in my mind.

I still needed time to research Courtney, the super fan, and meet Ian the Mouse King, before I could narrow my suspects, but Ava had means and motive. She had been the understudy, and that probably meant she wouldn't have set foot on stage in front of an audience—or those scouts at the end of the season. With Tiffany out of the way, however, Ava had become the star of the show. The fact they were both staying at the inn, and sharing my kitchen, meant she had means to tamper with the shake. George, the hard-nosed ballet master and possible secret lover, also shared my kitchen, and if Ava was right about the affair with Tiffany, his career was at stake. He didn't seem the type to go down easily. Something about his reaction to the murder put me on edge. Besides, wasn't it always the secret lover?

The audience applauded as the scene changed, and I took a moment to admire the elaborate details of the architecture under the new lighting cue. Gilded box seats on the next floor matched the ceiling and stage, each outlined in a pattern of curlicues and roses, all bathed in a golden hue.

Ray came into view upstairs as my eyes adjusted. The second-floor hallway wrapped the main auditorium, and my friend peered through one of the cutout sections between boxes. His location was great for admiring the stage, but whatever had his attention was at his level, not mine.

He turned his head slowly, watching something with great interest. Something that definitely wasn't onstage.

I swung my head around, seeking but failing to identify what held his interest. I slid off my seat and into a crouch without making the conscious decision to move. "Excuse me," I whispered, creeping past Libby to the aisle.

She cast me a curious look, but I shook my head.

"I'll be right back. Stay with Caroline."

I hurried up the aisle and into the lobby, then took the sweeping staircase to the second floor. I moved along the corridor outside the private boxes, then doubled my pace when I saw Ray slipping through a door marked "Staff."

"Ray," I hissed, hot on his heels.

He spun, eyes wide, in my direction. "Holy snowcaps, Holly." He pressed a palm to his forehead. "You nearly scared the concessions out of me."

I smiled at his goofy expression and word choices. He was truly the world's most loveable dork.

"What are you doing up here?" he asked.

"Looking for you," I said, a little out of breath and extra thankful I'd worn flats. "What were you watching a minute ago? I saw you but couldn't figure out what had your attention."

He grinned and tsked. "Always investigating. Even at the ballet."

"Just tell me," I implored. "Otherwise, I'll combust, and then what will you tell Evan on our wedding day?"

He looked at the little screen on his camera, touched some buttons, then handed the device to me.

I studied the silent video in motion. A recording of the ballet.

"There," he said, pointing to the screen.

A shadow grew at the bottom corner, and the camera followed it. Away from the bright lights of the stage and along the dimly lit hallway. When the figure passed beneath an emergency exit light, I recognized him. "George."

Ray nodded. "Keep watching."

George didn't stop moving until he reached the back of the theater and took the door marked "Exit."

"Where was he going?" I asked.

"Exactly," Ray said. "Where and why? Shouldn't the ballet master be present for the entire duration of the opening night performance?"

"He was downtown when Tiffany died," I said, testing my theory. "And the other dancers think she was seeing someone secretly. Maybe it was him."

Ray did a slow blink. "Yikes."

"Yeah," I agreed. "Care if I tag along and use that press badge of yours to gain access backstage? I'd like to talk to the dancer playing the Mouse King."

"Be my guest," he said, motioning me to take the steps ahead of him. "Any chance you want to tell Libby I'm here and mention how beautiful I think she looks tonight?"

"Already on it," I said, pulling out my phone to send Libby a text. "She promised to talk to you about what's been going on with her. So hang in there."

"You know?" he asked, grabbing my shoulder gently, to stop me in my tracks. "Tell me. Please." He looked handsome in his black suit and tie. His clean-shaven face emphasized the hard angles of his chin and jaw. In his eyes, hope collided with pain, and I felt it in my chest.

But I had an obligation to Libby too.

I shook my head. "I can't. It's her story to tell, and she said she will. So, hang in there. The whole truth is coming soon."

We started to move again, and I felt his eyes on my back.

"At least tell me she's okay," he said.

"She's okay," I promised. "And she'll be even better soon, now that she finally stopped hiding her problem."

"But there is a problem?"

I slowed as one of Evan's added security men appeared at the bottom of the steps. I recognized him from the parade. He'd been watching Evan closely while the sheriff and his deputies had handled the crime scene. I wondered again what had held his interest.

His eyes narrowed, and his arms crossed. "I need to see your credentials," he said, raising a hand to stop us. He was handsome, with tanned skin, striking gray-blue eyes and a fully shaved head. Dark stubble dusted his cheeks. His body was chiseled, and muscles strained against the fabric of his shirt and pants.

I wanted a picture.

For Caroline.

Ray raised his press badge. The man looked it over, then dipped his chin in acceptance before looking at me.

"I'm with him," I said.

His brows raised. "No one gets near the ballerinas without credentials. Those orders are coming direct from the sheriff."

I sighed in relief. "Oh good. It's fine then. I'm Holly White." I extended my hand. "I'm Sheriff Gray's fiancé. It's nice to meet you."

"You're Holly White?" Disbelief colored his tone as he gave me another once-over.

"I am." That was good, right? "You've heard of me?"

"Yeah," he said, ignoring my offered hand and pulling a cell phone from his pocket. "Sheriff Gray told me to call him when you showed up."

Ray snort laughed.

I frowned. "I'm sure he was joking," I said. "I can call him when the ballet ends. I'll only be backstage for a minute. Truly."

"He said you'd say that."

Ray made an obnoxious choking sound, and I shot him a dirty look.

"Holly!" Caroline's voice echoed around us, punctuated by the click-clack of her designer heels. "We were worried. What are you doing? You're missing the show." She stopped at my side, glaring for only a moment before her eyes caught on the security guy. "Oh," she said, a flush rising from her neck to her cheeks, then staining the tips of her ears. She rested a hand on her collarbone. "My."

Libby arrived a step behind her. She faltered and froze in front of Ray.

I craned my neck to see around the corner, where Ian the Mouse King was sure to be found. "I was hoping to talk to one of the dancers," I explained, though I wasn't sure anyone was listening. "But security won't let me pass."

Caroline made heart eyes at the bald giant, who seemed to have forgotten how to speak. "Aren't you going to introduce me to your friend?" she asked.

His big hand shot out before I could explain that this was the man refusing to let me carry on. "Zane Archer."

She accepted, then clung to his fingers daintily. "Caroline West. Mayor West's daughter. I'm sure he would appreciate it if you let Holly take a little peek backstage. She won't bother anything."

A heavy round of applause rose from the theater, and dozens of footsteps padded over polished wooden floors.

"Intermission," I said.

It was my personal jackpot. All the dancers would be together for a few minutes now. I could talk to any of them I wanted and watch how they interacted with one another in the process.

"I don't know," Zane said. "Sheriff Gray was pretty adamant I call him."

"You can call me," Caroline said.

I slipped away, thankful for the chemistry running wild, because Zane didn't seem to notice my vanishing act.

The space backstage was compact and crowded. Men and women in various costumes hurried in and out of passages and dressing rooms. I scanned each closed door for one that said "Ian" or "Mouse King."

I was still searching when I heard a woman scream.

A moment later, Ava appeared outside an open doorway, panic twisting her features into despair. "Rats!"

Security flew past me, and I kept pace on their heels.

Inside Ava's dressing room, a pile of rubber rats was stacked on the floor.

Chapter Ten

E van arrived at the theater a few minutes later. He'd been nearby when dispatch reported the disturbance. A pair of deputies appeared on his heels. Venue security took positions near the stage when intermission ended and the ballet began again.

"I don't know how the dancers do it," I said to Caroline, standing at my side. "Their friend was very recently murdered, and a dozen of the killer's calling cards were found in her former understudy's dressing room. But they're just going on as if it's business as usual."

"We're professionals," a willowy woman responded, popping up out of nowhere and dressed in layers of pink tulle. "It's our job to compartmentalize, focus, and perform." She kept moving as she spoke, then smoothly entered the stage with a line of others dressed like her.

I blinked. Her words and sudden presence were a reminder that there really wasn't any privacy backstage. Men and women worked the props, lighting, and curtains, watching and listening to everything acutely. Evan's added security men, along with the venue team, patrolled the crowded space, weaving among hurried dancers, some mid costume change.

Caroline sighed, gaze fixed to the ballerinas onstage. "We're missing the 'Waltz of the Flowers.'"

"How long do you think she was listening to us?" I asked. "And how many others were too?"

"Not long," Caroline said. "The dancers don't have a lot of time between costume changes. She most likely only caught the end of what you said as she approached. Besides, even if she'd been lurking for a while, you haven't said much. And nothing wrong."

Hadn't I? Because my mind had been moving a hundred miles a minute. I was sure I'd spilled my every suspicious and unfairly judgmental thought.

Ray circled the perimeter, sneaking photos of the hustle and bustle.

Libby leaned against a wall near Zane Archer, probably on the orders of her brother to stay within sight of one of his men.

I couldn't stop wondering if the threat against Ava meant she wasn't the killer. I hoped it didn't mean she would be next. Or for that matter, that I would. I'd received the ugly rubber rat threat too, but thankfully not an entire pile.

Caroline turned her gaze to Ray. "How do you think it went with him and Libby?"

"I don't think they had much time to talk before they were interrupted by the rats. Unless they talked after that but before now." I'd lost my ability to track time in any specific way. So much had happened so quickly, the evening seemed to be passing in chunks and little episodes, instead of any sensible or smooth way. The spaces between specific memories, like speaking to Zane, the arrival of Libby and Caroline, the appearance of the rats, then the cops, had melted into blurs.

A familiar cloud of white hair came into view, floating along in the distance, followed by a few faces I recognized from the parade. "Cookie's here!"

Caroline smiled, and we headed toward the sound of our friend's laughter.

She and her Swingers were dressed in white, flowing gowns and chatting up the stage crew. They'd set up a small table with drinks near the far wall and spoke sweetly with dancers coming off stage at the end of their performances.

Caroline chuckled. "Of course these ladies have stolen the back-stage spotlight."

"Cookie," I whispered-hissed, drawing her attention. "What are you doing? This is a crime scene."

"Oh, hi, Holly. Caroline." She darted over to us, eyes wide with concern. "My dance group and I were here for the performance, admiring all these fancy techniques and picking up ideas for our new choreography. Marianne's husband works for the theater, and he got us in. I was on my way to the rest room at intermission when I saw the cruiser pull up outside. I knew something must be going on, so I got the Swingers and came to help out."

Caroline hugged her business partner. "We're glad to see you. I'm surprised you were able to get backstage without any trouble. Where'd you get the trays and drinks?"

Cookie smiled. "Marianne's husband, Bud, is guarding the stage. He's worked here since the Reagan administration. They're like one big family around here. We borrowed the theater's kitchen to make drinks and to use their trays." She pointed to a thin, gray-haired man perched on a barstool near the stage entrance. "That's Bud."

He had a cup in one hand and was chatting with several other ladies dressed like Cookie.

"It's always good to know people," I said.

Caroline stepped back to admire Cookie's ensemble. "Look at these beautiful, matching gowns. I'll bet the other security people assumed you were part of the show."

"Husbands are handy too," Cookie agreed. "My first Theodore got me into all kinds of places on account of him being so handsome and connected." She looked a little bummed at the thought of her dead husband, but the moment passed quickly, and her smile returned. "I guess Theodore the goat does things like that too. Just this year we were backstage at the county fair for two of those big FFA events. The Future Farmers of America love goats. I'd never been backstage for anything before that."

Caroline nodded.

My soon-to-be husband had connections to local crime scenes, but he wasn't keen on taking me with him.

Evan exited Ava's dressing room, as if conjured by my thought, and marched in our direction.

Caroline, Cookie, and I stilled to watch, eager for whatever news he brought with him.

He rubbed his forehead before dropping the hand to his side. "Well, my team and I have spoken to just about every dancer and stage crew member. No one saw anyone enter or leave Ava's dressing room. Apparently the room belongs to the dancer playing Clara, so it was Tiffany's before tonight. And the theater's costume department confirmed they have a lot of those rubber rats in stock from some sort of Halloween event they held several years ago."

I absorbed this information, wondering if one of the ballerinas was gunning for the role of Clara and planning to remove every obstacle in her path. If so, hopefully the culprit wasn't the least qualified dancer, or this season would become the premise for a horror film. "Have you spoken to the guy playing the Mouse King?"

Evan nodded. "Yeah. He was out back taking a smoke break. Alone."

"No alibi." And apparently really resilient lungs. I couldn't dance half as long as any of these men or women, and I'd never had a cigarette in my life.

"He's not the only one," Evan said.

I recalled Ray's video and felt my eyes widen. "The ballet master."

"We're looking for George Ashton now."

"Ray and I saw him leaving the theater before we came back here and Ava screamed," I tattled. Did that make George innocent? He hadn't been here to plant the rats? Or had he arranged the threat while she was onstage, before he'd left, to secure his alibi?

Evan's keen eyes trailed over the busy scene around us. "When he turns up, I'll see what he knows. Meanwhile, tell me your scoop."

I grinned, and he frowned when he noticed.

"Out with it, White," he said, his Boston accent thickening. "I know you've picked up something that hasn't come my way yet, and I need to know what it is." He lifted one palm like a traffic cop. "To clarify, I am not encouraging you to continue whatever interference you're already involved in. The opposite. But if you have information, I want it."

I filled him in on the things Ava had told me about Courtney and the gossip among dancers about a secret romantic involvement for Tiffany. "I haven't had time to look the blogger up online yet," I said. "But I will. I just never seem to remember to do it at a time when I'm in a position to stop and use the internet." My gaze jumped to Caroline, a self-proclaimed ballet fan among us. "Do you follow the Bun Heads blog? Or know who Courtney is?"

She shook her head. "I don't spend much time online, other than marketing for the shop and managing the livestream."

I deflated a bit, realizing I'd hoped she could shed some insight.

"I wish you'd told me about the love interest," Evan said.

I didn't care for the note of frustration in his tone. I understood it, of course, but things didn't always go the way we planned. I'd wanted to tell him, and I'd wanted to research the woman online, but life was coming at me in full speed and technicolor these days.

I wasn't one hundred percent sure how I'd even found time to wear a dress or attend a ballet.

"Tell me more about the blogger. Where did you first hear about her? Before you asked Ava?"

I scanned the faces of dancers crisscrossing the space. In a stroke of luck, I spotted the woman I wanted. "Her," I said. "She's staying at the inn and mentioned Courtney at breakfast."

Evan moved in the dancer's direction. Cookie, Caroline, and I followed.

The ballerina froze, eyes wide, presumably at the large member of law enforcement staring down at her from a significant height difference and in full business mode. Then her gaze swept appreciatively over him, and a smile formed on her lips. "Hello, Officer," she cooed sweetly.

Caroline snorted.

I rolled my eyes. Sometimes I became so accustomed to Evan's ridiculous good looks, and the fact that everyone in town knew we were getting married, that I forgot he still stunned newcomers from time to time. Just wait until she heard that accent. Hubba hubba.

"I'm Sheriff Gray," he said. "If you don't mind, I have a couple of questions for you."

"Elise," she said. "Absolutely. Why don't we slip into my dressing room?"

"Right here will be fine."

She pursed her lips and slouched a bit, evidently disappointed, but willing to carry on.

"Can you tell me about Courtney?" he asked, leaving the question open-ended, for her to fill in all the details.

"Courtney?" She wrinkled her nose. "Why?"

"Humor me," he said, still playing his cards close to the vest.

"Okay." She blew out a sigh and tented her brows. "Courtney is a ballet blogger with a strong social media following. The fan base loves her, trusts her opinions, and looks to her accounts and posts for all the latest news, trends, and facts on ballet, specifically this conservatory. We all assume that makes her local, or at least from this state, but we can't confirm it and don't know anything for sure."

Evan nodded. "She reports on all your events?"

"All our events. Our practices. Our diets. The dancers." Her brows rose. "She was a huge fan of Tiffany's. A lot of people think her push and full backing of Tiffany online made her the fan favorite, and it likely skewed the opinions of those assigning roles following tryouts."

"You don't think Tiffany was the right dancer for her role?"

I felt my breath catch. If she said no, that would make the second of Tiffany's cohorts to say that today.

"No." Elise shook her head. "She wasn't even the first choice by the judges. Initially. But when the early performances began, Courtney started a petition to oust the other lead. The whole thing was unreal and unprecedented. And it affected ticket sales in a seriously unfortunate way. The story made state news."

"What happened?" he asked.

The dancer smirked. "Tiffany was placed in the role for one performance, to see what would happen if the ballet gave into the pressure. We sold out."

"And the other ballerina?" I asked, unable to help myself. "Did she end up in Tiffany's former role? Is she here now?"

"No," she said. "Violet left, and no one blamed her."

"Was she bitter?" I asked, earning a side-eyed glare from Evan.

"At first, sure, but she's the lead at a regional dance company now. She wasn't out of work long, and if you ask me, she's better off. It's no fun being in a competitive field where there's no competition because someone who isn't even part of this world makes the decisions on who gets to play the lead."

Evan shifted, watching the dancer for a prolonged beat. "Have you seen Courtney or Violet since you've been in Mistletoe?"

"No, and no one has ever seen Courtney. She only posts images related to ballet, never selfies. It's like I said: no one knows anything about her real life."

Around us, the space filled with dancers and applause soared beyond the curtain. Chatter and laughter energized the air. Apparently there was something to the idea of a performance high, because the dancers barely spoke when they were at the inn. Now, they were all exceedingly jovial.

"Cookie?" Elise said, turning to her with a wide smile. "Can I have another cup of tea when you get a minute?"

Cookie grinned. "Coming right up!" And she hustled away.

Evan and I exchanged a look. "How long have Cookie and her friends been back here distributing drinks?" he asked.

I bit my lip. "I don't know. Caroline and I just noticed them before you came out. They've been standing near one of the security guys and greeting the dancers as they came offstage."

Cookie returned with a disposable lidded cup.

Evan hijacked it on its way to Elise. "Pardon," he said, cracking the lid and inhaling the steam. His eyelids fluttered and he coughed. "That's whiskey."

"And Earl Grey," she said. "I was out of my schnaps, but Evie had a fifth of Jack Daniels in her handbag."

I covered my mouth as Elise and Caroline burst into laughter.

Evan's gaze darted around us—everyone had a cup and a smile. "Cookie," he scolded.

"What?" she asked, sincerely confused. "You're conducting interviews, and my tea is great at putting folks at ease. It loosens lips too, if you know what I mean." She paused for a dramatic wink. "Plus they're happy. Look at them."

"They're not happy," he grouched. "They're drunk."

Cookie stared, blank-faced, and I suspected it was all she could do to avoid quipping, *"You say potato/I say potahto."*

"Sheriff?" a deputy called, pulling Evan away.

He cast a stern warning look in our direction as he went to the deputy's side.

I hugged Cookie and nearly asked for some tea as well.

The rear stage door creaked open, and a gust of night air whistled in. Followed by a dancer in Mouse King garb.

I decided to skip the tea and make my move. "Be right back," I told Cookie.

Ian was tall and blond, with curly surfer hair and enigmatic blue eyes. His lips curled into a come-hither smile I was certain worked on most of the women he met. "Hello," he said, dragging his gaze appreciatively over me. "Backstage for an autograph?"

I struggled not to roll my eyes. "I was hoping to ask you about Tiffany."

His smile wavered, but he rallied. "Fan of Tiff's?"

"Just a curious local."

"Reporter?" he guessed.

"No. She was staying at my inn, and I was shaken by her death." *Her murder,* my mind screamed, but I was taking a cue from Evan and trying not to say more than necessary.

"She was a nice person," he said. "Sweet in all the right places, if you know what I mean."

My jaw dropped, and I suddenly felt twice my age. Had he really said that? Did he mean what I thought he meant? If he didn't, was I the one with the dirty mind?

"Holly!" Caroline called, spinning me on my toes. She pointed fervently to the open dressing room where Evan had gone with his deputy a moment before. "You're going to want to see this."

I turned back to excuse myself from the interrupted chat with Ian, but he was already ten feet away and moving quickly in the opposite direction.

I rushed back to Caroline's side and peeked into Ava's, formerly Tiffany's, dressing room, where the rats had already been collected and catalogued.

Evan stood near a rolling rack of costumes, which had been shoved away from the rear wall at an angle. Beside him, a door opened into a dark passageway and the beam from his flashlight swept the creepy, cobwebby space, illuminating large footprints in the dust on the floor. Frigid night wind whistled through unseen cracks, chilling everyone in its path.

"Who knew this passage was here?" Evan demanded, turning to stare at the crowding room. "It leads outside, which means anyone could've had access. Who knew?"

The mass of previously happy onlookers shifted and whispered, trading looks and speculation.

Cookie poked her narrow body between Caroline and me, an expression of concern on her soft, wrinkled face. "Uh-oh. Looks like I'd better make him some tea."

Chapter Eleven

Early the next morning, I carried my third cup of coffee and a plate of Mom's cutout cookies into my office and dropped back onto my chair. I'd been up late addressing the remainder of the holiday cards from our farm, and I'd risen early to stuff, seal, and add postage to the envelopes. Though it was probably a pointless endeavor. If I wanted the cards delivered by Christmas, I'd likely have to take them myself. Whatever I did, it needed to be done sooner rather than later, because according to the weather report, another storm front was headed our way. Hopefully it would follow in the path of its predecessors this month and skirt around Mistletoe completely instead of barreling through it. Evan and I had guests flying in from all around the country in a few days, a wedding to host in four days, and a murder to solve immediately. No time for delays due to overworked road crews.

Cindy Lou Who chattered on the windowsill at my side, hunting birds at the feeder beyond the glass. Tiny nose prints were visible on the pane, accentuated by the puffs of steam from her breath. The hair on her tail fanned out, and her chipped ear turned like a satellite, angling back when she looked ready to leap.

Donated toys piled high beneath the window, bookended by rolls of alphabet-block gift wrap. I'd left the French doors to my office open so I could hear the guests when they began to stir. I also hoped to appear welcoming and friendly instead of exhausted and suspicious.

Thoughts of myself as an innkeeper were still strange and new to me. I'd never imagined myself in a position like this one, and I wouldn't have chosen it. But my parents had insisted I'd be perfect, so I'd given it a try. Shockingly to me, I'd acclimated rather well, despite the fact I didn't have any suitable skills for the job or any previous desire to do it.

I wasn't a good cook, and I didn't bake, so guests had to walk or request sleigh rides to the Hearth for breakfast before it opened to the public each day. I only had to stock the fridge with drinks and snacks, then set them out twice a day. I typically arranged meats, cheeses, jams, nuts, and fruits on charcuterie trays, and opened bottles of red and white wine from a shop in town. Aside from cleaning and doing my best to keep guests happy, that was the job. Live and hang out at a gorgeous inn on the farm where I'd been raised. Surprisingly, I wasn't terrible at it, and I enjoyed the opportunities to meet people from all around the world and tell them about my incredible hometown. As a bonus, I had time to work on my jewelry creations and manage the online shop that sold them. I still wasn't sure where we'd live after the honeymoon, because Evan had left the decisions about our address up to me, but it was hard to imagine leaving Reindeer Games.

It wasn't something I expected to figure out today either, so I wouldn't try.

With the dancers on such a tight schedule, apparently thriving on protein shakes and determination, my job was impossibly easy. Which worked out, considering the number of cards that had to be sent, toy donations needing to be wrapped, and my wedding right around the corner.

Stalking Around the Christmas Tree

I shook away the oppressive thoughts and lifted my chin. The fatigue was getting to me. I needed a change of pace. And I should probably also lay off the caffeine and sugar before I had a colossal crash.

Cindy leaped from the windowsill when I stood, ready to beg for another treat or meal.

I carried my cup and plate back to the kitchen.

The sound of shoes on hardwood turned my head toward the sweeping staircase as a pair of men's legs came into view. I adjusted my trajectory for a better look up the steps to my second floor.

George turned the knob on the door to Tiffany's old room. He slipped inside and pulled the door shut behind him.

I hurried to the kitchen, to leave my things on the counter, then scooted back on silent, socked feet, undecided on what to do about his snooping.

I met George's eyes as I looked up the staircase again.

He pulled his hand away from the door he was closing and moved more swiftly into the hall. "Good morning."

"Good morning," I echoed, wondering if he knew he was busted or if he supposed I was a dunce. "Everything okay?"

He glanced over his shoulder at the closed door, then back to me. He'd dressed in black since the day Tiffany had died; today it was a turtleneck and slacks. "I was looking for a missing coat," he said. "One of the girls misplaced hers, and I thought it might've been in Tiffany's room." He paused to swallow before carrying on. "I know the police packed up her things, but the coats have the dancers' names embroidered above the pocket." He mimed the approximate location with one hand near his hip. "I thought the officers might've noticed and left it behind, if it was there at all."

"Would Tiffany have taken something that belonged to another dancer?" I asked, realizing I knew nothing about her character.

He moved toward the stairs on a labored sigh. "I don't know."

I stepped back.

"Maybe. Competition is tight in this industry, and the ladies can sometimes be mean. There's also the possibility she'd simply borrowed it, and the other dancer forgot. I'm executing my due diligence."

I let him pass as he moved into the hallway and removed his coat from a hook by the door. "Can I ask you something?" I said before thinking better of it.

He turned to raise a curious brow. "Depends."

"What do you know about Courtney?" I asked, holding my breath as I watched him intently for signs of dishonesty or distress.

George frowned as he wound a wool scarf around his neck, then spoke while he buttoned his coat. "Only enough to hope she isn't covering this mess, or our entire conservatory is doomed." With that, he decamped from the inn, leaving me standing gobsmacked in his wake.

I hurried back to my office and checked the time. I wasn't sure where George was headed, but the dancers would be downstairs for breakfast and rehearsal within the hour.

I sat at my desk and cued up the internet on my laptop, immediately searching for the infamous blogger and social media maven I always forgot about until I wasn't in a position to research. Now I had nothing but time, for at least an hour.

A plethora of images and results populated the page, and I hunkered down to learn all I could. Unsure where to begin, I started at the top. Courtney wrote weekly about her love of ballet in a blog called Bun Heads. She posted photos and little details about the images, her mood, opinions, and industry gossip daily on Instagram, Twitter, and Facebook. The profile pages identified her as simply Courtney. Her handle on every platform was BunLovingOne. As a marketing package, it was tight, cohesive, *and on pointe,* I thought, enjoying the mental pun.

My promotion efforts for the Reindeer Games Inn would benefit greatly if I followed her lead.

The Bun Heads blog posts were mostly serious, with a lot of information on things that went right over my head. I was a dance class dropout. Never a particular fan of the theater or ballet, though I had plenty of wonderful memories from both. My warm feelings related to the subject, however, stemmed from the people I'd gone to events with, not from my personal interest in what had happened onstage.

After a bit of scrolling, I turned my focus to Instagram, my favorite social media source. The pictures were usually beautiful or funny, and I enjoyed the reels with sound or commentary. I made good time there without needing a professional dancer to translate.

Courtney's photo feed was fantastic, featuring gorgeous shots of multiple theaters, the dancers in various states of concentration and performance. Her love for the art was palpable and moving, evident in every image, and I found myself eager for more.

No wonder her fan base had followed her with such dedication. People already devoted to ballet must've felt as if she spoke directly to their souls. Her shots put me on the stage, among the dancers, instantly at their sides.

I sat back in my seat, letting the thought take hold. What if Courtney had been right there? Was it possible she was one of the dancers? A member of the stage crew? Perhaps part of the conservatory's promotions and marketing team?

That would explain her ability to get so close to her subjects and know so many things about this particular bunch of dancers and their world.

I tapped a fingertip against my bottom lip, imagining various people in Tiffany's life as the blogger. Each adopting the false identity to cover their own. I wondered what had caused Tiffany to stand out to this person in a group so wholly talented? Was Tiffany truly superior, or was it something else entirely? Maybe she'd just been nice to Courtney when the others weren't.

If Courtney wasn't employed by the conservatory, then what had forged her utter dedication to this group? And if she was truly Tiffany's biggest fan, why hadn't there been a single post since Tiffany's death? Was Courtney too gutted to respond? Had Tiffany learned her secret and threatened to tell? Was Courtney on the run because she was the killer?

My phone dinged with an incoming text, shattering my endless web of questions, and I nearly hit the ceiling.

Caroline's number appeared on-screen.

I chuckled at my over-response, then swiped to see what she was up to. Apparently the only person awake as early as an exhausted innkeeper and a snooping ballet master was a baker.

The phone dinged again before I opened the first message. Then several more times while I read.

Caroline: *checking in*
Caroline: *dad's raging over last night's rats*
Caroline: *spent all that money to get the ballet here*
Caroline: *now he thinks he's cursed. Because of rats*
Caroline: *I mean, rats? Hello? Murder!*
Caroline: *U doing ok?*

I laughed as I pecked out a response: *I'm good. Noodling on all this*

Caroline: *don't noodle too hard*
Caroline: *you'll wind up threatened*
Caroline: *or worse*

Stalking Around the Christmas Tree

I thought about the rubber rats left on my truck and frowned before replying: *Too late,*

Caroline responded with a row of question marks, and I remembered I hadn't told her about the rats. The day had gotten away from me; then our night at the ballet had been a whole other level of distraction.

I sent her one more text: *Catch u up soon*

I realized belatedly, and with a smack, that this was a good time to poke around in Tiffany's room and see if I could guess what George had been doing in there. I just had to get a look around before he returned or the ballerinas woke. I checked my watch and cringed. The ladies weren't likely to make an appearance for another twenty minutes, but I wasn't sure how long George would be gone.

I moved into the foyer and peeked through the front window. No signs of George.

I turned and dashed toward the steps, sliding into the railing when I tried to stop.

Cindy Lou Who sat at the top of the steps, judging me as I hurried in her direction.

I gave her head a pat as I passed by on my way to Tiffany's door. Then I let myself inside.

Coincidentally, this room had also been in use by last year's murder victim. I pressed the thought aside and made a mental note never to say those words aloud. I'd have every ghost hunter and psychic on the East Coast lined up to tell me all about the home's checkered past and resulting bad juju. I had shoes older than the inn, and I didn't believe in juju.

I scanned the darkened space, letting my mind get the best of me. The massive, ornately padded headboard cast long shadows over the silver bedding and large pale gray rug beneath. The first hints of sunrise climbed the windowsills and stretched across the floor in my direction. Everything smelled faintly of a perfume that was likely Tiffany's.

A soft, shifting sound caught my ear, and I stilled, waiting for it to come again. It did not.

I shook my head and sighed. The inn was not cursed or haunted. I had an overactive imagination. Ask any of my elementary school teachers, my parents, and at least two of my college professors.

I turned back and reopened the door without bothering to wander around.

The floor creaked outside, and I saw my life flash before my eyes.

"Holly?" Evan stood on the stairs, curiosity wrinkling his brow.

I ran to him and flung my arms around his neck, thankful he wasn't a killer or a ghost.

He laughed. "What's this about?"

"I'm just glad to see you," I said, planting a kiss on his cheek as he wrapped me in his embrace. "I was scaring myself for no good reason."

"Well I'm here now," he said, dropping a kiss onto my nose. "And I brought stuffed Belgium waffles, if you have time to share breakfast."

I pulled back to smile at his handsome face, and his green eyes crinkled at the corners. "I do."

Chapter Twelve

Evan and I enjoyed breakfast in my private, first-floor living quarters. I left the door ajar so I could listen for the service bell I'd put in the kitchen. The dancers shuffled around, making their protein shakes for later and sipping coffee before eventually leaving for breakfast at the Hearth.

I slumped against Evan's side on my couch, full to the top from thick, buttery Belgium waffles stuffed with sliced strawberries, cream, and chocolate syrup. I'd have to start my plan for healthier eating after the wedding. It would've been rude to say no when he'd gone through the trouble of purchasing and delivering a delicious meal. "Thanks for breakfast."

"I know you've got your hands full," he said. "And I wanted to help."

He'd dressed in dark jeans, brown work boots and a green V-neck sweater that was warm and soft to touch. The color brought out flecks of gold and brown in his otherwise moss-green eyes.

"Speaking of which," I said, "you're busy too. Since there's been a murder, I can take some of those wedding chores off your list, if you need." I wasn't sure how I'd manage anything extra, but I knew his time was just as limited as mine.

He straightened, forcing me to do the same, and he swiveled on my couch cushion to face me. "I appreciate you, but I've got this."

"But—"

He shook his head. "If I ever need help, I know I can ask and count on you to step up. But I don't need help, and you need to know that you can count on me to pull my weight and figure things out."

I smiled, and my eyes stung senselessly with emotion. Maybe it was the fatigue or the week we'd had so far, but more likely it was the years I'd spent falling in love with him, and the fact that I knew in my heart every word he said was true. "I love you."

Evan's responding grin was enough to steal my breath. "I love you too."

Building a strong, lasting relationship and marriage like both of our parents had was a goal we'd agreed to faithfully work toward, and when I looked into his eyes, I knew we would succeed.

I lifted my teacup and finished the last tepid dregs. "Anything new on Libby's situation?"

He sank back to the cushion and rubbed a palm against his thigh. "I'm working with my old contacts in Boston to see what they can make of the greeting cards. They've shared images of known members of the crime family with my deputies and security team, so we can all be on the lookout. But there are a lot of people in town right now, and it's going to be a needle-in-a-haystack situation. I've also made a few calls to the jail where the man she testified against is being held."

"What was his name again?"

"Kellen Lance."

I nodded. "Why'd you call the jail?" I asked, understanding the other steps he'd taken, but not quite sure what this would accomplish.

Stalking Around the Christmas Tree

"I asked for a list of his most recent and frequent visitors. I'm interested in the people who are closest to him, the ones who'd be most negatively impacted with him behind bars. It's not uncommon for guys like this to continue running, or at least managing, their operations from jail. So if Boston PD is right, and his crime business isn't hurting, these cards are more likely personal. Either that or they're being delivered at his command, the early threads of a vengeance plan."

I cringed. "I don't like the sound of that."

"You and me both."

I lifted his hand with mine and laced our fingers together, hating to see him worried and hurting. I knew he'd do anything to protect his little sister. I would too.

Evan rubbed my back. "We'll figure it out, and she'll be okay."

"I know," I said. Neither of us could accept any other outcome. "What about this thing with the rats and ballerinas," I said, changing the subject to something that frightened my heart a little less. "Was Tiffany's killer only after her, or does someone have a beef with all the dancers? Or is it just about the Clara role?"

"I don't know," he said. "It's a competitive world. Could be an inside job, or someone on the outside looking in."

Like Courtney, I thought.

"Could even be the ballerina who was ousted by the blogger. She allegedly got a better gig, but that doesn't mean she's not bitter," he added.

I set the teacup aside and pulled my feet beneath me on the sofa. "What about that other dancer?" I asked. "Sophia."

"Who?" He cocked his head. "I've talked to a lot of dancers lately. You're going to have to be more specific. Don't tell me she's young, fit, or wears her hair up either." He grinned. "That won't help."

They did all start to look alike when they were in costume, but I supposed that was the point.

"You would've talked to her the other day at the Hearth. I sent her in to see you when you were talking with Libby."

He shook his head. "No one came in to see me. Lib and I had a long uninterrupted chat until the gamers came for their cocoas and cider."

"Hmm." Why wouldn't she have gone inside when the building had been right there, and she'd even walked toward it? "Okay. How about the Mouse King?" I asked. "You said you spoke to him during his smoke break? I'm not sure what his problem could've been with Tiffany and now Ava, but people are being taunted with his rats."

"The theater's rats," Evan corrected. "And I'm not buying the rubber rat lead. It's too counterintuitive for him to leave a calling card at a murder site, then use the same thing later as a threat, knowing it would lead directly back to him."

"He's kind of slick and icky," I said, recalling his obnoxious, overconfident wink and crude comment about Tiffany. "I didn't like him."

"I'm also not a huge fan, but there's nothing criminal about his behavior, icky or not."

"There should be."

"I'm not arguing," Evan said. "But I don't think Ian's dumb, and leaving a big red arrow that points to himself would be dumb."

"Fine." I smiled at Evan, enjoying the moment and the way he let me talk these things through with him. "Oh, I finally researched the blogger this morning. Have you had time?"

"Not yet. She doesn't seem particularly relevant to me, but if that changes, I'll dig in. Why? What's your take?"

"I'm not sure," I said. "I read a few months' worth of her social media posts, and I skimmed a few blog articles."

Evan squinted at me, as if trying to get a bead on what I hadn't yet said. "Something's bugging you."

"Yeah." I looked away, trying to get my head around the troublesome detail skating just outside my mental reach. Then it hit me. And it had nothing to do with all the posts and photos I'd reviewed. "Ava and Elise said no one's ever seen Courtney."

"Is that uncommon?" Evan asked. "I'm not a blog reader, and I've made a point of avoiding social media since the moment I knew I wanted a job in law enforcement."

I didn't spend a lot of time online either, and I didn't follow popular blogs or social media accounts. But something about Courtney's anonymity bothered me.

Then the trouble spot clicked into place. "Sophia told me Courtney was thin and blond. How could she know that if no one had ever seen her?"

Evan scratched his neck. "Sophia's the ballerina you thought came to speak with me at the Hearth?"

I nodded.

"That's interesting."

"Agreed."

He shifted in my direction, dropping his hands into his lap and catching me with his careful gaze. "What did this ballerina look like?"

Her image popped into mind, and my jaw dropped. "I think she was thin and blond."

"Sounds like I need to talk to Sophia," he said.

"What if she's the blogger?"

He shrugged. "I don't know. Maybe nothing. I'll keep you posted."

"Please do." I swiveled and leaned into him once more, my head on his strong, broad shoulder. The "thin and blond" description wiggled in my mind. More than half of the ballerinas fit that category, including the woman who'd given it. But if everyone in the ballet world knew about the blogger, why give a description at all?

"On a much lighter note," Evan said, "how are you feeling about the wedding? Are you getting anxious, or are you like me, ready to pack your bags every morning when you wake?"

I laughed. "I'm a little nervous about walking the aisle in those death-trap heels Caroline is insisting on. I don't want to face-plant and embarrass myself on our wedding day. Or wind up in the emergency room with a broken nose, my beautiful antique family gown covered in my blood and humiliation."

Evan laughed.

"I'm not joking. The dress is old. It's been worn by three women in my family. I can't be the one to trip and rip it or drop chocolate cake on it at the reception. It's so much pressure."

He stroked my hair and planted a kiss on my head.

"My honeymoon bags are already packed." I felt his smile against the crown of my head.

"Mine too, and you don't have to wear heels, you know. No one will see them during the ceremony if your dress is anything like the ones I've seen at other weddings. You'll probably dance barefoot through the reception anyway."

I straightened and made a show of looking alarmed. "Do not let Caroline hear you say that. She thinks a bride without heels is blasphemy. And I don't want to upset her—she's driving this bus. She's planning our day as if it's a royal affair. I'm shocked she even trusted us with the few things on our lists. She won't even let me see our cake."

"We picked out our cake," Evan said, confusion crumpling his brow. "I was there. I remember."

I wagged a finger. "We chose the flavor of our cake. She ordered it, and I don't envy whoever she hired to bake it. That's even more her area of expertise than the rest of this."

He blew out a little whistle. "Someday she's going to be the bride, and someone's going to have to do all this for her."

"That person cannot be me," I said. "I would fail her miserably. She'd disown me. I'm terrible at event planning. Luckily, I think she knows that, which is why she didn't leave me in charge of my own wedding. I'm the friend who's great at showing up and listening while she complains about all the other people who are mucking stuff up. And I usually bring sweets."

"Everyone has a role to play."

I laughed and smiled until my cheeks hurt. "How about your family? When will the rest of the Grays get into town?"

He tipped his head, looking first over one shoulder, then the other. "I was able to reach my mom and let her know what's going on with Libby. She agreed to wait until the last minute before heading our way. We don't want her to unintentionally lead anyone straight to Lib's door."

"Do you think there's something to worry about?"

"I'm using an abundance of caution," he said. "Taking the 'better safe than sorry' approach."

That was fair. "What if the storm comes?" I asked, recalling yet another problem. "We can't get married without your mom. Can she, at least, arrive ahead of the forecast? Just in case?"

Evan looped an arm around my shoulders and pulled me near, settling me against him once more. "I will work that out."

"I received a Christmas card from her yesterday," I said, resting my cheek on him. "I just opened it this morning. She hopes I have a merry holiday season and wonders when to expect her first grandchild."

Evan burst into laughter. My head bobbed on his chest. "She's so hard to read sometimes," he said sarcastically. "It's difficult to really know what she wants."

"I love that your family has no problem speaking their hearts and minds," I said. "Much better than trying to guess."

"She still shouldn't have put you on the spot about something so personal. If she wrote it in your Christmas card, you can guarantee she plans to follow up in person."

I pushed upright, and he tensed.

"I can talk to her ahead of time if you want."

"I already wrote her back," I said. "I emailed."

His lips twitched, but he didn't speak. "Yeah?"

"Absolutely. I told her I wanted a big family, and I hoped we'd get started soon."

His smile broke free, either at the talk of having a big family one day, or getting started soon on creating one. Probably both. "Really?"

I nodded and took one of his hands in mine. "If the stars align, and we work really hard, we might even have something for her to celebrate next Christmas."

Evan rose and walked toward the door to my quarters.

Confusion flooded my previously delighted brain. "What are you doing?"

"Have I ever told you?" he asked, pausing to flip the lock, a wolfish grin spread over his handsome face when he turned back. "I have an incredible work ethic."

A girlish laugh bubbled out of me as I rose and met him halfway. "Sweetie," I said flatly, winding my arms around his neck, "it's one more reason I said yes."

Chapter Thirteen

I spent the afternoon in a sweet holiday haze, driving around the outskirts of Mistletoe in my Reindeer Games pickup, tucking Christmas cards from the farm into mailboxes of homes I suspected the postal service wouldn't reach in time for the holiday. The rest of the cards, destined for locations closer to the center of town, or too far to make it regardless, would go into the mailbox outside the post office.

I decided to give myself a break and accept that a handful simply wouldn't make it before the big day. I was only one person, and I was doing the best I could. Not an easy thing to accept from a people pleaser like me, but I was trying to grow a little where I could. And considering the fact I was going to share my life with someone very soon, it seemed like the right time to focus on letting more things go.

I cranked the local radio station, playing nothing but holiday tunes until the new year, and bopped along to my favorites as fat snowflakes flipped and turned through the air outside. The predicted high temperature for today was near freezing, which meant some of the snow was melting in the sun, and it was relatively warm for all the shoppers walking the streets of downtown.

I suspected I'd find people out in droves. Furthermore, the farm would be flooded with folks who took one look at the fabulous day and decided on an impromptu road trip. I slid sunglasses over the bridge of my nose and smiled at the sparkling white canvas beyond the windshield.

My phone rang, and I turned the radio down to answer. Ray's number showed on the screen. "Hello?"

"Hey, Holly," he said, sounding a little more down in the dumps than I would have preferred. "Any chance you have an update on Libby?"

I smiled sadly, though he couldn't see it. I felt his disappointment across the line. And if I was being honest, and Evan was in trouble like Libby might be, I'd probably want to implode. Especially if he wasn't keeping me in the loop. "Hasn't she talked to you?" I asked, remembering her promise but unsure if she'd kept her word.

"She gave me the wiki version," he said. "Apparently breaking up with me was her way of putting a safe amount of physical distance between us to protect me if someone tried to hurt her. I want to be infuriated, because I thought we were a stronger couple than that, but I probably would've tried the same thing in her place."

"And she wouldn't have given up on you either."

"Yeah," he said, sounding lighter. "I'm glad she told me, but I still feel as if she's keeping me at arm's length, and I don't like it. I thought you might know something more. Or maybe you could give me a tip on how to be useful to her. I don't know. Something. I haven't even been able to reach her today."

I considered his request, understanding how hard it was to be a bystander, but not knowing how he could help. "Evan's using all his old connections to figure this out," I said. "There isn't much left for us to do except wait and be there for her. He's giving her situation as much of his time as possible, all things considered."

Ray gave a humorless chuckle. "You mean like the murder at the parade he needs to solve and all the rubber rat threats? Christmas on the way, tourists everywhere, and his wedding this week?"

I grunted because words did not do my thoughts justice. Our proverbial plates overflowed. "Why don't you come to tomorrow night's reindeer games?" I asked, changing the subject and hoping to distract Ray from the things he couldn't control. "You'll be near enough to Libby to see she's safe, and she can see you aren't going anywhere. Plus, you and I can have fun like old times. There will be whoopie pies."

There was a long pause before Ray responded. "I've been so focused on Libby I haven't played a single reindeer game this year. That's not like me."

"It's not," I agreed. "But someone you love was hurting. It makes sense that you're distracted. Come and eat cookies with me. It'll be fun."

"I haven't even started Christmas shopping," he said.

"You and most of the other men in this world," I teased. "Don't worry about that. Tomorrow night is Holiday Bingo and Cookie's calling, so you know she'll use her British accent." That was always a hoot. "She's leading Carol Karaoke afterward. We can drink eggnog and swivel our hips to 'Blue Christmas.'"

He barked a laugh. "I'm trying to win Libby back, not scare her away forever."

"Please," I said. "Besides, you never lost her. She was protecting you. And I think we could all use a little normalcy right now. Bring your mom and Pierce."

"Would if I could," he said. "But they're celebrating their first wedding anniversary with a second honeymoon. They took a cruise to Alaska because, apparently, Maine isn't cold enough."

I smiled, holding my tongue on several comments. Then I thought of a surefire way to get Ray to come over. "I'm going to bring a load of my jewelry orders and envelopes. I could really use some help getting things sorted and packed. If I ship them overnight, they might still arrive in time for the holiday." Several of the deliveries would require a Christmas miracle to arrive by New Year's Day, but it was Mistletoe and stranger things had happened this time of year.

"You need help?" Ray asked, his excellent friend skills getting hung up on the exact word I expected.

"Yep."

The road curved back toward town, and a smattering of old hotels and diners came into view, popular in decades when the railroad still brought the bulk of visitors to Mistletoe. A familiar SUV idled near a copse of trees, only a few feet from the parking lot of a rundown motel.

I suddenly had a better idea of why Ray hadn't been able to reach Libby.

"I'm going to have to call you back," I said. "See you tomorrow night!" I disconnected and pulled up behind the SUV, then cut my engine. I climbed out and knocked on the other vehicle's window.

Libby screamed and pointed a pepper spray at the glass. She wore a black motorcycle jacket and a deep auburn wig with jet black tips.

I made a face at her and shook my head. "What are you doing?"

She set her phone and weapon into the console's cupholder and powered her window down by an inch. "I was scrolling gift ideas for Ray."

"And you thought you'd find inspiration in your vehicle outside the local Cap and Kerchief?"

Libby glanced at the outdated one-story building with a flickering "Vacancy" sign. "I was thinking about getting a room."

"Lies," I said, moving around to the passenger seat and motioning her to unlock the door so I could climb inside.

She rolled her eyes but pressed the button.

I hoisted myself in, kicking snow from my boots. "You want to tell me what's really going on? Or do I have to wait here until something happens?"

Libby stared straight ahead, disgruntled and annoyed.

I made a show of getting comfortable. "I was just on the phone with Ray. He's worried about you."

She muttered something under her breath that sounded a lot like, this town is infuriating.

"Don't blame Mistletoe," I said. "This is between you and everyone on your team."

She looked away, staring into the distance at passing cars. "No. It's this town. In Boston, people mind their own business. We look the other way when folks have public spats or emotional outbursts. Here, everyone has to know everything about everyone, and no one can leave anything alone."

"That's true," I said solemnly. "We are a meddling people."

She turned exhausted hazel eyes my way.

"But we're your people." I nudged her arm with a playful punch.

Libby blinked and tears appeared. "Whatever." She pulled her phone from the cup holder and swiped the screen.

I looked through my window, wondering what had caused her to park so near the old *'Twas the Night Before Christmas*–themed hotel.

"See this?" she asked, pushing her phone in my direction.

I turned to find an image of the teal sedan on the screen again. "You saw the car here?"

"I followed it this far," she said, pointing through the trees to the edge of the hotel's lot. "There's a smokey cover over the plate, which made it impossible to read, but it's the same car. Same Suffolk County Theater sticker."

"Have you told Evan?"

"Not yet. I want to know who's driving. I thought I'd take their picture and send that to Evan. He already asked a friend at Boston PD to help. If he forwards the image to the detective, maybe it will help confirm whether I need to worry."

I squinted in the hotel's direction, unsure about her plan and theory. The ballet was in town. It seemed possible the car's driver, someone she'd spotted visiting Mistletoe throughout the year, was a regular who'd returned to see *The Nutcracker*. I set my hand on hers and waited for her to meet my eye. "How are you doing?"

She squeezed her eyes shut, and a tear fell. She reopened her eyelids and swiped the renegade drop from her cheek. "Awful," she whispered. "I know Evan's looking into this now, and he doesn't seem very concerned, but I can't eat. I don't sleep. I've pushed everyone away. I broke up with Ray. I'm never at ease, and I'm a real jerk to the people who care most about me. I don't even feel like myself half the time. I just want this to end, and I don't know how to make that happen without the whole thing blowing up in my face."

"For starters," I said, "why don't you follow me into town and leave your car in a visitors lot. Then ride with me to run some errands. We'll talk. Get a bite to eat and figure this out." I motioned to the hotel. "I'm sure it would only take a phone call to get the names of all the guests staying here."

Her expression turned aghast. "Not without a warrant," she said. "Privacy laws prevent places like this from divulging those details, and we don't have enough precedence to make a case for a warrant."

I grinned. "This isn't Boston. We can start with a little good cheer and a piece of peppermint pie. People have talked for less."

Libby sighed, then motioned for me to get out. "I'll follow you into town."

Stalking Around the Christmas Tree

I hopped back behind the wheel of my pickup and led her to a crowded parking lot near the square. We left her SUV and rode together the rest of the way. After the cards were all delivered, and the rest taken to the post office, we visited the pie shop. I'd hoped Evan would be there, but this time it wasn't to be. Libby and I grabbed a booth in the corner and ordered, then settled in for a heart-to-heart.

The space was busy, but not crowded. Some waitresses spun and smiled behind the counter, taking and delivering orders. Others raced over black and white checkered flooring, ferrying trays of pie and coffee each time the little service bell rang.

"Evan loves this place," Libby said wistfully. "I've only been here once or twice."

"When I first met him, he told me it was a good way to get to know his new town, but I still find him here regularly. I'm sure it has a lot to do with the pie."

"He's here because it's the best place to overhear locals spilling tea and trading gossip," she said. "Most folks probably don't realize the local sheriff knows their deepest transgressions and embarrassments."

I grinned. "He also says the staff uniforms remind him of your mom." My gaze tracked a waitress in an old-fashioned pink uniform and white apron.

Libby watched as another hurried past. "I was too small to remember those days."

"She's looking forward to seeing you at the wedding," I said.

Libby nodded, her fearful eyes sweeping my way. "I hate that coming here for your wedding could put her in danger. It's starting to feel as if the right thing for me to do is leave town. Then everyone will be safe, and no one I love will be in danger because of something I did."

"Oh, no you don't," I said, sliding off the bench on my side of the booth and moving around to block her in. I pushed her shoulder, and she twisted to face me. "I've never had a sister before, but I know sisters don't run when one is in trouble. They fight."

Libby's bottom lip trembled, and the months of anxiety were suddenly visible in every crease and line of her face.

"You did the right thing," I said. "You did a brave thing by testifying against that man. I'm not sure most other people would've done that. You stood up for your friend who couldn't stick up for herself. You named her killer. You told the truth about what you knew of his role in her death, and you let the courts decide what to do with the facts. You made it possible for them to do the right thing too.

"I'm really proud of you," I continued, surprised by the wave of emotion that overtook me as I spoke. "I can't imagine what that meant to Heather's family and all the other women who've been victimized by him."

Heather was a good girl from Utah who'd fallen in with the wrong crowd, then in love with the man who'd gotten her hooked on drugs before selling her to someone across the country. Libby had chased her, but she'd been too late, and Heather hadn't survived.

"You changed lives that day, Libby."

The waitress arrived, and we tore wads of napkins from the metal dispenser on the table, wiping our eyes. "Two coffees and two slices of chocolate peppermint pie."

"Thank you," I said, giggling slightly at the waitress's quizzical expression. "It looks so delicious."

She smiled and took her leave.

Libby laughed, and I slid off the bench, returning to my side of the booth.

I would definitely add a generous amount for the gratuity on our bill.

Stalking Around the Christmas Tree

We dug into our slices of pie, sipped our coffees, and smiled. It was the kind of easy, comfortable moment I hoped to repeat frequently with her in the future.

"Who would've thought life in a Christmas town could be so dangerous and dramatic?" she asked. Her fair skin was pink and splotchy. The effect was dramatic against her latest disguise.

I forked a big bite of pie and pointed it at her. "Not me—and I grew up here. But let's be honest. Nothing's as bad as that wig."

She burst into laughter, and I joined her.

"Please stop with the costumes," I said. "It's like living on the set of a music video. I never know who you'll show up as next."

Libby took a slow, easy breath and formed a small but natural smile. "I guess Libby Gray will be next," she said. "Since my sister insists."

Chapter Fourteen

We finished our coffees and slices of pie, then headed back into the day, feeling refreshed.

"Do you mind if I make a couple of quick stops?" I asked. "I still need to pick up gifts for Mom and Cookie."

Libby froze and scanned the bustling sidewalks. Resolve slowly replaced the indecision on her brow. "Where should we start?"

"The fudge shop," I said. "Millie and Jean are holding back a pound of their cherry cordial for me. It's Cookie's favorite, and I get it for her every year."

"I love that place." Libby jolted forward, clearly embracing our day out. "Their sweets are so addictive they should be illegal. The air always smells so good, I think I gain three pounds just shopping. And I shop often."

Memories of the rich fudgy scents hit with a blast. My mouth watered and my feet grew lighter in anticipation as we traversed the snow-lined sidewalk.

We halted impatiently at the corner and waited for the light to change.

A few moments later, we were swept across the street with the crowd. We broke right on the other side and headed for the festive little fudge shop. Libby opened the door for me to pass, and we sighed in unison as we entered. Rich scents of chocolate and peanut butter mixed with salty caramel and warm butter in the air.

Oh! Fudge was Mistletoe's only fudgery, and it was beyond adorable. Run by two best friends, Millie and Jean, there was always a line, and the products never disappointed.

"Oh my goodness." Libby moaned. "We have to move fast, or I'll need a new pants' size hanging around in here."

I laughed, still floating high on the delectable scents and not caring if it meant bigger pants.

White twisted-iron tables and chairs lined the shop's perimeter. Pink and white striped wallpaper covered the walls. Paper doilies shaped like snowflakes topped a counter, and silver trays with bite-sized samples topped each doily. Little signs stood before the trays, identifying the treats in neat red script.

"I love the sample counter," I whispered.

Libby pressed her lips into a tight line, but resistance was futile.

Jean and Millie stood behind a sparkling display case at the shop's center, helping customers and ringing up sales. They wore matching red blouses, tan slacks, and pearls. Millie was taller, but they both had blue eyes and kind smiles.

Libby and I taste-tested our way along the counter, moaning softly and our eyelids fluttering in pure delight. When we took our places in line, we both had chocolate on our fingers and smiles on our lips. We waited contentedly for our turn at the register.

Millie grinned when she noticed me. "There she is! The bride-to-be!" She reached below the counter and lifted two boxes into view. One had a golden seal and a receipt stuck to the top. "For Cookie," she said. "Thank you for calling in the order. I had to pry the last pound of cherry cordial out of another customer's hand."

"She did," Jean agreed, never losing a beat as she rang up the next guest in line. "My mother was livid."

"Your mother shouldn't be buying fudge here," Millie said. Her puffy apricot-colored hair bounced against her round face as she shrugged. "You should make your mother fudge."

"When?" Jean asked. She pulled narrow, half-framed glasses to the end of her nose and stared over them at her friend. "In my spare time? Like it isn't Christmas in Mistletoe, and I don't already live at this shop?"

"Always exaggerating," Millie said, turning back to me with a dismissive wave of her hand. "She's so dramatic. And sensitive about her mother. She should've been a thespian. Or a writer. They're always making stuff up."

Jean sniffed. "I'd write you with a pointy nose. Maybe that would make your prying a little easier when you start sticking it where it doesn't belong."

"See what I mean?" Millie asked, hooking a thumb in her friend's direction. "I told her trying to diet in December was a bad idea. It's making her mean."

Jean tucked sleek silver hair behind her ears as she scowled. "My mother likes to buy the fudge from our shop. She thinks she's helping us stay afloat. It makes her feel useful and supportive."

I traded looks with Libby and pulled Cookie's gift across the counter. "You said you have two things for me?" I asked, slightly confused. I'd only ordered the cherry cordial. "What's the other?"

At this time of year, it wasn't uncommon for Mom to place orders for me to pick up, but typically she told me about them. Then again, life was busy at Reindeer Games. Maybe she'd forgotten.

The ladies grinned, and Millie set a hand on the second box. She lifted a finger, indicating I should wait, and watched as Jean finished her transaction.

"Merry Christmas," Jean called after her customer. "Come back in the new year. We make fudge then too."

Millie opened the second box to reveal a stack of large golden rings. "They're pretzels," she said. "Dipped in white chocolate, then coated in pretty golden dust. It's edible," she said. "We thought you and Evan might enjoy them as a fun little snack to get you in the mood for the big day."

Jean motioned another customer to her register, then turned her eyes to me. "It must be hard to get properly worked up about your ceremony this time of year. Especially around here. Most folks stick to traditional spring weddings so they can enjoy the process."

She was right about the added hustle and its impacts. It had been tough to stay in the wedding mindset lately, but that had more to do with Tiffany's murder and the threats that followed than the holiday. Regardless, a spring wedding would never have worked for me. To me, Christmas represented love. Things like family, devotion, and faith were at the very core of the whole season, so being married at the farm on Christmas Eve was a must, and I didn't feel at all as if my day was being overshadowed by the busyness or holiday. I was thrilled to make our big day a part of the joy. Though, I could understand why the timing wasn't for everyone.

"I guess I just love this time of year too much not to have my wedding now," I said. "Thank you for this gift." I made eye contact with each woman and offered an appreciative smile. "These pretzels are perfect, and they'll make our next date night all the sweeter."

Millie crossed her palms over her heart.

Jean looked to Millie, then Libby, before landing her eyes on me. "How about the other thing?"

"What other thing?"

She finished her sale and wished the customer Merry Christmas, then glanced around the shop before leaning over the counter in my direction. "The ballerina who died. She was staying at your inn, wasn't she? You must be digging into that mess by now. We heard it was murder, and with it happening right underneath your nose, we know you can't resist."

I frowned, not liking her implication that I needed a pointy nose like Millie, but knowing she was right. "I've asked some questions," I said. "But I'm not sure what to make of the answers. I don't suppose you've seen any of the dancers in here?"

"In our fudge shop?" she deadpanned. "No."

"Right. Well, I'll keep you posted if I make any sense of things."

Jean closed the register drawer and leaned against the counter. "Check the love interest," she said. "It's always the spouse or lover."

Millie's brows rose. "Did the ballerina have a lover?"

"I think she might have," I whispered, wondering again who that might've been.

The women nodded confidently, as if that was my answer.

"Well, good luck," Millie said. "If anyone can get to the bottom of a local murder, it's you and your sheriff."

Libby put a pile of sweets on the counter in front of Jean.

"Hi, Libby," Jean said. "Did you find everything you were looking for?"

"I don't suppose you sell bigger pants?"

Jean puckered her brows, and I stifled a laugh.

We said our goodbyes and made our way back into the snow a few minutes later, our boxes of goodies tucked into little logoed shopping bags.

Traffic crept along Main Street, thick and slow. Our two-lane roads, lined with quaint shops and parking spaces, were painfully slow moving two months of the year, but everyone made do with a lot of patience and walking. Some groups parked and trekked for blocks to converge on the overcrowded sidewalks and past-capacity shops.

Thankfully, Libby and I were only going next door.

Wine Around occupied a small historical building on the corner, with a deep purple face and hunter-green trim. Broad black window boxes brimmed with holly, and a pine-cone wreath hung below a "Welcome" sign on the door.

Shoppers flowed in and out ahead of us, toting handled bags and wearing broad, satisfied smiles. We blended into the crowd and pushed our way inside.

The air smelled of fresh pine and berries—as festively scented as the fudge shop, but with far fewer virtual calories. The scents here were courtesy of candles and wax melts.

The owner, Samantha Moss, was at the counter, likely pointing shoppers to her most expensive bottles of wine while enchanting them with her delicate beauty and gangster attitude. She wore wide-legged black dress pants, with high-heeled boots and a slinky silver blouse that dipped low in back. Large diamond studs adorned her ears, and she'd arranged her dark waves into an elaborate updo with loose, curling tendrils. A bracelet of clear glass snowflakes dangled from her wrist. A gift from me.

Libby headed for the display of dessert wines from around the world. I stepped into place behind other customers at the register.

Samantha's shop was lined in dark wooden shelves and wine racks, featuring vintages of every kind of wine from every region. Displays near the shop window held accessories like fancy glasses, decanter sets, and charcuterie boards. A row of shelving down the center stored more wine.

I inched forward with the line, mentally reviewing the gifts I had at home and the ones I still needed to buy. I'd started early in case wedding planning made shopping difficult later, and I was thankful for the foresight now. This trip would wrap up the buying portion of my holiday. The actual wrapping was another story. And I had a lot of toy drive gifts that still needed my attention as well.

Samantha rolled her eyes when she saw me, a ritual I now considered a hug. From Samantha, an eye roll was as close to a hug as anyone would ever get. "You," she said, moving a small box onto the countertop. The sound of a thousand broken things rose through the cardboard. "More for your jewelry. The Winers donated another case of bottles last week, but I was in a mood last night, so I broke them all. I felt guilty at first, but now they fit into this, so I guess you're welcome."

I smiled. "You're a true friend."

The Winers were her wine club members. They met at her store monthly for a tasting and pairing night, when she served all her newest imports and a selection of cured meats, cheeses, fruits, and crackers. I'd bought Mom an annual subscription to the club a couple of years back, and she still looked forward to attending every month, so it was a definite repeat gift from me, good until the day she lost interest. Given the amount of wine and cheese she typically hauled home, I doubted that would be anytime soon.

As for the bottle breaking, Samantha's counselor had suggested she find an outlet for her anger issues. She'd recommended knitting or cross-stitch as a way to refocus troublesome thoughts and negative energy. I'd suggested CrossFit or Krav Maga. Samantha preferred to seethe, scream, and break things as needed. Who could argue with a system that worked, I guess.

She pulled a certificate and envelope from beneath the counter. "You're here for your mom's club renewal?"

"I am."

She rang me up and pointed to the total on her register. "How's your investigation coming along?"

Libby snorted from the wine rack behind me.

I ignored her. "What investigation?"

"Come on. The dead dancer was staying with you. You can't resist a puzzle thrown at your feet like that," Samantha said. Her expression changed as I formulated my rebuttal. "Ya know, this makes four in four years. Most of those were linked to Reindeer Games. It's like your place is cursed. The whole farm, I mean, not just the inn."

"Nothing is cursed," I said, darting my attention around the shop and brightening my smile. "Everything is great."

"Well, it's some serious bad luck then," Samantha countered. "Have you been threatened yet?"

I deflated because she was right. There were definite patterns. "Not specifically," I said, and I squirmed a little as I recalled the rubber rats on my truck.

Samantha stared at me for a long beat. "Not to pile onto the cursed angle, but you know there's a massive storm coming in for your wedding."

I passed her my credit card. "It's most likely going to bypass us like all the others have this month."

She ran my card, signed the certificate, and gave me a receipt. "Always with the silver linings. That's good. The world needs more people who ignore all the signs like you."

I narrowed my eyes as I moved away so she could help the next person in line. "Let me know if you have any requests for the DJ. I'm expecting to see you on the dance floor for the funky chicken."

"It's not too late to rent shovels for guests instead of chairs," she called after me.

"I'll send a sleigh for you if necessary!"

Then something unexpected happened.

Samantha smiled. The expression only lasted a fleeting moment before she schooled her features back into the bored superiority of a runway model, but I'd seen it. And that made my smile wider. "Shut up," she said.

Libby met me at the door, raising a hand to Samantha in good-bye. "You guys have a weird friendship."

"Yeah," I said.

"Nice to see you again, Lady Gaga," Samantha hollered at Libby as we returned to the snow.

I laughed. "It really is time to stop with the disguises."

Libby made a face. "I know. I know."

We got back in line to cross the street, and a familiar blond head moved through the crowd on the opposite side.

"What is it?" Libby asked, instantly tuned into my tension.

"I think I see the ballerina I wanted Evan to talk to." She wasn't wearing the pink coat this time, but it certainly looked like the same woman. "Sophia."

"I don't know how you can pick out anyone in this crowd. It's like a Where's Waldo puzzle, only everyone's moving."

"Let's see if we can catch her," I suggested. "Maybe I can get some more information and pass it along to Evan or set up an official meeting between them at the inn. Assuming he or his deputies haven't talked to her about the blogger yet."

"What blogger?"

I craned my neck to see around the people before me, straining for another glimpse of Sophia. "There's a social media influencer named Courtney tied to this somehow, and one ballerina said no one has ever seen her, but Sophia, the one we're trying to catch up with, told me Courtney was thin and blond."

"Aren't they all thin and blonde?" Libby asked.

"Kind of," I said. "More than half, for sure, but still, if no one's ever seen her, why would Sophia have said that? Why'd she describe her appearance unless she knew her?"

Stalking Around the Christmas Tree

The light changed, and I grabbed Libby's coat sleeve, towing her into the street, past the crush of shoppers oblivious to my rush.

Sophia, or her lookalike, was gone when I reached the opposite sidewalk.

"Ugh!" I rose onto my tiptoes and struggled to see over the tourists.

"Gone?" Libby guessed.

I fell back to earth with a sigh. "Yeah."

Libby nudged me forward, moving toward my truck. "If that was really one of the ballerinas, why was she downtown? Shouldn't she be at the theater? Was rehearsal cancelled?"

"Not that I'm aware of, but lately it seems like those dancers are peeling away one by one. I saw Sophia at the farm the other day, and George was downtown the morning Tiffany died. He left the building before the rats turned up in Ava's room. Ian—that's the Mouse King—takes smoke breaks alone outside. It's impossible to keep track of them."

"Did everyone staying at the inn leave together as usual?" Libby asked.

"Yeah, but the rest of the ballet's cast and crew are staying elsewhere, and I never know what they're doing."

A street vendor filling paper cups with warm candied pecans came into view, and Libby squeaked, "Yes, please." She got in line and bought two, then passed one to me.

"Thanks." I slid the handle of my bag from Oh! Fudge around one wrist and tucked the box of broken glass under the opposite arm.

Libby tipped her cup against mine in cheers. "To wrapping up our mysteries before Christmas."

"Here here," I said. "Oh! Kettle corn!"

We made a second stop for bags of sweet and salty popcorn before continuing. My box of glass shards slipped beneath my elbow, but I caught it before it hit the snow.

Libby laughed. "Nice reflexes, but let me help." She tucked her cup of pecans into a coat pocket and took the box.

"At least if I dropped it, everything inside is already broken."

Libby smiled at me as I tipped my cup and shook out a mouthful of pecans. "I'm glad you pulled me away from the hotel. I needed an afternoon like this more than I realized. I've been cooped up inside my head for too long. And I don't have any real reason to think I'm being followed. Receiving random greeting cards is hardly a threat. I might've been making a problem where none existed."

I bumped my hip gently against hers. "I know why you did it," I said. "You testified against a man so scary no one else would. You were brave, and you irritated a crime family. You helped put a killer behind bars. That's huge, and I don't think we've taken the time to fully appreciate that. No wonder you've been on edge. The cards and the suspicious sedan just compounded it all. Everyone who loves you understands why you pulled away, because they'd have done the same if they thought it would keep you safe."

She leaned against me as we walked. "Thanks for saying that."

"What are sisters for?"

A few steps later, she straightened. "Not to get you going or anything, but what do you think is happening with the ballet? It's a lot, right? A murder. An online stalker. Rubber rat threats. A hidden dressing room passage." She wrinkled her nose. "What on earth?"

"Agreed, and don't forget the obsessed blogger has suddenly gone radio silent."

"Tell me more about her."

I gave Libby the rundown on Courtney.

She frowned. "That's really strange. All of it. The dedication. The anonymity. The sudden silence."

"Yeah, and the images she used in her social media posts were amazing. They made me feel as if I was in the middle of the action. So much so, I can't help wondering if she's one of the cast or crew."

Libby performed a long, slow whistle. "That could explain why she's going after the leads one by one."

I nodded. "Ian, the man who's dancing the part of the Mouse King, seems a little sleezy and a lot like a womanizer. One of the other dancers said the group thought Tiffany might've been seeing someone secretly. I hope it wasn't Ian, but something he said made it seem as if it could've been."

"What does Evan say?"

I sighed. "He doesn't think Ian would keep leaving rats at the crime scenes, because they'd implicate him."

"What if that's the point?" Libby asked. "Maybe he's counting on everyone to assume he wouldn't do that, and really he's enjoying watching us chase our tails?"

I cringed at the possibility because that would make Ian a whole other level of wicked. "I don't know which theory to pursue," I admitted. "But at this point, I'm trying to just be happy I've only gotten a couple of rubber rat threats. It could be so much worse." Sadly I spoke from experience.

"Maybe, with everything else going on, the killer hasn't had time to threaten you properly."

I laughed. "Hopefully there won't be any more warnings, and this gets wrapped up before it goes any further."

"Hey, what's on your windshield?" Libby asked when my truck came into view.

My stomach sank before I saw what she did. Nothing left on my truck had ever been good news.

We hurried to the pickup, where a large piece of white paper was wedged beneath my windshield wipers. Images of small, cartoon-like toy blocks, apparently cut out from the wrapping paper Christopher left for the toy-drive donations, were arranged into an old-timey, serial killer–style message.

You should've minded your own business

Chapter Fifteen

Evan met Libby and me at the inn after the dancers went to the theater that evening. The performance began at eight, and they'd packed up after a round of showers and a light dinner they'd ordered in. The home was peaceful and quiet in their absence. Exactly what we needed for our discussion.

I left the door to my living quarters open several inches so I could listen for anyone returning unexpectedly. Then I set a tray with sweets and tea service on my table, where Evan and his sister were already lost in speculation on the intent and meaning of today's threat.

Cindy Lou Who curled near the fireplace, eyes drowsy and expression content.

"I don't like it," he said, scrubbing a hand over the top of his head. "I can't believe you're both being followed. I don't know where to start to fix this. Who's in the most immediate danger? I have no way to know how to divide my time and resources."

"What?" I asked, settling in to join them.

Libby poured a cup of tea and blew across the top, dissipating the steam. "Evan thinks the message on your truck window might've been for me. Assuming I was right to worry about the teal sedan and greeting cards."

My gaze flicked to Evan. Libby and I had just discussed that possibility and decided she was overreacting. Why was he reigniting this flame?

Unless he'd heard something from Boston PD and knew more than he was saying.

"Evan?" I asked.

"It wasn't a rat," he said, looking as if he might combust. "The message was vague. And the two of you were together. It makes more sense that the message was for Libby than for the killer to suddenly change up their lazy leave-a-rat MO and write a note. That took time."

I set a hand on Libby's shoulder, to comfort her, and furrowed my brows at the sheriff. I willed him to be overthinking instead of right. I much preferred the idea I was the target, but what he said made sense.

My heart sank for him. Now he had two dangerous individuals to find in Mistletoe, a town currently bursting at its seams with people. And a murder to solve.

Libby patted my hand on her shoulder, attention fixed on her brother. "I think I saw the car again today at the Cap and Kerchief. I was watching it when Holly found me and took me shopping."

Evan pressed his lips into a thin line and swung his gaze to me. "What were you doing at a hotel on the edge of town?"

"Delivering holiday cards from the farm." I dropped my hand away from Libby and glared. "Why? What do you think I was doing at a hotel on the edge of town?"

He blinked. "Interrogating some new lead. Maybe a member of the ballet's stage crew."

"The ballet's crew is staying there?" I asked, my thoughts running amuck all over again. I looked to Libby.

"The sound and lighting team," he said.

"So, it's possible the car you've been seeing is related to the ballet. They might've been in town throughout the year to check things out before and after accepting the mayor's bid." And if that was true, Libby wasn't in any danger.

And the note was for me.

Evan stilled. "Can you confirm it was the same car?"

"Same make, model, and color," she said.

"And the plate?"

She shrugged. "It's got one of those smoky license plate covers."

He pressed his fingertips to his forehead. "Those are illegal. I'll call the hotel and see if they ask for plate numbers or issue passes to park in the lot. If not, maybe their security camera caught the driver getting in or out."

"What about you?" he asked, returning his hand to his lap and tired eyes to mine. "Why do you think the threat could be for you? You're not still asking around about Tiffany Krieg's killer, are you?"

I poured some more tea.

Evan groaned. "Who've you spoken to?"

"Everyone I could backstage last night," I said. "Plus you and Libby, Caroline, and Ray."

"Jean and Millie at Oh! Fudge," Libby said. "And Samantha from the wine shop."

Evan's eyes narrowed. "Would it have been quicker to tell me who you haven't asked about the murder?"

I sipped my drink.

"Do you know how many people could've overheard you?" he pressed.

"I didn't bring it up when I was shopping," I said. "Millie and Samantha did. I'm innocent."

The back door rattled slightly in the kitchen, a common occurrence when someone opened the front door while the wind was blowing. It created a little suction in the home.

I raised a finger to my lips and stood, moving quickly out of my private quarters. "Back so soon?" I called out brightly, wondering who'd returned already and why.

The inn was silent around me save for the steady ticking of our foyer's grandfather clock. I crossed the hardwood floor and craned my neck for a look up the stairs. No lights were on. No movement perceptible.

Evan and Libby crossed into the space behind me.

"Who was it?" Libby asked.

I stared at the tuft of fresh snow on the mat, where the door had opened and closed. "I don't know, but I don't think they were on their way in. I think they were on their way out."

Evan cursed and passed me in the foyer, threading his arms into his sheriff's coat on the way. "Hey." He backtracked to plant a kiss on my lips. "Stick together. I'll call later."

I nodded, and he was gone, chasing the ghost of whoever might've just overheard a whole lot of things they shouldn't have.

* * *

I sat across from Ray the next night after dinner while Libby glided through a crowded Hearth with ease, managing the tables of the busy café while Mom filled orders behind the counter. I'd worn an ugly Christmas sweater and jeans with my comfiest boots and pulled my hair into a low ponytail for ease. My top had a picture of a frowning cat wearing a Christmas sweater. I imagined it was how Cindy Lou Who would look if I could stuff her into clothing.

Stalking Around the Christmas Tree

I knew, undoubtedly, that ten seconds later the shirt and my arms would be shredded if I tried.

Ray had dressed nicely, and he arrived quickly after his shower, while his hair was still dark with dampness and his skin still smelled of soap. Poor Libby wouldn't stand a chance.

I bopped my head to the holiday tunes on hidden speakers while Cookie stood behind a podium turning the handle on a metal cage filled with brightly colored bingo balls. Claiming she'd have a better view of the audience, she'd moved the podium onto a corner stage that would soon be used for Carol Karaoke. I was pretty sure she just liked being onstage.

"What's she wearing?" Ray asked, nodding toward Cookie as he noshed on Mom's famous snickerdoodles and waited for the game to begin. "She's usually decked out in red and green."

"Or dressed like Mrs. Claus," I said.

He laughed. "Exactly."

Tonight Cookie wore a pink wool dress that covered her knees, and a matching pillbox hat with a white feather and a mini veil.

"She told me the look was inspired by Elizabeth."

Ray frowned and set his cookie down. "Let me guess. Elizabeth, the Queen of England?"

I nodded, and he barked another laugh. Cookie's love of all things English, specifically the royal family, was legendary and seemed to grow in intensity every year.

"Whatever happened to her plan for adopting a corgi last spring?" he asked.

"Didn't work out," I said, offering my most serious expression. "Theodore was allergic."

"Bummer." Ray retrieved his cookie and took another bite.

I sipped my steamy mug of apple cinnamon tea and grinned.

We each had a bingo card before us. A little bucket of red and white striped mints sat at the table's center. The mints were meant to be chips for the game, but Ray had eaten two since he'd sat down, and put another in his hot chocolate.

As promised, I'd brought a box of finished jewelry orders, packing lists, and envelopes to prepare for shipping. I'd made it clear on my website that I couldn't guarantee delivery in time for the holiday at this point, but I thought it was worth a try. Anything I finished tonight might still make it with overnight shipping. There were three more days until Christmas Eve. Regardless, it would be nice to get ahead on work and come back from my honeymoon to as few backorders as possible.

"How can I help?" Ray asked, tracking Libby visually around the room. He casually pushed the sleeves of his nicely fitting black V-neck sweater up his forearms.

Libby noticed and stared every time she bustled past, hazel eyes flicking from his sweater and forearms to his face before her cheeks went repeatedly pink.

I shook my head and stifled a smile, because Ray wasn't playing fair, and he didn't even have a clue.

"What?" he asked, returning his eyes to mine when Libby was out of sight again.

"Just making a plan to knock these out tonight." I lifted the box into view, then stowed it back on the seat at my side. "If I stack the products and packing slips on the pre-addressed envelopes, will you stuff and seal them for me?"

He pulled a ready pile across the table to him and watched me as he packed it up. "Like this?"

"That's all there is to it. Now, pull the strip off the adhesive and fold the flap over to seal it. Give it an extra pinch so all my hard work won't fall out somewhere between here and Timbuktu."

He made a show of gripping and releasing the sealed end, smoothing a palm over it on the table, then turning the envelope upside down for a shake.

"You're so extra," I said, fighting a laugh. "When all the orders are packed, we can put them back in the box, and I'll run them to the post office tomorrow."

"I can take them with me," he said. "I live in town, so getting there is easier for me than you. And I don't mind," he added. "You're getting married in, like, five minutes. Let me help."

"Fine. I accept, but I want to reciprocate when I can, so don't be shy."

His attention was back on the redheaded server. "Have you talked to Libby?"

"Yeah," I said, mind immediately conjuring images of the latest threat on my truck. "Have you?"

Was my truck some kind of threat magnet? Or did driving a giant red pickup with a Rudolph nose and antlers just make it easy for criminals to find me? Maybe switching vehicles would reduce the number of mean notes and mutilated rubber rodents I received. Then again, with my luck, the same stuff would just show up at my door.

"We haven't spoken since the ballet," Ray said, interrupting my reverie. "But she invited me over tonight after her shift. That's good. Right?"

"Right," I said, warmed by his hopeful expression and her willingness to open up more fully. If these two lovebirds sorted things out, Evan and I could be attending Libby and Ray's wedding next year.

He pushed long fingers through the hair slowly drying across his forehead. "How's Evan holding up?"

"Okay," I said. "All things considered. The threat on my truck didn't improve his stability, but you know—par for the course."

"What threat?" he asked. "The rats?"

"No." Though he hadn't loved those either. I flipped my phone over on the table and brought up the image of the note. "I forgot I haven't talked to you since it happened." I turned the screen to face him. "Libby will tell you more about this tonight, I'm sure. But we were shopping together, and when we got back to the truck this was there."

His eyes widened, then narrowed, and his lips parted. "First," he said. "We've been sitting here for thirty minutes. You should've led with this. And second, you should've called as soon as it happened. Why am I suddenly the guy no one talks to?"

"You're not," I said. "Everything's just upside down right now, and we called Evan first."

He scratched one eyebrow, not appearing appeased. "Wait." His eyes met mine again. "You were with Libby when this threat came?"

"Yeah."

"So, was it meant for you or her?"

I lifted and dropped a palm. "That's the million-dollar question," I said. "Evan asked the same thing, but it hadn't crossed my mind it might be for her until he said something."

"And now?"

"Now I'm not so sure. The ballet-related threats seem to come in the form of rubber rats. I'd just taken Libby away from a stakeout at the Cap and Kerchief, where she thought she saw that teal car again. And the wording of the note could go either way."

"Did Evan ever figure out who was sending those cards? Or at least get a lead?"

I shook my head, and he turned his eyes back to the image on my phone. "This looks like an old-timey serial killer made it."

I grimaced. "That's what I said. Let's hope we're wrong."

He released my phone. "Now what?"

"Evan's speaking with Boston PD. Trying to sort the ballerina threats and finish his wedding to-do list in the next three days."

"Anyone stand out to you? Someone you think is capable of all this?"

"I'm not sure. The ballerinas are a closed-off group. The dancers staying at the inn barely talk to me. It's like they're in full concentration mode all the time. Evan and the deputies have interviewed most of them at this point, I think. I suspected Ian for a while—the one playing the Mouse King—because he's rude and icky and has a connection to the rats, but that isn't panning out." Mostly because Evan thought he was too obvious. I still hated that Ian had left our conversation the moment I'd taken my eyes off him backstage. I had more questions.

"Who else?"

I puffed my cheeks, releasing a labored breath. "There's the mystery blogger, Courtney. She's a possibility, though there's no way to find or question her. And the understudy is out, since she was threatened." My head tipped toward one shoulder as I grew more pensive. "Then there's George. I've been looking at the other possibilities, but my thoughts keep circling back to him."

"The ballet master?"

I nodded. "Tiffany snuck out the night before she died, maybe to meet someone. Maybe him. He was downtown instead of at the theater when she died. He had access to her and her food. She wouldn't have questioned the contents of a protein shake from her choreographer and trainer.

"Or possible lover," Ray added.

I made a mental note to research the side effects of cyanide poisoning, then passed him another set of jewelry orders. "We saw George leave during the performance the other night, right before the rats were left for Ava. And we know there was a hidden entrance to Tiffany's room. He could've used that to be with Tiffany without anyone knowing, when they wanted to be alone. And he could've used it to deliver the rats."

Ray unwrapped another mint from the bucket and popped it into his mouth. "The footprints in that passageway were big too. Had to be made by a grown man."

"'Ello!" Cookie crooned into the microphone, creating a peal of feedback. She adjusted the volume and chuckled. "Let's try that again, shall we?" Her accent was delightfully inconsistent, as always.

I grinned and waved.

People stared.

"All righty then. Welcome to Holiday Bingo! I'm Cookie Cutter, and I'll be your hostess, game caller, and entertainment tonight. So get your cards and markers ready, and let's start rollin'!"

Ray gave a small smirk and placed a mint on the free space at the center of his board.

I pushed more orders and envelopes in his direction.

"So you think George is the killer?" Ray asked.

"Maybe."

"Let's explore that," he said, beginning to stuff and seal the envelopes. "What's his motive?"

I wrinkled my nose. "It's always the lover?"

He shook his head. "Got anything else?"

"Not really. Unless she was also involved with Ian, and George had a fit of jealousy."

Ray seemed to consider the theory. "Okay, running with that. Why would he then harass the other ballerina?"

I pursed my lips, still stumped.

"B-ten," Cookie called. "B for my favorite clock tower, Big Ben. Ten for all the stars I would give the architect."

Guests went to work, exchanging curious looks and soft giggles.

I put a mint on my card, then matched up another order, packing list, and envelope. "I saw him go into Tiffany's room the other day before everyone else was awake," I said. "He knew I saw him."

Ray's brows rose. "What did he do?"

"He claimed to have been looking for a jacket; then he went out for a walk." And I hadn't seen him return. I'd been having breakfast with Evan when the dancers left for the day. I hadn't seen George again until that night.

"What happens when the show ends and the ballet leaves town?" Ray asked, crushing the mint with his teeth.

"I don't know. I guess Evan will continue to work the clues from here. He can always reach out if he needs more information."

Ray stretched back on his seat. "Sounds like he needs to wrap this up in the next few days, or his odds of closing this case go to squat."

"Pretty much," I said.

And a killer would get away with murder.

Chapter Sixteen

Caroline appeared at the door a short while later, and I waved her over. She stripped off her coat as she made a beeline for our table. Her dark-wash jeans and cable-knit sweater were the picture of casual cool. She'd coordinated the outfit with tan ankle boots and the red gumdrop earrings I'd made her last Christmas. "Sorry I'm late." She hung the coat on a hook at the edge of the booth then took a seat beside Ray. The sides of her hair were pulled back with bobby pins, and she looked like she belonged on the cover of a holiday magazine for Christmas chic. "I changed outfits ten times, and my hair wouldn't cooperate. It's been a day."

"We're just glad you're here," I said warmly, but I was wondering what had gotten her worked up. It wasn't like Caroline to lack confidence in the hair or wardrobe department, but maybe it'd been a tough week all around.

Cookie waved from the podium.

Caroline blew her a kiss.

"I-thirty-one!" Cookie called.

"I love when she does the accent," Caroline said. "It confuses the daylights out of tourists when they come into our shop after this, and she sounds completely different. Sometimes they mention it; most of the time they don't."

Ray wrinkled his brow. "What does she tell them when they ask?"

Caroline stole a mint from the bowl, further depleting our resources. "That she likes to class things up when she can." Her lips curved into a small smile. "So?" she asked. "Today was your final dress fitting."

I grinned. It's been a good day all around. "Fits like a glove. It's hanging in my closet now. All I have to do is manage not to ruin it, and maybe one day I can pass it down like Mom and Grandma did."

Caroline stomped her feet under the table and covered her mouth with both hands to stifle a squeal of delight.

I bit the insides of my cheeks, fighting the urge to do the same. Instead, I paired my last jewelry order with its packing list, then stuffed both into a corresponding envelope and placed it back into the box for shipping.

Ray noticed and picked up his pace until he'd finished his stack as well.

Hooray for friends and progress. I mentally checked the task off my to-do list, then moved his completed envelopes into the box as well.

Libby arrived at our table and grinned. She'd held true to her promise and ditched the wigs. Her red waves ran free over her shoulders, and her usual uniform of long-sleeved T-shirt with the Reindeer Games logo, jeans, and sneakers was back in place. "Hey, Caroline. What can I get you?"

"Salted caramel hot chocolate and a basket of wedding cookies for the table," she answered without missing a beat.

"Coming right up." Libby's gaze moved briefly to Ray and his forearms before she turned and headed for the counter.

Caroline followed Libby's not so sneaky glance and set a hand on her collarbone. "My, my, Mr. Griggs." She lowered the fingers to his arm and squeezed. "Be careful with these things, lest your poor lady collapse in a swoon."

"What?"

I laughed.

Ray wrinkled his brow and looked from me to Caroline and back. "What?" he repeated.

Caroline offered a sad smile. "You poor, sweet man. Just keep doing this." She motioned to his air-dried, fluffy hair; the sweater; the arms. "And you'll be just fine."

Ray ate another mint, looking unsure if we were serious or teasing him. And not in any mood to find out.

Libby loaded sweets into a basket behind the counter. Mom's Mexican wedding cookies were the best I'd ever eaten. Like with most of the items on the menu, she started with a traditional recipe, then put her own special spin on it—in this case by adding dashes of cinnamon and nutmeg to the buttery pecan treat.

Caroline shifted, crossing her legs beneath the table and leaving Ray alone. "I can't stay long, but I've been craving those cookies all day. How's Evan holding up?"

I made a mental note to circle back and ask where she was hurrying off to, but she'd successfully warmed and distracted me with her question. I loved that my friends worried about Evan. Especially since he'd felt like an outsider when we met. Now he had his own little crew. My crew. And it struck me with joy whenever I thought of it. "He's Evan," I said. "He's managing. Determined. On edge and exhausted, but this is his sweet spot. Every time I'm sure he's had all he can take, he has a breakthrough."

Caroline bobbed her head. "Hopefully he gets there fast, because the ballet is leaving soon."

Ray lifted and dropped a palm on the table. "That's what I said."

Caroline's blue eyes caught mine. "How mad is he that you're meddling again? I don't want you two fighting before your big day."

I sipped my cider, thinking of how I would answer. Evan hated when I looked into cases like this, because the process usually put me in danger, and he always wanted me safe, but we'd slowly come to an understanding. "I think he accepted his fate before the proposal," I said lightly. "Unyielding curiosity is probably not his favorite quality of mine, but no one's perfect. And I've accepted that he's much nicer if I keep him informed as I go, so I'm working on that. It's going more smoothly this time. Turns out that when I'm not sneaking around to accomplish things, and he provides me with a little feedback, we make a pretty good team."

Libby returned with Caroline's cookies and cocoa. "I'll be back to chat when I can," she said, sliding the mug and basket onto the table before zipping away.

"I wish I knew how to help her," I said, trailing Libby with my gaze as she moved on to the next table. "I don't know what to make of her situation, but I know it's not good, and I hope the note on my truck wasn't meant for her."

"Me too," Caroline said, eyelids fluttering as she sipped her rich chocolate and caramel drink.

Ray balked, staring at our friend as she drank. "You know about the note?"

She set the mug down slowly, looking deeply satisfied and a little irritated at Ray for ruining her hot cocoa moment. "Sure. Holly sent me a photo."

Ray slid his eyes to me.

I cringed. "She messaged me while I was waiting in the truck for Evan to arrive, so it was on my mind."

Caroline turned to Ray. "What's your plan?"

"What do you mean?"

"To protect Libby," she said. "I know you have something cooked up in that big head of yours."

"She invited him over after her shift," I said.

"Oh?" Caroline wagged her brows. "That sounds promising."

Ray twisted on his seat, resting his back against the wall and facing Caroline more directly. "I'm hoping we clear everything up, and she takes me back when I finish begging, because I want to stay the night."

Caroline choked on the cookie she'd just put into her mouth. "What?"

"Not like that," he scolded. "I mean I want to stay over and help keep watch. For as long as it takes for Evan to find the person tormenting her and arrest them."

I smiled at the powdered sugar stuck to Caroline's lip gloss and blanketing the area around her mug. Her sudden cough had sent half the coating from her cookie all over the table. "I'm sure she'll understand and accommodate you," I said. "She grew up with a protective older brother. She'll want you to feel comfortable, and if that means keeping watch over her, so be it."

"I hope you're right," he said. "Because if she kicks me out, I might sleep in my truck outside her place. I can't stand the thought of someone wanting to hurt Libby, let alone actually getting their hands on her."

Caroline and I reached out to him in unison, patting his fingers on the table.

He looked mildly uncomfortable at our mothering and turned his eyes to Caroline. "Where are you rushing off to? Already planning to leave before you sat down. That's curious. Isn't it, Holly? Or do you already know what she's got planned?"

I shook my head. "I do not, and thank you for reminding me."

Caroline's cheeks darkened. "Don't read too much into this, because it's just coffee, and definitely no big deal, but—"

I leaned forward, eyes widening with her every unprompted protest.

"Ooooh," Ray cooed, steepling his fingertips beneath his chin. "Dramatic pause? What's this?"

I pressed my lips together to keep from smiling.

The red in Caroline's cheeks spread over her entire face and down her neck. "I'm meeting Zane later for a very casual, friendly get-together—nothing more."

Ray mouthed the word *Wow*. "Zane, the security guy?"

"It's just coffee," she said, repeating her prior protest and not answering the direct question.

I bit the insides of my cheeks to stifle a smile. "So you said."

She slid her lips together over the shiny gloss. "Not that it matters at all, because our meet-up is genuinely nothing, but I thought he was really nice. Didn't you?"

"He was handsome," I said. Not to mention incredibly fit and slightly mysterious, meaning not from Mistletoe, so we didn't know everything about him, which would make locals nervous.

"We don't know anything about him," Ray argued, and I nearly laughed.

We Mistletoe folks were so predictable.

Her dad was sure to hate him. So, that was a vote in his favor from me.

Caroline frowned. "Evan hired him as extra security for the month, which means he would've vetted him before inviting him into town. I assume anyone who gets a green light from our sheriff is at the very least not a known criminal or outwardly ridiculous in some way. Zane made it through the interview process, so if he is a terrible person, he's also conniving enough to fool Evan, but I don't think many people do."

I looked from her to Ray. "That's true."

"And he was so cute," she said. "Those dreamy gray eyes and that strong jaw."

Ray made a nauseous face.

"Bingo!" someone called.

I started, having forgotten anything was happening outside our little booth. Compartmentalization was becoming a strong suit of mine.

"Please don't be weird about this," Caroline said. "I haven't been on a real date in years. Dinners and appearances arranged by my dad for publicity, yes. An outing requested directly by a man with interest in me as a woman? No. Not in an eternity. So I want this to go well."

I felt her need for connection from across the table. Caroline wanted a partner in life just like I always had, and dating in a small town where her father was a control-obsessed political figure made meeting new people organically nearly impossible. "Won't he leave in a few days?" I asked carefully, because when Christmas was over, her life would still be here. Unchanged. And this man, who she might really like by then, would be gone.

It begged the question: Was it better to hit it off with someone on his way out of town? Or to never hit it off at all?

Caroline shrugged. "He only lives about forty-five minutes outside Mistletoe. He commutes."

A round of applause rose through the café, and Cookie passed a giant cellophane-wrapped cutout cookie to a woman in a blue and white snowman sweater. The woman raised her prize overhead like a champion and powered on her light-up reindeer antler headband.

"Congratulate our winner!" Cookie cheered. "Then clear your boards if you're ready for some more!"

"I think that's my cue," Caroline said, finishing her hot chocolate and rising to her feet. "I'm going to run home and change."

"You changed ten times before you came," I said, repeating her words from earlier.

Worry strained her pretty features. "Maybe you're right, and this is pointless. I should cancel."

"Nope." Ray shook his head and grabbed her wrist. "You were excited when you came in here, and we ruined it." He looked to me.

I made my most apologetic face. "He's right. We should've said congratulations and asked you to tell us everything instead of putting a big gray cloud on your happiness."

"You didn't," she started.

"We did," I said. "And that's on us. Can we start over? Do you have five more minutes?"

She looked to Ray, who offered her a snickerdoodle. She accepted, and a smile curved her lips. "Okay." She retook her seat, a grin forming instantly.

"Tell us everything," I said.

Ray kicked back once more. "How'd your friendly coffee appointment get scheduled?"

"Zane asked if he could call me on the night we met. I gave him my number, and he texted before I got home. He said it was nice to meet me, and he asked how long I'd lived here. That was it. We've been texting casually since then. He stopped into the cupcake shop on his lunch break yesterday and brought me a cup of my favorite vanilla soy latte from the Busy Bean. I'd mentioned it in one of our exchanges, and he remembered.

"He's funny, sweet, and thoughtful. He thinks I'm smart and strong. He's told me I'm beautiful, but not as often as he tells me how amazing he thinks it is that I went after what I wanted and opened Caroline's Cupcakes. Even when it meant defying my folks, who are basically Mistletoe royalty.

"He thinks chasing our dreams and pursuing our callings is important. And that it takes a big brain and lots of fortitude to make a new business succeed. He wants to open a private security firm one day. He was in the military, and he liked protecting people. So, after he came home, he started taking jobs like this one, to build a network and more experience in the civilian sector."

I found myself nodding along. Everyone told Caroline she was gorgeous, because she was, and appearances meant everything to her family. Not enough people saw past that, and I instantly appreciated Zane for the way he'd reminded her of things she never seemed to let sink in when we told her. "I noticed him watching Evan closely at the parade's crime scene. I wondered what that was about."

Caroline nodded. "He mentioned that! He said he admired the way Evan took charge and handled things. He knew what to do, and everyone respected him by falling in line. He said it marked a real leader, and he wanted that, except not as a lawman, because he doesn't want to be held to the same level of accountability as a deputy or sheriff." Her cheeks flushed again, and her grin widened. "He wants to be able to go a little rogue, as needed."

And there it was. She saw the handsome stranger as dangerous, and that had been one of her dream-guy requirements.

She illuminated as she told us everything she could remember about Zane, and there was something in her voice that said so much more. The tone and cadence of her words spoke to my heart because I sounded like that sometimes too. When I talked about Evan.

She and Zane hadn't known one another for very long, but I suspected they'd made the kind of connection that caused a person to second-guess their every life choice, because suddenly their world has tilted. Expanded. To make room for one more.

It might've been far too soon to think so, but I also suspected this "not-a-date" was going to end in one of two ways. Either we'd reference this conversation in a toast at their wedding reception one day, or Caroline was going to be gutted when it ended in any other scenario.

"Anyway," she said, looking more than a little embarrassed for saying as much as she had. "I really think he's nice, and I want to get to know him."

Ray tipped his head in her direction, eyes fixed on mine. He recognized the tone too.

I nodded.

"We get it," he told her, eyes moving back to Libby. "If things go well tonight, you should invite him to tomorrow's reindeer game. Give us a chance to get to know him too."

Caroline's brows rose. "Yeah?"

I smiled, and she looked as if she'd won the lottery.

Caroline stayed until bingo ended, then slipped out with a broad smile and her fingers literally crossed.

Ray and I stayed straight through Carol Karaoke. We watched countless tourists, young and old, get hopped up on sugar, don costume pieces from Cookie's prop trunk onstage, and bellow all their holiday favorites.

It was a pretty terrific night.

I kissed Mom and Dad on their cheeks at closing time and walked with Ray and Libby to the halfway point between my house and hers.

"You okay to finish the trip on your own?" Ray asked. "We can walk you there before heading to Libby's place, if you want."

I swept my attention to the guesthouse across from the inn. It was close enough to see, but still a several-minute walk. Maybe a football field's length. A narrow road looped between the structures, with light poles illuminating a large area near each of our front porches.

"No, I've got this," I said.

"We'll still keep an eye out," Libby promised. "Is Evan coming over after work?"

"Thanks. I'm not sure, but if he does, he'll find me wrapping toys in that creepy serial-killer paper."

Libby cringed. "Literally. I will never look at a toy alphabet block the same way again."

She and I both.

In fact, maybe I'd just put the toys in gift bags.

Chapter Seventeen

I woke with the sun the next day, exhausted from a restless night's sleep and too many pressing things on my mind. I shuffled through the quiet inn on socked feet, preparing a tray with a tea service before carrying it to my office. I sipped and scrolled on my phone for long minutes, perusing Courtney's Bun Heads blog and attempting to process the few details I knew about Tiffany's murder before the ballerinas and George made their morning appearances.

Evan had called to say goodnight long before I'd fallen asleep, and he'd let me know the official coroner's report was in. As predicted, Tiffany's cause of death was poisoning. And toxicology reports had confirmed cyanide as the culprit and her fruity protein shake, the vessel.

The newest information was the most interesting. Based on the full autopsy and blood workup, it seemed as if Tiffany had received more than one dose of cyanide. In fact, she might've ingested smaller doses for several days before finally succumbing to the poison.

My thoughts had run immediately to George. He'd mentioned Tiffany's recent complaints of headaches, dizziness, weakness, and fatigue—all signs of a professional dancer running on a low tank of food and sleep, but also, I'd learned, symptoms of cyanide poisoning.

How long had those symptoms been occurring? How long had she complained? Only on the morning she died? Or had this been going on since before her arrival in Mistletoe? How many poisoned protein shakes had she consumed?

Related questions piled higher from there. Where did someone get cyanide? What exactly had gone into her protein shakes? Was the killer wearing a medieval ring with a secret poison compartment, like a cartoon villain? Had the killer purchased capsules online, like those ones television spies cracked between their teeth to avoid divulging state secrets?

The ballerinas used my blender every day. Should I toss it? Could cyanide withstand the dishwasher?

I'd had a multitude of fruits and vegetables delivered by courier at the start of their stay, courtesy of our mayor. I'd seen the dancers mix packets of powders into the fruit, along with plain yogurt, almond milk, and ice. Was the fruit poisoned? Or was the poison in the packets? And if all the women used the same products, and one of the foods was tainted, wouldn't all the dancers fall ill? Or worse?

They hadn't, which meant Tiffany's shakes had been targeted.

But how?

It didn't take long for me to find an interesting article online about cyanide and apple seeds. I read it twice for good measure, because apples were a popular ingredient in the smoothies being made in my kitchen. According to the internet, apple seeds contained tiny levels of cyanide. An adult person would have to consume between 150 and thousands to die, but given Tiffany's petite size, and the fact she might've been consuming them for a while, the mass of fruits in my refrigerator suddenly felt a little ominous.

Cindy Lou Who leaped onto my desk, and I squeaked. She knocked her head roughly against mine.

Stalking Around the Christmas Tree

"Goodness. Ow." I scratched behind her ears. "I love you too, but you need to give me a little warning. I nearly had six consecutive strokes."

She leaped down and headed for the kitchen, pausing outside my office doors to see if I was coming.

"There's food in your bowl," I said.

She glared.

Sometimes I daydreamed about adopting a cat who'd covet my attention and lie all over my desk, maybe snuggle in my lap, like all the lovely cats online. Then I remembered Cindy Lou Who would probably eat that cat and move on.

The sounds of shuffling feet and quiet voices drew Cindy's attention to the stairs. I felt my muscles stiffen as dancers bounded into the kitchen.

I listened intently as my single-serve coffee maker whirred and brewed. The refrigerator doors opened and closed. And the blender pulverized fruits and veggies.

One of the members of this ballet troupe, or the obsessed social media influencer associated with its dancers, was a killer and roaming free in Mistletoe. Someone had to stop them.

The thought was almost as unsettling as the fact that the ballet would all be gone tomorrow. The dancers. The crew. The choreographer. And the guilty party would become infinitely more likely to get away with these crimes.

George appeared in the foyer and knocked softly on my door frame. "Excuse me."

I tensed, forcing a too-bright smile that likely appeared maniacal or fully unhinged given my frame of mind. "Good morning."

He tried and failed to smile back. His pale skin and long face seemed more pronounced today than before. He was still dressed in head-to-toe black and appeared somehow smaller.

"What can I do for you?" I prompted when his gaze became distant and he didn't speak again.

"Sorry." He squinted and gave his head a little shake. "The dancers are doing some press this morning in preparation for our final performance tonight," he said. "Normally, I buy them flowers." Regret flashed over his increasingly gloomy features. "I wondered if there's somewhere I can order five bouquets for delivery to the theater and a couple dozen individual long-stemmed roses as well."

"I can handle that for you," I said.

"I would appreciate it. My card's on file with the reservations. I listed the number for incidentals. You can charge the flowers to that. I'll bill the conservatory when we get home."

"No problem." I reduced the size of my smile to something more compassionate and less perky.

George was clearly distraught, and I could only hope his reason was the loss of a dancer, and not guilt over her murder.

The front door swung open in a burst, sending a whoosh of icy air through the foyer and straightening George with a shiver.

Cookie appeared on the welcome mat, pushing the door shut behind her. She set a load of bags at her feet. "Morning!" she said, stomping snow from her boots and unwinding the thick wool scarf from her neck. "It's a doozy out there this morning. Roads are slick. The crews are on it, but give yourself a little extra time," she told George. "Theodore nearly did the splits on the walk from my car."

George lifted a hand in acceptance and walked away.

Cookie spotted me and grinned. "Hello! Hello! Are you ready for your big day?"

The sense of dread I'd felt when speaking with George washed away at the reminder of my coming wedding. "One hundred percent. Only two days to go."

Cookie rolled her eyes. "Not that," she said. "I meant the bridal luncheon. I'm here to help set up. Your mom, Caroline, and Libby are on their way, and we're going to do as much prep work as we can before the Hearth and cupcake shop open. Then we'll meet back here around noon for the party. I sure hope the farmhands can get the lot cleared before then. We got another four inches last night."

My heart fluttered, and a strange set of tingles raced over my arms as I gave her bags another look. I'd completely forgotten about the luncheon, but it was exactly what I needed to recenter myself on the things that mattered. "What can I do to help?" I asked, pushing onto my feet as Cookie shucked off her coat and plucked the snow-covered cap from her head.

She wore a nice knit dress that reached her calves. The front was designed to look like an elf in red and gold. The pattern stopped at the neckline, leaving Cookie's smiling face and crown of white hair to finish the character. Even her dark tights and black boots matched the cartoon figure. "Nothing. What do you think of my new dress?" she asked. "I found it at the thrift store! I can't imagine anyone wanting to give this away, but it's mine now."

"Love it," I said. "I wish I knew what I should wear."

She puckered her brow. "I don't suppose you have anything like this?"

I shook my head.

"I didn't think so. This is really one of a kind, but it's too bad. We could've been twins. Only thing better than one elf dress is two."

"So true," I said. "Can I get you some coffee?"

"No thanks. I'm ready to get to work. I left Theodore at the barn with the horses. He needed a little break from all this wife hunting. It's beginning to take a toll."

"It's not going well?"

She sighed. "No one has been quite right for him. But we've got high hopes this year's calendar will draw in some real quality ladies. I'd hate to think I got ordained for nothing."

I leaned against my desk, delighted by the topic at hand. Theodore's calendars were always a hit, and since Cookie gave the proceeds to charity, it made an already good thing even better. "Oh yeah? Are you doing anything different this time?"

"Yep. Ray's touching up some of the initial shots this afternoon. He thinks we can get the products printed in time for the new year. We'll miss Christmas, which is too bad, but Theodore and I got sidetracked with all those indecent proposals."

"The requests for stud service?" I asked, making sure I was keeping up.

She blushed. "Can you believe folks would just come out and ask a thing like that?"

I could, because I'd spent my share of time around farmers and livestock, but Cookie walked a thin line with Theodore. Sometimes I wasn't sure she knew he was a goat. Other times, I wasn't sure she knew goats were animals. Regardless of how she thought of him, Theodore was family, and I supposed it would be rude for someone to ask one of my family members for stud service.

The front door opened again, and Caroline darted inside, shaking snow from her coat and hair. She pulled a small canvas-sided wagon behind her, like she was a little league mom on snack duty. A multitude of bags and boxes tipped precariously as the transport rocked to a stop.

"Hello!" She hung her coat on a hook near the door, then took Cookie's coat and hat and did the same with them. "How are you?"

"Good." Cookie and I chorused, leaning forward to hug our guest.

"I was just telling Holly about Theodore's wife hunt," Cookie said.

I nudged her with an elbow. "Now we have to ask Caroline about her big date."

Cookie's mouth opened. "I didn't know you had a date."

Caroline blushed furiously as she glanced toward the bustling kitchen, then moved into my office to chat. "Because it wasn't a *date*, and I wasn't telling anyone until I knew if he was worth the bother."

"And?" I asked.

She gave a deep dramatic sigh and clutched her hands at her chest. "He's divine, and I'm a goner."

Knew it.

"Who?" Cookie asked.

"Zane Archer." Caroline spoke his name like a teenager sharing the name of her favorite musician or film star. "He's kind and smart and loves all the most important things. His family's in politics too, so he knows what my life has been like. No one ever understands that."

"Really?" I asked, my cynical side breaking through. "His family's in politics?" What were the odds?

She nodded. "His mom was the governor."

"Of Maine?" I asked, voice squeaking. "Seriously?"

Her smile widened. "Yeah. She started as a PTA president in their little district when Zane was small, then got involved in the local chamber of commerce when he played middle school sports. She was mayor for a while and parlayed that into a seat as governor while he was in high school and college, but she retired last term when her husband got sick."

"Zane's dad?"

"No." Caroline's expression lit. "His dad left when he was small, which is terrible, but his mom did everything on her own, and now he's all about female empowerment because he saw what she overcame. He knows what women are capable of, and he sees all the inequalities so many people—like my dad—pretend don't exist. He's so proud of her. Also unlike my dad, Zane's mom supported him when he wanted a military career. She didn't complain or care when he was discharged and wanted to work in private protection either."

Cookie reared her head back. "I like him already!"

"Me too," Caroline said, a note of misery in her tone. "I just hope he feels the same."

"If he doesn't, he's a nitwit and you dodged a bullet," Cookie said.

Caroline's smile returned. "Well, if he does, he'll have to survive my father's utter disapproval. It might've been different if his mom had stayed in office, but now he's just another potential suitor who won't add leverage to Dad's campaigns. He'll probably have Zane thoroughly investigated the minute he hears about our date."

I knew she was right and hated it for her. I couldn't imagine not being allowed to choose my own dates or having to worry someone asked me out for unscrupulous reasons, like an inside scoop on one of my parents or a leg up in society. "I thought you were meeting at the cupcake shop after hours," I said.

"We did, but he invited me to dinner at the Bistro tonight."

"Your dad will definitely hear about that," I said.

She frowned. "I know."

"Well," I said, hoping to see her smile return, "I think it's safe to say he likes you. Anyone who wasn't interested wouldn't have asked you out again or remembered your favorite latte just so he could surprise you with it."

Her expression softened, and so did my heart.

"We'd better talk while we work," Cookie said. "Time's getting away, and we've got decorating to do."

Caroline waved as she followed Cookie into the formal dining space that was more for show than actual use. I didn't cook at the inn, so beyond the occasional small event or book club meeting, I only went inside the room to dust and sweep. "I have the rest in my car," she said as Cookie pulled the pocket doors closed behind them.

I grabbed a towel from my office and tossed it onto the floor, then used a foot to remove the watery tire tracks left by Caroline's wagon.

Excitement for the luncheon slowly built in my chest. Not only would I soon be surrounded by all my favorite women, but the luncheon signified the nearness of the wedding, and that made me want to dance.

The doorbell rang, and I went to answer. I played a silent guessing game on my way through the foyer. It was early, and no one close to me ever knocked or rang the bell. All my inn guests were in the kitchen. That left a possible delivery or a member of the farm crew who didn't want to come inside but had a message to convey.

I was wrong on both counts.

A uniformed deputy I recognized as Deputy Mars stood on the porch. "Ma'am," he said, tapping a fingertip to the brim of his hat. "Morning, Holly. I'm here to collect the remainder of Tiffany Krieg's things for her family."

I opened the door widely to let him pass. "I thought you'd already collected her things."

"We took several items as potential evidence but left the remainder."

I glanced down the hallway toward the kitchen. I'd been in Tiffany's room after spotting George in there a couple of days back, and I hadn't noticed any of her things.

As if on cue, George strode into view, a cup of something steamy in his hand. He stopped at the sight of the deputy.

"Deputy Mars is here for Tiffany's things," I said, watching closely for his response.

The deputy moved past me, hand outstretched. "Nice to meet you . . ."

"George."

"George," Mars repeated. "You're one of the dancers?"

"A choreographer. I moved Tiffany's things to my room." He tipped his head toward the steps and led Deputy Mars to the next floor.

I gaped after them. Why would he have done that? Was he even allowed to move her things?

I went to my desk and grabbed my phone, then texted Evan details on the exchange.

Small bouncing dots appeared onscreen immediately, and I relaxed. Evan was responding.

Evan: *It's fine. We took what we needed earlier.*
Evan: *Forget that and try to enjoy your luncheon.*
Evan: *Love you!*

I stared at the screen, then sent another text: *How'd you know about the luncheon?*

Evan: *Caroline sends me push notifications with daily wedding calendar updates.*

I grinned.

Me: *I'll send pics. Love you too.*

The ballerinas headed back upstairs as a pack, getting their things together and preparing for another day at the theater.

Stalking Around the Christmas Tree

I waved goodbye as the deputy tipped his hat on his way out.

George stood alone at the bottom of the staircase, staring blankly at the closing door. He turned away slowly a moment later and returned to the kitchen.

I rose from my desk and beetled after him.

I'd expected to find him refreshing his drink, but he set the mug on the counter and walked through the back door, sans coat.

I grabbed my parka from the hook and followed.

His gaze darted to mine when I opened the door. A look of exhaustion crossed his pinched face.

"Just me," I said. "Sorry to interrupt your . . ." I waved a hand, but left the sentence hanging, unsure what he was doing in the cold without a coat.

"I just needed a minute before returning to professional choreographer mode," he said. "I know how much these performances mean to the dancers. It's their final rehearsal before the big show back home, but I'm tired."

I frowned at the reminder that Mistletoe's big event was little more than practice time for this particular group. Then I refocused and pressed on. "Everything okay?" I inched casually closer. I had a question or two, and the group was leaving tomorrow. This was possibly my last chance to speak privately with him.

He eyeballed me. "I wanted a moment alone," he said more slowly, as if I'd somehow missed his message the first time.

"I won't keep you long," I promised. "I was just hoping to ask you a few things."

He shook his head. "You ask a lot of question. Anyone ever told you that?"

"What do you mean?" I was a generally curious person, but I'd barely asked George anything. I'd hardly even spoken to him, if I didn't count the morning of the parade, the time I'd caught him in Tiffany's room, and when he'd asked me to order flowers.

His brows tented in a supreme get-real expression. "I mean you're everywhere, and you're always asking questions. Downtown at the parade. Backstage at the show. At the café. The pie shop. The fudge place. I thought it would be nice to do a little shopping for my family one afternoon, but everywhere I went, there you were, asking more questions about Tiffany's death, when all I wanted was a moment's reprieve from the constant reminders. Don't you have anything better to do? Aren't you getting married?"

I gasped openly, then attempted to school my features. "How do you know that?"

"Oh, I don't know," he said, sarcasm mixing with the obvious irritation. "Maybe because I've spent five minutes in this town, and that's all it takes."

I frowned, unclear what he was getting at.

"Come on," he said, looking as if I'd grown an extra head. "You have to know. Your wedding is all everyone is talking about. It's a more popular topic than Tiffany's murder. And she died on a parade float in front of everyone!" His voice ratcheted up a few decibels, and his tone hardened.

I took a step back, gaze flicking to the door behind me and considered how long it might take to reach it if needed. Or whether Cookie and Caroline would hear me scream.

A choked, grunting sound turned me back in George's direction, hands raised in defense.

He'd crumpled onto a snow-covered patio chair, elbows resting on his knees, hands cradling his face. The moan that escaped was something like the noise Cindy Lu Who made when she brought me a dead bird or mole.

"George?"

"Go away," he croaked miserably. "Just give me this moment of peace I need before I have to go pretend the only thing that matters in life is ballet. Just. Give. Me. This."

I teetered, because I had manners. But also questions.

"Can I get you anything?" I offered. "I can ask one of the farmhands to drive the dancers to the theater in the transport so you can have more time."

He lifted his head on a labored sigh and rubbed long fingers against his temples, then fixed me with a placid expression. "Just ask whatever it is that's keeping you there. Then go."

I pulled my lips to the side, debating for a moment. "What do you know about Courtney?" I asked, unable to pass up an opportunity.

"The blogger?"

I nodded.

"She's some online personality obsessed with Tiffany."

"Have you ever seen her?" I asked.

He shook his head. "As far as I know, no one has ever seen her. Why?"

"I'm not sure," I admitted. "It bothers me that she's been silent since Tiffany's death."

"I think we're all just . . . stunned." He shook his head, as if the very possibility one of his dancers had died was simply beyond his comprehension. "She was too young. Too strong and fit. She wasn't doing anything dangerous or wrong. And she's just—" He turned tortured eyes to mine, peering pathetically from beneath a brush of thick, dark lashes, cheeks pink for more reasons than the relentless cold.

Then I saw it. The same look I'd seen in Caroline's eyes when she'd verbalized the possibility that Zane didn't like her back. George was in love with Tiffany. It was there in the deep lines around his sunken features and on his lips, if not in so many words.

I steeled my nerve, needing confirmation and deciding on the direct approach. "How long were you romantically involved with Tiffany Krieg?"

His mouth opened, then snapped shut. The red in his cheeks spread over his face, and his jaw clenched. He didn't speak, didn't deny it.

"Did you love her?" I asked.

George swung his tortured expression away and nodded. "Yes."

Chapter Eighteen

A shiver rocked down my spine. This was the exact scenario I'd discussed with Ray. But we hadn't worked out George's motive for murder. Was it jealousy? Betrayal? Had Tiffany been wooed by Ian's good looks and overconfidence? Was that the reason behind the rats? I'd interpreted them as calling cards, but maybe they were allusions to the reason for her death. Hints released by a broken and guilty heart.

George watched me, frame rigid, likely regretting his confession.

He'd loved Tiffany, and now she was gone. No wonder chatter about my wedding had irritated him. His happily ever after could no longer be.

The rear door to the inn opened, and I jolted, spinning in the direction of the sound.

One of the ballerinas appeared, tucking a protein shaker into her pack. "We're ready," she told George.

He levered himself off the snowy chair and ran his bare hands down his undoubtedly wet backside, then glared at me a moment. I'd stolen his only opportunity for privacy, and now I knew his secret.

I stepped out of his way as he passed, moving through the open door.

"Thanks, Sophia," he said softly. "Give me a minute to grab my coat and a change of clothes."

I blew out a shaky breath, unable to ignore the fact I might've just been alone with a killer. If George was guilty, he'd have it in for me now for sure, and the group had another night at the inn. Still, I couldn't stop myself from asking one more question. "She snuck out to be with you the other night, didn't she?" It would've been tough for a couple to spend time alone together when traveling in a group like this. Suddenly the strict time for lights out made more sense. Not because George thought the dancers were children, or beneath him, but because he needed to assure the rest of them stayed in their rooms. Meeting off-site practically guaranteed he wouldn't get caught with Tiffany.

He dipped his chin stiffly and walked away.

I dithered on the patio, giving him space and time to change and leave. Silhouettes passed through the kitchen, a series of shadows beyond the window's curtain. All of them too small to be George.

I paced a little, replaying my conversation with the choreographer and asking my gut if his tears were born of grief or guilt.

The transport revved to life a few moments later, and the silhouettes poured away from my kitchen. I listened as the front door opened and closed, gently rattling the back door a few feet away.

Snowflakes landed on my cheek and nose, then melted. I wiped away the icy drops with the back of one freezing hand. Then something new crashed into my mind like an avalanche.

George had called the ballerina who'd come for him "Sophia." But that wasn't the same woman I'd spoken with outside the Hearth. Her jacket had that name embroidered above the pocket, but it wasn't the same woman.

I lurched forward, darting back inside and through the house as quickly as possible, hoping to catch the transport before it rolled away.

"Where's the fire?" Cookie called, tipping her head into the hallway as I wrenched the front door open.

"Be right back!"

"Where's she going?" Caroline asked.

I had no time to explain.

The vehicle was in motion, turning away from the narrow lot outside the inn and onto a partially plowed road toward the Hearth as I slipped and slid down the walkway.

"Wait!" I called. "Wait!" I waved my hands overhead, catching the eyes of two ballerinas through the windows.

Brake lights cast red streaks over the snow as the vehicle slowed to a stop.

I huffed a breath of relief and hurried to the passenger door, pressing a palm against the stitch in my ribs. I hadn't gone far, but walking in the snow was effortful, and doing it in any kind of hurry was work.

George powered down the window.

"Hey!" I panted. "Is there a Sophia staying with us?" I asked. Her name hadn't been on the list I'd been provided upon securing the reservations. I didn't have a stocking hung for her on the mantel. And that was the least of my concerns.

"Just last night," a woman called.

I set my forearms on the open window frame and leaned in, searching for the source of the voice. The woman speaking raised her hand to wave. She was the same one who'd called George away from the patio, the one I hadn't spoken to before.

This woman had a round face coated in freckles and hair as thick and dark as mine.

"You stayed at the inn last night?" I asked.

"After the show," she said shyly. "I came to look for my coat, and time got away, so I stayed with these guys. I hope that's okay."

Two of the other dancers winced, as if they'd just realized it might be frowned on to have had an overnight guest.

"No, it's fine," I said. "I hope your stay was comfortable. Did you say your coat was missing?" I flipped my gaze to George.

"I already told you that," he said, obviously still irritated with me and my questions.

"You didn't tell me the ballerina missing her coat was named Sophia."

"Why do you care?" he asked, biting off each word.

Because Sophia wasn't the woman I saw wearing the coat, I thought. *Because whoever I spoke with was masquerading as a member of the ballet and likely up to no good. Because whoever had stolen Sophia's coat might be a killer.*

Unless . . . "Do you have two dancers named Sophia?" I asked, eliminating any simple, reasonable explanation for the conundrum.

"Just me," Sophia said.

So who was the person I'd spoken to?

Courtney's name flashed through my mind. Could the blogger be in Mistletoe, stalking the ballet? Had she gotten too close to the object of her obsession and become confused? Maybe even homicidal? Had she been close enough to tamper with Tiffany's shakes? The photos she'd taken certainly made it seem as if she was moving among the ballet troupe.

I dropped my hands away and stepped back, more confused than ever by the way evidence was mounting.

George stared across the vehicle and through the open window for a long beat before powering up the window and shifting into gear. No goodbyes.

Stalking Around the Christmas Tree

I watched them roll away, before turning back to the inn. My breaths came in icy cloud bursts for new reasons on the return trip. Adrenaline coursed through my veins as I weighed my top suspects, George and Courtney, against the thin facts. Both had loved Tiffany. Possible motives were unclear.

I stumbled over densely packed snow as I moved along, attempting to stay upright while texting my thoughts to Evan.

Farm crews were visible in several directions, bulldozing the fresh powder off paths and asphalt. Mini tractors dispensed salt onto cleared spaces to prevent ice from forming. Further away, village road crews were audible, doing similar jobs on a larger scale, clearing the main roads for travelers.

I said a little prayer for commuter safety and tucked my phone away, wishing I'd worn gloves.

A familiar figure came into view on the inn's porch, and I waved.

Deputy Mars's cruiser idled on the road out front. "Hey, Holly," he said, raising a hand. "I came back to see if it was too late to add a plus one to my RSVP for your wedding reception. You weren't here, but Caroline just said it was okay. You don't mind, do you?"

Caroline stood inside the door, holding it at an angle to limit the amount of the icy air that blew inside.

I shook my head, still processing Sophia's lost jacket and mysterious imposter. "Of course not. The more the merrier," I said.

Mars flashed a toothy grin, bringing me back to the moment. "That's great. I've been seeing someone special, and I thought it'd be nice to spend the holiday with her, but I don't want to miss the sheriff's wedding. And yours," he added.

"It's really no problem," I assured him.

Was everyone in Mistletoe pairing up and falling in love? Or did it just seem that way to me because I was so head over heels for Evan?

"Who's the lucky date?" I asked.

"Jessica Post. We were high school sweethearts, but she left for college, and long distance never works. We didn't talk for a few years, but she's back now, working at her folks' farm, and we've been in touch quite a bit. A Christmas Eve wedding might be the perfect setting to spark things up a notch."

I patted his icy sleeve on my way inside. "I can't wait to meet her. Do you want to come in and warm up before you head out again? Maybe take a cup of something warm to go?"

"I tried," Caroline said. "He's a tough one."

My phone buzzed, drawing my attention.

Evan: *Almost there and I have pie!*

I cocked a brow at the message and laughed. I had details about an ongoing murder investigation, and he had pie. We truly were a real power couple.

Caroline pushed an individual cupcake box in Mars's direction. "At least take one of these to Jessica, and say you were thinking of her. Guaranteed gold star for thoughtfulness."

He bobbed his head and offered a reluctant look of acceptance. "If you're sure. I know she loves your cupcakes."

"*Everyone* loves our cupcakes," Cookie called from the dining room.

Age had not affected her hearing.

Evan's cruiser rolled into place behind Mars's, and he climbed out, a white pastry bag in one hand, a tray with two disposable cups in the other. "Oh, hey, Mars," he said.

"See?" Caroline asked. "Bringing food to your significant other is always a good idea."

I laughed and welcomed Evan with a kiss on his cheek.

"Hey, Sheriff," Mars said. "I was just on my way out."

"Well, drive safely," Evan said. "The crews are making progress, but it's still dicey in some areas."

"Will do." He thanked Caroline for the cupcake and headed carefully down the steps.

I led Evan to the kitchen while Caroline closed up behind us.

"Need help clearing breakfast?" he asked, nodding to the dirty blender, cast-off fruit cores and peels in the sink, and the array of unwashed mugs on the counter.

"Nope. Those go in the dishwasher, and that goes in the garbage disposal. I'll have it done in two shakes, and I'm not going to worry about it until after you leave." I took a seat at the small nook near the back door, where a white table and chairs sat before a matching, built-in bench. Red plaid cushions topped the seats, and a wooden box with faux mistletoe and holly centered the table. I shoved the decoration out of our way.

We sloughed off our coats and dug into the cooling meal.

Evan unpacked the bag while I removed the lids from our hot chocolates. "All right," he said, "what happened this morning?"

I forked a bite of my new favorite, 'Tis the Season Turtle Pie, and released a shamelessly satisfied moan. "This is so good. It's unfair. I would eat this for every meal if it was legal."

He grinned, sipping his drink and waiting for my story. "It's probably not a great idea for your general health, but you won't be arrested."

"Good to know." I forced the fork out of my grip after two more bites and licked bits of caramel from my lips. Then I started my story by telling him about George's admission to a romantic involvement with Tiffany.

Evan leaned forward, forearms anchored to the table as I spoke, wholly engrossed. "And you think this blogger, Courtney, is in Mistletoe?"

"I don't know," I admitted. "It's just a theory."

He hadn't been overly concerned about the social media guru the last time we'd spoken, but his opinion seemed to be changing.

"I'm still hung up on the protein shakes," I said, tipping my head toward the cluttered kitchen. "I've assumed someone staying here made the shake that killed Tiffany, probably George. But I saw a dancer tuck a shaker into her bag this morning, and now I'm wondering how many of those things they drink a day and where else they might store them. Could the poison have been added at a secondary location? Do they put their shakes into a refrigerator or something while they practice?" If so, that didn't exactly help narrow my suspect list.

The walkie-talkie on his shoulder made an abrupt fuzzy sound. "Sheriff?" someone asked.

Evan lifted a finger, indicating I should hold my next thought. Then he squeezed the small device and turned his head in that direction. "Yeah."

"This is Deputy Mars," the crackly voice replied. "I'm down here at the farm's entrance, and I think you're going to want to take a look at this."

The air seemed to be sucked from the room as my eyes caught Evan's. We were on our feet and in motion before Mars spoke again.

"What's going on?" Evan asked.

We shrugged back into our coats, abandoning our breakfast and rushing to the front door as quickly as possible.

"I'm going out!" I called to Cookie and Caroline on my way past the dining room again.

The walkie-talkie crackled, and Mars's voice returned. "Someone left a whole lot of notes down here."

"I'm headed your way now." Evan clutched my hand as we hustled along the lane toward the Hearth, slipping and crunching over ice and snow.

My face and lungs burned as we reached the parking area outside the Hearth and crossed to the farm's main entrance.

Deputy Mars's cruiser was parked lengthwise at the bottom of the driveway, lights on. Sirens off. Thankfully, it was still early, and tour buses wouldn't begin to arrive for another forty-five minutes.

Mom and Dad were at the gate with Deputy Mars and bundled head to toe. I suspected Dad had been working, and Mom was on her way to help Caroline and Cookie set up for the luncheon. From the expressions on their faces, whatever had rerouted them to the gate wasn't good.

Deputy Mars lifted his chin when he noticed our approach. "Whoever did this acted fast. They were here and gone in the time between your arrival and my departure. I made a pit stop to say good morning to the Whites, and this was here when I reached the gate."

Evan and I finished our trek to join them, then stopped.

Dozens of papers were stuck to the farm's wooden gate. The thin white corners of each page batted and curled in the frigid wind.

Two words were printed across each sheet.

Found you. Found you. Found you. Found you.

Evan cursed, and I squeezed his hand more tightly, feeling his pain in my heart. Everyone knew *I* lived here.

These messages had been left for Libby.

Chapter Nineteen

Caroline met me in the foyer when I returned to the inn. "Whatever happened out there, if no one was hurt, the drama has to wait."

I felt ill and speechless as she took my elbow and towed me toward my room.

"Well? Was anyone hurt?" she asked, turning, hands on hips as she closed the door to my private quarters?

"No."

She released a deep breath of relief without changing her determined expression. Ever poised, ever ready: Caroline West. "Good. Then local law enforcement can handle that. You have a party to attend."

I collapsed onto my couch and rolled my eyes up to meet her gaze.

"I love you," she said. "And you love everyone, so I'm sure whatever happened feels like it's your problem somehow, but you need to tell that big heart of yours that a whole lot of people are on their way over here to see you. They've been waiting for this luncheon for weeks, and they want to bring you good tidings. It will ruin their day if they get here and you look miserable. So suck it up. For them. Okay?"

Stalking Around the Christmas Tree

I arched an eyebrow, impressed with the number of words she could manage on a single breath, then nodded, knowing she was right. The luncheon was technically about me, but it was also a moment for my family and friends to spend time with me before the wedding, and it meant a lot to them too. "Okay."

Caroline lowered onto the cushion at my side and wrapped an arm around my shoulders. "You're a good egg, Holly White."

I laughed.

"I had another speech prepared, but we really are on a tight schedule," Caroline said. "You need to shower and blow out your hair. Use the big-barrel brush I bought you for volume. Your mom's friends are coming in an hour to do your hair and makeup. They'll also paint your nails and bring you tea, snacks, and whatever you need. You just have to stay in here until the luncheon begins. Cookie, your mom and I have more work to do out there. No peeking." She checked her watch and sighed. "I have to run to the cupcake shop and meet the workers covering the next shift, but I'll be back before your guests arrive."

My heart swelled, and I pulled her into an embrace.

"What's this for?" she asked, hugging back tightly.

"You're doing all this while running back and forth to town to handle your business. You probably spent more time than I can imagine planning this luncheon. And I've never properly thanked you or Mom or Cookie—or anyone else who's spending their time with me three days before Christmas."

"Nonsense," Caroline whispered against my hair. "Holly, you thank us every day. You just don't always know you're doing it."

A small sob of emotion broke on my lips, and Caroline rubbed my back. "It's okay," she cooed. "You're in the middle of a lot. Let yourself cry. Let yourself do whatever you need to get centered. But put some cold compresses on your eyes before they do your makeup."

I laughed, and she let me go.

"I have to hurry, and so do you. Remember. Stay in this space." She motioned broadly, indicating the general area. "Not the main inn."

"Got it."

"I steamed your dress and set out everything else you need, so you won't have to hunt for it."

"Thank you," I said, meaning it from the bottom of my heart.

Caroline nodded and then she was gone.

I followed her instructions, showering and pampering myself, pushing thoughts of everything except this luncheon and my local lady friends out of my head. Caroline was right: the rest could wait. All my problems would still be there in a couple of hours when I put my jeans back on.

Meanwhile, I used the big round brush, as instructed, and blew out my hair to twice its normal size. Then I slipped into a dress I'd nearly forgotten purchasing last month on a shopping excursion for that exact purpose.

The cream-colored material hugged my chest and torso in flattering, feminine ways, emphasizing the narrowest part of my waist before flowing more freely to my knees. Delicate black embroidery at the hem, cuffs, and neckline formed a small repeating pattern I loved. The heels were comfortable and short, also in cream and black. And when Mama's friends arrived, they painted my nails a deep crimson with marvelous shine.

One woman worked through my thick, oversized hair with a giant-barreled curling iron until the slight twist in each section looked strangely natural instead of utterly intentional. Another lady applied makeup from four palettes in various shades of tan until I looked like myself, but also not at all so. Her work brought out the flecks of amber and green in my brown eyes and complemented the shape of my cheekbones and jaw. I was polished and pretty and a little in love with what I saw in the mirror. I couldn't wait to see Evan's reaction. And I hoped I looked this pretty on our wedding day.

I listened with sweaty palms as the others finished their work and welcomed guests beyond my closed door. Anticipation churned in my belly. I had no idea what to expect out there. I'd so fully trusted Caroline that I hadn't asked any questions. I'd just planned to show up and say thank you.

A small knock sounded on the door, and my mom stuck her head inside. She wore mascara and lip gloss. A pair of small diamond studs twinkled in her ears. "Ready?" she asked. "Oh my!"

I stilled as she slipped inside, unshed tears suddenly glistening in her eyes.

Her ladies gathered their things, making a quiet exit as Mom lifted her soft palms to my cheeks. "You look so beautiful."

"So do you," I said.

And she did. She'd abandoned her jeans like I had, trading her usual sweater and apron for black slacks, a pale green blouse, and a white cardigan. Her hair was tucked behind both ears, and blusher pinked her cheeks.

"You're getting married," she said.

"I am."

"You're going to be very happy." She dropped her hands and smiled warmly. "I've seen you and Evan together when you think no one is looking—watched your relationship grow these last few years, and I can see the bond and friendship there. You make a great team. You lean on each other and accept one another. You're going to do just fine when hard times come, and they will. But you'll get through them because you know how to work together. And you do it so well."

A lump wedged in my throat, and my eyes misted. "Thanks, Mom."

"Oh." She grabbed a box of tissues from the vanity and passed one to me. She pressed another to the corners of her own eyes. "I didn't mean to get sappy. It's just that a mother worries when her only child takes a major step in life like this. And I'm so proud to know you're choosing wisely. If things go right in this life, you'll outlive me by a quarter century." She smiled. "And it fills my heart to know that one day, hopefully many, many years from now, when your father and I aren't here to cherish and protect you, you won't be alone. You'll be in very loving and capable arms."

And with that, the tears ran full and fast on both our faces. We laughed as we mopped them, trying to erase the paths they made over our powdered cheeks.

"Ready?" Caroline asked, marching in merrily amid our mutual breakdown. "For the love of Christmas. What are you doing? Martha? Kate!"

The makeup ladies returned and separated Mom and me.

Caroline shook her head with a laugh. "I'll get the guests started on their words of wisdom."

I had no idea what that meant, but I was thankful for the treasured moment I'd shared with Mom. And for friends like Caroline and everyone else who'd carved out time to have lunch with me before my wedding.

Ten minutes later, Mom and I were righted, and I hooked my arm in hers as we left my private quarters.

The kitchen had been cleared of the blenders and fruit—and the pie and hot chocolates I'd shared with Evan. In place of those messes was a multitude of gorgeous blooms. Every surface was heavy with spring and summer flowers. Punch bowls on the countertop held lemonade and other brightly colored drinks that had ice cubes with flower petals or mint leaves frozen inside. An easel displaying a large white canvas near the window announced *Holly & Evan, your love is a work of art.*

Beside it, a three-tier cake in pale blue fondant dripped with additional buds and blossoms, the overall look reminiscent of Monet's water lilies. He'd painted them a hundred ways, and I loved every one. Never had I ever imagined the art as a cake.

Dozens of friendly faces smiled as I marveled. Their voices quieted to let me take it all in.

Millie and Jean stood near Cookie and her book club. Libby and Samantha leaned against the staircase. Childhood friends and their mothers, owners of the art studio where I sometimes sold my jewelry, and a collection of local women I'd simply known all my life crowded into the kitchen, hall, and space beyond.

I wasn't sure I could form the words I needed, and tears stung my eyes once more. "Thank you all for being here," I croaked. "I'm speechless. And so very grateful."

A low murmur rolled through the crowd, followed by a number of voices calling, "Cheers!" Mom's ladies dispersed, refilling drinks and straightening trays of tiny cupcakes and cookies shaped like flowers in every shade of icing, from rose to gold.

"It might be winter in Mistletoe," Mom said, "but this is the spring of your new, married life. Caroline thought the analogy, and the connection to your favorite paintings, was a good theme for your luncheon."

I spun on Caroline and hugged her abusively.

She laughed and the room broke into motion once more, chattering and enjoying the buffet of drinks and finger foods. Everyone thoroughly enjoying the day.

A table near the fireplace had been covered in white eyelet and now overflowed with gift-wrapped packages in every shape and size. A small wooden wishing well on the coffee table, made by my grandpa for my parents' wedding, was filled with cards. Classical music played softly beneath the voices of my guests. The event was everything I could've asked for and one hundred times more.

"These are your words of wisdom," Caroline said, pointing to a picnic basket filled with cards, a bottle of champagne, and two plastic flutes. "For you and Evan to read together some day while sharing a toast. Everyone here wrote something nice to keep in mind, advice they wished they'd been given, or a word of praise for the happy couple."

I pressed my hands to my chest, certain my heart would burst from fulfillment if it could, and deep appreciation that it wouldn't. Because I couldn't wait to get started on the next few decades of wonderful adventures. I mouthed the words *thank you* to Caroline again. I wasn't sure I'd ever stop saying that. And I kept my promise to focus only on the luncheon, leaving my fears and concerns about local crime out of my mind for a while.

A couple hours later, Libby came into view near the fireplace as I said goodbye to the first few guests. She'd chosen a satin periwinkle top with dark jeans and black kitten heels for my party, and she looked perfect. Her long red hair hung in waves over her shoulders. She cradled a glass teacup filled with punch, but her expression was worried, her stare distant. She'd been threatened, or at least tormented, again this morning, yet she'd gone home, gotten changed and arrived on time to my party. She'd put her large personal crisis aside to have lunch with fifty people she'd probably never met. The handful of us she did know also knew about the messages left for her at the gate this morning, and we were all behaving as if it hadn't happened.

I closed the door and slipped into the living room, crossing the room to her side.

Libby smiled brightly as I approached, dumping the distant expression she'd worn a moment before. "Hey, Holly. This was such a fun afternoon. I'm so glad I was here."

"Me too," I said softly, appreciating all the effort she'd made for me when she was clearly and understandably wrecked. "How are you holding up?"

Her smile increased, and her free hand wrapped around her middle. "I'm great. I think this little bit of normalcy was exactly what I needed. I don't want to miss out on any of your wedding festivities. Big brother's only getting married once."

I certainly hoped so. "True," I said. "But this party doesn't erase what happened this morning, or your rightful concerns about it. You don't have to pretend with me. I've been freaking out all afternoon too."

Her smile fell. "Really?"

"Yes. I didn't want to put a damper on the party or make anyone think I wasn't glad to be here, but I'm scared. Someone came to the farm to let you know they were here. That can't be good."

"Right?" she said, stepping closer and whispering. "What will happen next?"

I offered a sad smile. "I don't know."

This was the game someone had been playing with her for months. Sending cards. Letting her know they were getting close. No real threats. Just continuous contacts to keep her aware and on edge. She was being watched. Whoever it was couldn't be arrested for sending unsigned greeting cards or even for leaving all those flyers. The former wasn't a crime, and the latter was litter at most. But combined, the acts felt like psychological warfare, and they'd long ago taken their toll.

"Holly?" Mom called, leading another group of guests toward the door.

I smiled and waved, then turned to Libby. "Call Evan and see how he's doing on this while I say goodbye to my guests. Then we'll meet him for coffee."

She pressed her lips together as she freed her phone from her pocket.

I straightened and worked up a cheery grin before going to thank my friends for coming.

When the last guest had gone, Libby reappeared at my side, my coat in hand. Her coat was already on. "I don't mean to rush you away from your party," she said, her Boston accent thick with nerves, "but Evan's got reason to believe that car I saw at the Cap and Kerchief was something to worry about after all. He's headed back there now. I want to meet him, and I could use the moral support."

I looked to Mom and her friends, who'd already begun tearing down decorations and packing up leftovers. Caroline and Cookie rounded the corner into view, wide-eyed and open-mouthed. Apparently they'd heard Libby too.

"Go!" Caroline said. "We've got this."

Mom frowned. "Be careful and stick together. Actually, stick with Evan."

I kicked off my heels and shoved bare feet into wool-lined boots, then donned my coat and hat, not bothering to take time to change. "I'll fill you in as soon as I can," I said, speaking to the group.

One of mom's friends signed the cross from her place in the kitchen.

And I followed Libby through the front door.

Chapter Twenty

The drive to Cap and Kerchief was slow and grueling. Many of the roads outside of town were still covered in last night's snowfall. Crews had tended to the downtown area first, then moved into neighborhoods and other places with the highest amounts of traffic. The more rural and less traveled streets were last to be addressed.

We passed more than one car angled half off the road, hazard lights flashing as it waited for a tow. I stuck to the center of the snow-covered asphalt when no one was coming in the other direction. The yellow line dividing the lanes was invisible, as were the lines marking the road on either edge, and even in my big pickup, we slid more often than I liked. If the hotel hadn't been quite so far from Reindeer Games, and if I hadn't been wearing a tea dress, it would've been faster and safer for Libby and I to take a snowmobile.

Eventually our destination came into view, along with a set of cruisers parked outside.

I navigated my pickup into a fully cleared lot and hopped out.

Libby met me at the grill with a look of determination. We entered the lobby with our chins high, facing together whatever awaited. A bell rang above the door, announcing our arrival.

The interior was critically outdated and in need of a thorough revamp. Golden carpet stretched wall to wall, and twinkle lights lined every flat space. A rocking chair was angled in the corner, centered on a round crimson rug. Before it, a giant fake fireplace, lined in threadbare stockings, held a pile of firewood with a painted cardboard fire.

"Wowza," Libby said, apparently reading my mind.

"Yeah," I agreed, moving slowly in the direction of the welcome desk.

Evan stood with a deputy, watching us approach. His grim, all-business expression turned to surprise when he saw us. Apparently Libby hadn't told him we were coming.

An older man, with wire-rimmed glasses and a striped dress shirt, exited an office behind the counter. "Welcome to Cap and Kerchief. I'll be right with you." His smile was tight as he spoke, and his attention moved from us to the lawmen before he spoke again. "All right. I've got the key, but it looks as if the guest checked out this morning."

A printed image of the teal car Libby had followed to the hotel sat on the countertop between the men.

Evan took the key as the older man returned his attention to Libby and me.

"Can I help you, ladies?"

"They're with me," Evan said. "Has the room been cleaned?"

The man stilled, giving us a closer look before responding to the sheriff. "Hard to say. Housekeeping is making their way around to the empty rooms now. They report as the rooms are finished. Could be that they haven't gotten there; or they have, but haven't finished."

"Thanks." Evan moved in our direction, arms parted to corral us toward the exit.

The deputy stepped up to the counter. "Just a few more questions, if you don't mind."

Stalking Around the Christmas Tree

We hustled back into the icy day, keeping pace with Evan as he headed along the exterior corridor, past a dozen closed doors. "I'd ask what you're doing here, but I suppose that's obvious."

"I had to know what was happening," Libby said. "I brought Holly for moral support. What'd we miss?"

He cast his sister a hard sideways look.

"I saw that picture on the counter," she continued. "Did the manager recognize the car?"

"Yeah," Evan said, raising the collar on his sheriff's coat against the biting wind. "Boston PD got a hit on the car. It's registered to an elderly man on the south side, but it's been captured in multiple surveillance images taken outside known hangouts for Kellen Lance's criminal organization over the years."

I shivered, not completely from the cold. "Who rented the room?"

"The reservation was for J. Doe. Whoever that was paid in cash, and the desk clerk who helped them check in is out of town for the holiday. The manager is trying to reach him by phone to see if he remembers if J stood for John or Jane."

I traded glances with Libby, who looked ill.

"Was the person alone?" she asked.

"Unknown," he said. "Again, we're waiting to speak with the clerk. We were able to confirm this room wasn't one of those covered by the mayor."

"So, not one of the ballet's stage crew," I said.

Evan nodded.

Libby's expression grew pensive and her gaze distant.

Evan slid the key into the lock on room 123 and raised a hand, warning us to wait while he entered.

Libby and I crowded into the doorframe, watching as he cleared the empty room.

A queen bed stood, unmade, at the center, its reindeer-patterned duvet haphazardly askew. A nightstand, dresser, and television completed the amenities.

Evan passed a set of large portraits on his way to the open bathroom door. Mrs. Claus on the left; her husband, Santa, on her right. Evan checked behind the shower curtain, visible from where we stood, then motioned us inside.

Libby closed the door and froze, a strange expression on her face. "Whoever has been tormenting me was just here a few hours ago. This was their private space."

I rubbed a hand over her coat sleeve. "You were right about the car."

Her gaze snapped to mine.

"You were right to be on alert," I continued. "Right to worry."

"Wrong to keep it from me," Evan grouched, snapping blue crime scene gloves over his hands.

"I didn't want to be right," she said. "I'd hoped to confirm I was wrong."

The heater rumbled to life, and warm air poured through vents overhead, circulating familiar scents inside the room. Coffee. Soap. The faint burnt-hair aroma of an ancient furnace.

A whiff of something fruity pulled me toward the bathroom. "I think I recognize that shampoo," I said, passing Evan on my way. A pile of towels lay on the floor near the tub, and I stopped beside them, crouching to inhale. "I do. I used this for years."

Evan ducked into a squat beside me. "That's not a very masculine scent. No judgment," he added. "Good hair is good hair."

I smiled. He was right on all counts, but the light peaches-and-cream aroma definitely wasn't one I'd imagine for a hitman from a Boston crime family. Though in fairness, I knew very little about hitmen, Boston, or crime families.

"We requested a phone log to see if that creates any new threads. It's unlikely any calls were made from the hotel phone, but it's worth a try. My deputy is requesting an interview with the staff member who cleaned the room when it was vacated. They might've gotten a look at the occupant or seen something else that will give us an indication of who was here."

Libby moved to the bed, bending at the waist to examine the pillowcases.

"Don't touch anything," Evan warned.

"Not even this?" she asked, plucking a long blond hair from the pillow.

Evan moved in her direction. "I'll take that."

I went to the small closet, where extra blankets and pillows were typically stashed. "Can I open this?"

He spun in place, looking as if he might regret allowing us here. "Use your toe under the door so you don't add prints." He pulled a plastic evidence bag from his pocket and took the hair from Libby.

I slid the tip of my boot beneath the folding closet door and tugged. The slatted wooden barrier slid on its hinges, bending at the center and moving aside, out of my way.

As expected, extra blankets and pillows filled the shelf overhead. A safe sat on a bench nailed to the rear wall, and a single pink silk coat hung on the metal bar. Embroidery above the pocket spelled the name, Sophia.

"Is that—" Evan began.

"Sophia's missing jacket."

He rounded the end of the bed once more, crossing the room to my side, cell phone in hand.

I looked to Libby as Evan spoke on the phone. "I talked to someone wearing this jacket outside the Hearth on the day you confessed what's been going on to Evan. I told her to stop in and talk to him, but she didn't. Then I learned this jacket had been stolen. I'd assumed the person who stole the jacket was impersonating a ballerina to get close to them, and I thought that person was someone named Courtney, an obsessive blogger."

"Any chance Courtney is from Boston?" Libby asked hopefully.

"I don't know," I admitted. "No one's ever seen her, and her social media accounts are thin on personal details. It's possible, I guess. But also . . . I might've talked to the woman who's been harassing you."

Evan disconnected his call and turned to us, hands on hips. "I've got an APB out on the car. I'm going to need a full description from you of the woman you saw wearing this coat."

I cringed. It'd been days since I'd spoken to the fake Sophia, and her features had faded somewhat in my mind. "She was thin, petite, blond."

Evan glanced at the tiny coat in the closet, and I thought of the long hair on the hotel bed's pillow. We already knew she wasn't big if she fit into that jacket, and her hair was currently in evidence. "Anything else?"

"Brown eyes," I said. "Fair skin."

"Can you guess her age?" he asked. "You believed she was one of the dancers. Did she appear closer to twenty or thirty?"

"Twenty, I think." I tented my brows apologetically. "She didn't have a Boston accent."

"The city's a melting pot," he said. "College kids. Tourists. Newcomers. Sixth generations. Doesn't matter. She could still be our stalker. And the information helps."

My gut clenched with irrational guilt. "She was on-site, probably looking for Libby, and I tried to send her inside to meet you."

Libby came to stand at my side. "You didn't know. And if she had listened to you, Evan was with me, so it's not as if she could've hurt me."

Stalking Around the Christmas Tree

Maybe not, but it would've still felt as if I'd fed Libby to the wolves. "I guess this means at least half the mystery is solved," I said. "We know the person messing with you is a small, blond female in her early to mid-twenties, but we don't know who she is or why she's doing this to you. And if the person who took Sophia's jacket was your stalker, and not connected to Tiffany's killer, then I've lost a clue as to who threatened Ava and me."

Libby nodded, and Evan grunted.

He stepped closer, stripping off the gloves before taking my hands in his. "Maybe let me worry about the rest of those things. I'm in uniform, and you're still dressed for a party."

I looked down at myself. "I left in a hurry."

"I see that." He leaned in and planted a kiss on my temple. "You look beautiful."

"Thank you."

He tilted his face to my cheek, the tip of his nose brushing my ear.

I bit my lip against a soft sigh.

"Please go home," he whispered.

I jerked away and frowned.

He grinned and mischief danced in his eyes. "Take Libby and drive carefully. Keep an eye out for the car, and maybe give Ray a call. Hang out as a group, and I'll be there as soon as I can."

Libby moved forward and hugged her brother. "I have to work tonight. There's another indoor reindeer game, so the place is bound to be packed. I'll call Ray on our way back and invite him."

Evan nodded.

I pulled the truck keys from my pocket. "Fine, I'll go," I told him. "Whatever else happens, just keep coming back to me safely."

"Back at ya."

Chapter
Twenty-One

The crowd was wound up at the Hearth that night. Mom had initiated a new set of quick games and encouraged folks to fill every seat. Each table and booth became a team. Then the nonsense began.

Cookie was back on the corner stage with a mic, announcing the rules to the first game while Mom delivered bowls of her homemade chicken noodle stew and baskets of warm bread to my table.

Ray, Libby, and I thanked her profusely. We'd settled in for dinner just before Cookie had insisted the room get quiet.

Mom's friends were acting as waitresses tonight.

"Everyone get that?" Cookie asked, sending a peal of feedback through the microphone. "First, you touch your nose to the Vaseline on the plate, then use that stickiness to adhere a red pompom to your nose. No hands!" she warned. "Then, move the red pompoms to the pictures of Rudolph we set up along the perimeter walls. Every table has a number. Put your noses on the Rudolphs with that number. The first table with every member to move their noses to the corresponding Rudolph wins a new basket of snickerdoodles. Ready?"

The giggling began immediately.

"Go!" Cookie called, and the patrons dove face first at their tables.

Ray snorted a laugh as he spooned soup into his mouth.

Libby's gaze was glued to the door. She tensed each time it opened.

"He'll be here soon," I told her, drawing her worried eyes to mine.

"I'm not sure if I'm more anxious to see Evan's face or afraid the mysterious blonde will walk in and confront me," Libby said. "I don't even know what she wants. Could she be a female hitman? Hitwoman?"

"Assassin," Ray said.

I shot him a warning look.

He cringed, then set his spoon aside and wiped his mouth on a green linen napkin. "I know something that will take your mind off everything else." He dug a file folder from the brown leather satchel at his side and set it on the table.

Libby watched with narrowed eyes. "What is it?"

"I have never-before-seen images of the third annual Goat for All Seasons calendar," Ray said. "Bride-hunting edition."

Libby's lips twitched. "Did you say bride-hunting? Like a bridal bride?"

Ray laughed. "Yes. Exactly the kind Holly will soon be, except Theodore is hunting for a goat version." He frowned. "I think."

I reached for the folder, but he planted a palm against it, holding the cover closed. "Wait a minute now. I'm required by the legally binding contract I signed with Cookie to tell you that these images are top secret until the official reveal. Fortunately, I have prior written permission to show them to both of you, Holly's parents, Evan, and Caroline—but no one else. You cannot knowingly reveal them either. Do you understand and agree to these rules and limitations?"

"Yes," we answered.

He removed his hand with a wide smile and returned to his soup.

Libby and I split the stack of images and started flipping through our sheets.

My pile was everything I'd hoped it would be and more. Images of Theodore in tuxedo pants and a bow tie, no shirt. Theodore standing beside the open door to a black stretch limousine, as if waiting for his date to climb aboard. Near a table for two at a crowded, high-end restaurant, a bottle of champagne in a bucket of ice, with two crystal flutes behind him. In the lavish lobby of the historic theater where the ballet was performing.

Each of the images was printed in striking, glossy, black and white, with a single, dramatic pop of color. A glimmer of blue off the marquis sign, reflecting on the snow. A red rose in a vase near the champagne. Rainbow-colored glints from a string of chasing lights reflected in the onyx paint of the limo. "Very artsy," I said, stealing a look at Ray's proud face. "Who knew Theodore was such a high-class goat?"

He tipped his bowl to gather another spoonful of stew. "This photo shoot made me love our town even more. Tell me where else on earth I could've gotten five minutes in a crowded restaurant like the Bistro with a goat."

"Well, he was wearing a tuxedo," I said.

Libby laughed, and my smile rose as well.

Relief washed over Ray's face at the sound. "What did you think of your pictures?" he asked, hiking his brows at her.

"Trade," she said, swapping her stack of images with mine. "I think my shots show his softer side."

I was giddy with anticipation. "Oh, goody."

The second round of images did not disappoint. In the new set, Theodore had swapped his tuxedo pants and tie for a pageboy cap and britches. He lay beside a red and white checked blanket and picnic lunch on a grassy hill beneath a tree. He strolled near a lake, looking intrigued by the brilliant blue sky, a trail of puffy white clouds seeming to take the shape of hearts overhead. In one image, he appeared to be in a rowboat, one hoof hung leisurely over the edge as a mama duck and a row of ducklings paddled heart-shaped waves in the still water.

"How much of this calendar was green screen and creative editing?" I asked, peeking over the tops of the photos at Ray.

He leveled a hand before me, tilting it left, then right. "They're all really pictures of Theodore," he said.

Libby slid her stack of shots back into the folder. "Was he really wearing tuxedo pants?"

Ray set his spoon beside the newly emptied bowl. "No, but I'm sure he would've loved an opportunity to *eat* tuxedo pants."

She snorted.

"He wore the bow tie."

Libby appeared delighted. "You're right. This was a great distraction. Now I can't stop imagining that goat chewing off his own clothes. What a surprise for his future bride."

The café cheered around us, and Cookie plunked the mic against an open palm in applause. "Let's hear it for table one! Mrs. White is coming around with your snickerdoodles now. The rest of us are moving on to game number two!"

"What's game number two?" Ray asked. "I don't like this. I liked the old games. One per night, maybe a little karaoke at the end. I knew what to expect. What happened to Gingerbread Goes to Hollywood? I had a whole *Stranger Things* setup in mind, with gumdrops for lights on the wall."

"You missed it," I said, letting my gaze flicker to Libby. Ray had been sulking while she'd avoided him earlier this month, and he'd missed half the games as a result, not to mention most of the late-fall farm shenanigans.

"Oh, right," he said, cringing slightly at the memory. "What's going on now?"

I followed his eyes to Cookie, who looked like the cat who ate the canary as she paced the dining area, microphone in hand.

Each guest's attention riveted on her small form.

"For this challenge," she said, "we're going to need a few volunteer Santas. Don't worry—I have the costumes and your jolly bellies. Can I please see one member of each team on the stage?"

"This can't be good," Libby said. "What did she mean she has their bellies?"

"I think this is the one with the painted Ping-Pong balls," I said.

"What?" Libby and Ray asked on husky laughs.

"Just watch."

Cookie welcomed the volunteer from each table, then handed every one of them a Santa coat, hat, and beard. Once they'd all donned the costumes, she came back with a cube-shaped tissue box obnoxiously gift-wrapped in green and gold. "I have a box for each of you, and it's full of Ping-Pong balls I decorated for the holidays." She lifted a ball painted like a Christmas tree ornament, as an example, then tucked it back inside its box. "I'm going to come around and help you get these on." She lifted a giant red Velcro strap and slid it through a fold in the box's wrapping paper, like a belt loop. "You can let me know if you want to wear it on your tummy or your backside."

The crowd erupted in laughter as she moved from Santa to Santa. Audience members called out suggestions. Eventually each contestant made a decision, and Cookie tied the boxes around their middles.

"Now," she said, finishing the last belt, "when the music starts, your jobs, Santas, is to shake your bodies until all ten balls pop out. First one with an empty box wins drinks for the table. Ready?"

Libby joined in on the hooting and hollering.

Ray clapped.

I hoped no one would dislocate something they'd need later.

"Go!" Cookie cranked up "Jingle Bell Rock," and the Santas started shaking.

The café door opened, and my gaze swung in that direction, as did the eyes of my table mates. A moment later, we released a collective sigh and traded awkward smiles. We were all on edge, but we were in this together. Better still, the newcomer was Caroline.

She stepped onto the welcome mat and waited, peering occasionally through the window.

I put my photos of Theodore with the others, then waved a hand overhead, in case she hadn't noticed us.

She waved back, stance tight with concern.

"What's she doing?" Libby asked, tension rolling off her once more.

"I'm not sure."

The door opened again, and Zane walked inside.

Libby sucked in a breath. "That answers that."

I supposed it did. Caroline had brought Zane to a very public Mistletoe event. There wasn't any scenario where her dad didn't hear about this by morning. She'd made the decision, knowing the consequences, so Zane had better be worth it.

I hung on the incoming couple's every interaction. Watched as they shared smiles and eye contact when she spoke on their way to our booth. He nudged chairs and people out of her way and held her purse while helping her remove her coat.

They'd dressed alike, and I wondered if it was intentional. It seemed early for them to have planned coordinated outfits, which made the whole thing more adorable. Both had chosen dark-washed jeans and dress boots with gray turtlenecks. His top was dark and fitted; hers was light and oversized, with a massive cowl neck, but a turtleneck, nonetheless.

My heart did a little flutter on Caroline's behalf. She looked truly happy.

"Hi, everyone," she said. "You all remember Zane."

Ray rose awkwardly from his place in the booth and shook the other man's hand.

I scooted against the wall, making room for them on my side, across from Libby and Ray. "I'm so glad you guys are here. Can I get you anything?"

Libby rolled her eyes. "How are you going to do that from back there in the corner?" She rose and took her server position at the table's edge. "What'll it be?"

"Coffee?" Zane asked, gaze sliding from Libby to the shaking Santas, on repeat.

"Peppermint hot chocolate," Caroline said. "And a sampler basket of cookies."

Libby winked and headed for the counter.

"That was Libby," I said. "Do you remember our names from the other night? I'm Holly and this is Ray. That's Cookie." I pointed.

Zane reached across Caroline to shake my hand. "I remember, and I've heard a lot about you over the last few days."

"I see," I said, sliding my eyes to the blonde between us.

She beamed.

"I'm glad you got a little time off and were able to visit tonight."

"Me too." His gaze returned to the Santas, who were getting tired now and starting to bend over with effort. "What are they doing?"

"Trying to shake the junk out of their trunks," Ray said.

Zane's brows rose.

"Ping-Pong balls and tissue boxes," I clarified, "but yeah."

Libby returned with the drinks and cookies, then retook her seat beside Ray.

A tall, lanky Santa threw his hands over his head and made a winded but victorious sound.

The crowd cheered.

Cookie checked his tissue box and declared it empty. "Table five is the winner!"

"So," Ray said, shifting forward and projecting his voice over the crowd. "What are you guys up to tonight?"

Caroline smiled. "Meeting you. Officially." She spoke the words with meaning, and Ray's gaze hopped to mine.

"Last game," Cookie said, drawing a small *boo* from the room. "After this one, we'll take a break and see what happens." She set the mic down and helped Mom pass out baskets of gingerbread men.

Cookie stopped at our table and grinned at Zane. "Well, hello."

Zane offered his hand. "Zane Archer."

"I know who you are," Cookie said. "Caroline hasn't stopped talking about you."

"Cookie!" Caroline hissed.

"All good things, I hope?" Zane said.

"Mostly she told us how you're good-looking, but not very good at holiday games played in large groups."

He barked a laugh. "That's oddly specific and nothing like anything I've told her."

Cookie shrugged. "She said you're a little dull and not very competitive either, but you seem nice to me. I don't know why she's like that."

Caroline laughed, a big, boisterous sound I rarely heard from her. "Stop."

Zane opened and closed his fingers, indicating he'd like to participate in the next game. "I guess I'd better make sure everyone's clear that I'm not always dull, and I can be competitive on occasion, especially if it impresses Caroline and/or her friends." He winked at Caroline, who promptly blushed.

Cookie set a basket of cookies on the table. "Atta boy."

She returned to the counter and grabbed the mic.

Caroline passed the cookie basket around, and we all took one.

"Don't eat it," Libby said, knocking Ray's from his mouth.

Part of the gingerbread man's leg fell from Ray's lips. "Why?"

Libby rolled her eyes, and the rest of us laughed.

"This is one of the original quick games," Cookie said into the microphone, climbing back onto the stage. "Everyone take a cookie, tilt your head back and set the gingerbread fellow on your foreheads. When the music starts, you have to move the cookie to your mouth and eat it without using your hands. If it falls off your face, you can pick it up, but you have to put it back on your forehead and start over. The first table with everyone's cookie eaten wins. Ready?"

We got into position.

The familiar opening notes to "Santa Claus Is Coming to Town" rose through the room, and the game began. I finished before the rest of my table, but in fairness, I'd played this game a lot. Libby's cookie fell and broke on the table, leaving her with two pieces to manage. Caroline and Zane were head to head in the race and holding hands on the table as they worked. Their giant smiles weren't helping their cause, but they were adorable.

When another table won, the couple at my side gave up and straightened to clap. They leaned against each other, looking as if they'd won Olympic gold instead of lost a cookie race.

But it was official. I liked Zane.

Caroline caught my eye, seeking that information, and I nodded. This time she was the one mouthing the words *thank you*.

Chapter
Twenty-Two

The café cleared out after the games. Dad and the farm crew lined horse-drawn sleighs outside the Hearth to take guests for rides around the property.

Everyone at my table settled in to discuss our lives.

I praised Caroline, my family members, and friends for a beautiful and meaningful luncheon.

Libby and I broke the gag order on Theodore's pictures by sharing them with Caroline, which meant allowing Zane a peek as well.

"If this guy's really on the hunt, I know the perfect goat for him," Zane said, earning a shove from his date. He rubbed the spot where Caroline had pushed him, as if she'd truly caused his bulging bicep pain.

She giggled.

"Seriously," he said. "Her name is Jasmine, but her people call her Jazzy. She lives with my mom's former administrator and his husband. They're fantastic humans, and Jazzy would rock this guy's world." He tapped a finger to the image of Theodore having a picnic in his britches and newsboy cap.

Caroline raised a palm. "World rocking won't be enough. Cookie wants a wife for Theodore, so the she-goat will have to live with them."

Zane relaxed against the back of the booth. "Well, never mind. They won't let Jazzy go. She's family."

Libby raised a brow. "Did you say she-goat?" She asked Caroline. "I'm a city-girl, but that doesn't sound right."

Caroline looked apologetic but unsure.

"The boys are bucks or billys," I said. "The females are does or nannies."

Caroline bobbed her head and raised her cooling cocoa. "Good to know. What else have I missed?"

Libby caught my eye, then turned her gaze back to the woman at my side. "A lot, actually."

"Well, let's hear it."

Libby and I filled Caroline and Zane in on the findings at the hotel. The couple looked equal parts interested and displeased.

Zane straightened, resting his forearms on the table. "I heard about the flyers at the gate this morning, but I hadn't heard about the coat, car, or hotel." He peered around Caroline to me. "You're still going strong on this case, huh?"

My required response felt like a trap. I recalled Evan's instructions for Zane to alert him if I meddled at the ballet, and I knew Evan preferred I not get involved in any of his investigations. But we all knew I was up to my eyeballs in Libby's stalker case as well as Tiffany's murder, so I answered honestly. "Yep."

"Good for you," Zane said, drawing the eyes of everyone around the table. He lifted a hand and shook his head. "I'm not saying it's good you're getting mixed up with a killer or obstructing an ongoing criminal investigation. I'm just saying I get it. I'd do the same thing, and I think Caroline would to. Probably both of you." He motioned to Libby and Ray, who nodded. "When we've got real friends—people we love and care about—we do what we can. However we can. Even if it means sticking out our necks. Sometimes, especially then. I get that, and I can see this group is a lot like my friends back home. One thing I've learned—through my time in the military, traveling, and seeing my mom rise and then walk away from her career, to be with her sick husband—is that not everyone gets people like these in their lives. It's an honor and privilege to serve and protect them."

If Caroline hadn't been between us, I might've launched myself against him in a hug.

"Thank you for saying those thing," I said. "I always feel so guilty for worrying Evan. I know I shouldn't, but I can't stop."

He nodded. "Like I said, I get it. I'm guessing he does too. Honestly, I don't know the guy that well, but he's probably just trying to protect you. He doesn't strike me as the kind of man to want to stop you from being who you are." His eyes slid in Caroline's direction, and I realized he was speaking about his feelings for her too. He just wanted to keep her safe, like the rest of us.

My heart melted a little further.

Ray's arm went around Libby's shoulders, and she leaned against his side.

The café door opened, and Evan appeared. He spotted us immediately and moved in our direction.

"This is getting crowded." Libby said.

"Scooch." Evan smiled at his sister, nodded at Ray, then scanned my side of the booth. "Zane."

Caroline bristled. "He's my date at the moment, so you have to be nice."

"I'm always nice."

I waited eagerly for Evan's attention as he took the seat beside his sister. "What have you learned?"

"For starters, Deputy Frank's wife is pregnant, so I'm losing a deputy in the spring. I know that's not what you mean, but he picked the worst day to make this big happy reveal. I just stared at him. I'm having an all-hands-on-deck moment, and he's leaving. I owe him a pie and a more enthusiastic response as soon as I can formulate one."

Libby rubbed his back. "Sorry. That's tough."

He slid a bland look at her and grunted.

She dropped her hand into her lap and frowned. "Now that we've got your problem out of the way, maybe we can focus on mine. Since I'm still waiting to hear if Kellen Lance sent a member of his crime family to make this my last Christmas."

Evan scrubbed a hand over the top of his head, a look of earnest exhaustion aging his features. "There's no news yet. I talked to Boston PD this afternoon, and they're trying to get a list of individuals who drive the car, since it's unlikely the elderly gentleman it's registered to is the one following you. BPD is also looking into the family and extended family of Kellen Lance. His side goons—sisters, friends, cousins, and anyone else in his world who fits the description of our ballerina impersonator."

The heat left Libby's eyes, as did the light. "We still have no idea who's after me."

Evan nodded. "I'm so sorry, Lib."

I set my phone on the table, ready to try my hand at online investigating once more. "Okay. Has anyone checked to see if Kellen Lance is maintaining his social media?"

"He isn't," Evan said.

I typed his name into a search engine, then followed some related links to his friends' lists.

"Bingo," I said, grinning. "I found his mother. That's better than having his updated account. Moms tell everything, and it looks like she and her boyfriend are in Honolulu for the holidays." I turned the phone to the gawking people across from me.

Ray smirked. "Facebook. Spilling everyone's tea since 2004."

I winked and pointed at him. Then I turned back to my phone. I examined the woman's friends, specifically those who posted regularly on her timeline.

"Isn't tech already doing this?" Libby asked.

Evan shifted. "Lib, in Mistletoe, tech is one of our deputies with a computer science degree. And we're all scrambling with the murder and high traffic right now."

"What about the guys at Boston PD?" she asked.

"I hope they're working on it," he said. "Especially now that we have the car as a link to show there's reason to allocate resources to the cause."

"You *hope*?" she asked, voice ratcheting up.

Caroline shifted forward. "Why would she pretend to be a ballerina?"

"Probably to blend in," Evan said. "If she thought she might be recognized. With the ballet in town, and two dozen dancers running around, all dressed alike, there's nothing to notice."

I waved a hand in their direction, eyes fixed on a blond baby. "Hold on." I flipped backward through the timeline, watching the baby as it grew younger—until it was born a few months back, around the time Libby's weird greeting cards began arriving and only a short time before she'd first noticed the teal car in town. "Did you know there's a baby in this family?"

The table stilled.

"No," Evan said.

"What do you mean?" Libby asked. "Who has a baby?"

I raised my eyes to find everyone rapt. "Someone. Her image is on this woman's feed consistently."

"Lance's mom is too old to have a baby," Evan said.

"And he's an only child," Libby added.

"You sure?" Evan asked.

Libby nodded. "I remember talking to Heather about him in their early days of dating, and she specifically said she hated that he was an only child, because having siblings was so important to her."

"Well, someone had a little girl," I said. "Her name is Antonia Grace." I passed my phone around the circle, wondering why I hadn't looked up Kellen Lance and his mom sooner.

Evan held the phone when it reached him. "The mother is tagged in some of these photos. Looks like she was romantically involved with Kellan, but her relationship status says it's complicated."

If she'd had Kellen Lance's baby, her entire life was probably complicated.

Libby leaned in for a closer look as he scrolled, and examined the images. "I'm not sure."

Zane leaned on the table, seeking my face. "What about you, Holly?"

Evan turned the screen to face me, and a petite blonde in tight jeans and a halter top pouted moodily from the device. Her gaze was distant, and her pupils dilated. She looked exhausted. A lot like the mother of a baby might. "This is the woman I spoke to outside the café." I was certain of it. Even with all the eye makeup and her long hair worn down in the image, I recognized her.

"She looks like Heather," Libby said. "Not the hair or anything, but that vacant expression. The empty smile. She's probably high. I saw this look on Heather for months before she vanished." Libby's cheeks darkened. "This is what happens to women who fall in love with Kellen Lance. They become shells of who they used to be."

Evan turned to wrap his little sister in a hug, but she spun away, planting her face in the crook of Ray's neck.

Ray's arms came around her protectively, and he rested his cheek against the top of her head.

Evan sighed. I could see it was hard for him to watch Libby turn to someone else for comfort. They'd lost their dad when Libby was young, and Evan had filled all the traditional patriarchal roles for her until now.

His eyes met mine, and he nodded, probably knowing I saw what he did. She'd chosen Ray to take over some of the jobs Evan had done for many years. Comfort was one of them, but Ray would forever have a partner in his role as Libby's protector. Evan wouldn't give up his part in that, this side of the grave. Even then, he'd probably haunt anyone daring to upset her.

And because Ray loved her, I knew he was glad for the assist.

Ray tipped his chin at Evan, and her brother gave a slow nod.

I smiled at the unspoken exchange between the men.

Whatever happened, Libby was going to be okay.

"We'll find her," Evan said. "And we'll set her straight. I hate to arrest her if she has a baby, but there are certainly grounds for it if you want to press charges."

Libby met her brother's eyes, expression tight and pained. "What's her name?"

He turned the phone to her. "Gina Dupree."

The café door swung open, and a gust of snow and wind swept inside.

Every member of our table jumped.

Dad appeared, looking like the Abominable Snowman. He dusted flakes from his coat and stomped his boots on the mat. "It's really coming down out there. Folks are heading home before the roads get slick again."

Mom emerged from the kitchen and went to hug him, snow and all. "I heard we could get up to thirty inches in the next twenty-four hours!"

Together, they approached our booth, pleasant expressions on their faces.

217

The café was quiet around us.

"Who have we here?" Mom asked, her curious gaze fixed on Zane.

Caroline made the introductions, and my parents took turns shaking her date's hand.

"Can we get you anything?" Mom asked, looking at each of our faces in earnest. "Sounds like you're my last guests for the evening, and I have plenty of everything on the menu. I'm happy to whip up something else if none of that suits."

"We're good, Mrs. White," Caroline said. "Thank you." She turned to Zane and smiled warmly. "The Whites are the parents I never had, and they extend that service to anyone in need."

He smiled. "The town's lucky to have you."

"Oh." Mom said, leaning against Dad's side and basking in Zane's kind words. "We have plenty of everything to go around. That counts for hugs and acceptance as well as beds, food, and shelter."

"Good thing," Dad said, tucking his gloves into the pockets of his parka. "I hate to break it to all you lovebirds, but this storm's a nor'easter, and it's not going to miss us like the others have." He looked from me to Evan. "Could end up with more than four feet of snow before your big day. Your family's going to want to get here before it hits. We'll make room—just let them know it might be now or never. Or at least, not until after Christmas. Tomorrow morning will be their best chance, after the road crews get things clear. If they wait any longer than that, they'll likely miss the wedding."

I looked to Mom.

She nodded sadly. "It's true. The ladies and I are setting up the wedding and reception first thing in the morning, just in case they can't get here after that. I've already called in a rush on things that weren't scheduled until the day of. Better to have them here and worry about proper storage and preservation than to wait and find we can't get them."

Zane frowned. "I hope you don't have to cancel your wedding."

Caroline guffawed. "They are not canceling. Not even a nor'easter can stop true love."

Zane glanced around the table before offering Caroline an apologetic smile.

"The storm could still pass," I said.

Evan looked from Dad to Libby. "I'll call Mom tonight. Let her know to get moving."

My parents relaxed visibly, and I wondered why I hadn't seen the full weight of their concern before.

I sighed at their relief, but I wasn't worried about the fancy wedding we'd planned. All I needed was Evan, and he was right here with me. I was concerned, however, with the fact that the ballet would leave town tomorrow night, and we still hadn't named the killer.

Chapter
Twenty-Three

I t was still dark when I rolled out of bed the next morning, too wound up to sleep. My wedding was only twenty-four hours away, and my inn guests would check out after their final matinee performance at the Mistletoe Grand. Then they'd make their way back to the capital for their big Christmas Eve show, killer and all.

I dressed in my most comfortable jeans and softest sweater, then piled my hair on top of my head in a messy knot and made a pot of tea. I curled onto the couch in my living quarters with a cuppa and my phone, determined to unmask the obsessive social media maven Courtney. If I couldn't unmask the killer, I could at least give finding the blogger's real identity another try. Something about her had bugged me from the beginning, and everything since then had made the feeling more pronounced. Why had no one ever seen her? What was the point of protecting her identity? Wasn't the point of massive social media pushes like hers to bring some amount of fame? Or at least recognition?

Her dedicated anonymity made me wonder if, perhaps, Courtney was an alias. A cute little name to hide behind because she was actually a man. Maybe even George. The large footprints found in the hidden hallway beyond Tiffany and Ava's dressing area could easily have been his. I'd thought it before, and the idea circled back to mind with determination. Maybe he'd used the passage to meet with his love secretly. Then again to leave the rats for Ava. He couldn't openly advocate for Tiffany as himself, so a pseudonym and alternate persona would have been the perfect cover.

The theory worked logically with the information I had available, but still I waffled. Because George had loved Tiffany, so why would he kill her? It hadn't been an act of rage or an argument out of hand. She'd been slowly poisoned over multiple doses. Did he intend to keep her slightly ill? Just enough to need him? Had his secret advocacy caused her star to shine too brightly, and he feared she might leave him, so the poison was intended to counteract what he'd done? That theory seemed unnecessarily bizarre. More like the plot of a movie than real life. Even less sensible was the idea of him leaving rats on my truck and in Ava's room afterward. What had Ava done?

Whoever Courtney really was, she wasn't the petite blonde I'd spoken with the other day. That was clear enough now. Boston PD was looking for Gina Dupree, Antonia Grace's mother and Kellen Lance's girlfriend. I wondered if Libby had slept any better last night, finally knowing who was tormenting her. Identifying the culprit meant she could now be found—eventually, and I hoped that had given my friend a small measure of relief. I hoped it wasn't too late for Gina to get the help she needed, maybe even extricate herself and her baby from Lance and his criminal ties.

I stretched my neck and scrolled through Courtney's social media posts, marveling at the beautiful imagery she'd caught with every snapshot. This time I strained to catch a glimpse at the person behind the camera, zooming in on every reflective surface and pane of glass. But Courtney was careful, and her features were never visible. Occasionally a small red gleam was visible but unfocused, perhaps a reflection of stage lighting or the setting sun. I read the caption beneath each photo as I scrolled, and examined the lists of her friends and followers.

By the time my teapot was empty, I'd exhausted all the available material on her social media sites and was forced to return to her blog. I blew over the steam on my last cup of tea and got comfortable. The blog was verbose and packed with terms I didn't know. I had to settle in for a long haul if I wanted to get through it.

Hours passed and the sky outside my window put on its daily show, moving through all the colors of blue as the sun burned away the night. I made a second pot of tea and dug into my stash of cookies when my back started to cramp from my curled-up position on the couch.

The fiery amber and red hues of sunrise climbed my windowsill as I carried my sugary breakfast back to the couch. My gaze caught on the tattered copy of *The Count of Monte Cristo* as I moved through my private space, and I smiled. It was my favorite novel, and I read it each year at Christmas. On the night I'd met Evan, I'd learned it was his favorite too. He had a copy in his cruiser when he drove me to the Hearth. His dad, an English teacher, had shared it with him before his death.

I returned to the couch and let the warm memory of our first meeting settle over me. I'd been shaken after finding a body, but Evan had been strong and calm. Most importantly, he'd been kind. Even when he'd insinuated my dad or one of our farmhands was the killer, he'd been transparent about his process, and everyone had trusted him to do the right thing.

I'd thought he was handsome at first sight, but it hadn't taken long for me to understand he was so much more. Evan was made of all the best stuff, like honor, compassion, and integrity, and he was continually striving to be better. Having the option to build a life with him was mind-boggling, and I couldn't wait to get started.

I bit into a cookie and returned my attention to Courtney's blog in earnest, pausing to look up the terms I wasn't familiar with and noting how many there were. For a fan, she certainly knew the lingo and everything else about ballet. I supposed that was true with sports fans too. Some had even played in high school or college, making them excellent at describing what happened on the courts and fields. Was that true about Courtney too? Had she been a dancer at one time? Was she the current choreographer?

I thought again about the magazine I'd seen at the parade. Then I opened a new window and searched for the article online. A time-line of photographs accompanied the words, highlighting Tiffany's rise to fame.

I flipped back and forth between the significant moments noted in the article and Courtney's posts from the same time periods. It was easy to see Ava had been right about the blogger's level of influence and power. The fervor of her posts seemed to spawn direct changes within Maine's ballet industry. Specifically with regards to Tiffany, but also in other ways as well. For example, a quote from Tiffany about how she came to ballet late in life, in middle school instead of in diapers, because she was from a lower-income family, had spurred the creation of accessibility programs for arts in under-served communities. It was as if Tiffany spoke it, Courtney championed it, and the change came into fruition.

That was some pretty amazing teamwork.

My fingers froze on the screen as that thought settled in. Was it possible Tiffany and Courtney had been a team? Could they have known one another? Was she who Tiffany had snuck out to meet on the night before her death?

The familiar sounds of brewing coffee and a blender alerted me to the time.

I set my phone aside and went to greet the dancers, hoping irrationally one of them might have the word *Guilty* written on her forehead.

"Morning," I said, returning my tray to the counter. "Anything I can help with today?"

The group smiled politely, shaking their heads as they worked through their morning routines, likely wondering why I was standing there when I rarely made an appearance before they left for breakfast. I'd kept out of their way as much as possible when George was still an overwhelming presence in the earlier days of their stay. Now, I was slightly less intimidated by him—and infinitely more motivated to find answers before they left town.

George leaned against the counter with his coffee, cautiously watching me.

"Would you like anything special set out this afternoon?" I asked. "Something to celebrate your last show here, or a light meal of some kind before you hit the road? I can arrange a fruit and cheese board. Maybe nuts and chocolates?"

The ladies exchanged hopeful looks, their collective gazes traveling quickly to George.

"That's fine," he said. "Thank you."

The dancers beamed and tittered, then took their coffees into the living room.

I smiled.

George eyeballed me. "What are you up to now?"

"I'm just being an excellent innkeeper. Hoping to help the dancers celebrate a series of great performances in Mistletoe."

He took a slow drink from his mug. "Uh-huh."

"How's everyone holding up?" I asked. When he didn't answer, I backpedaled. "Sorry. Of course everyone is grieving and shaken. It was nice of you to allow a small celebration today. I've ordered the flowers you requested. They're being delivered to the theater. And I'll have everything here when you return. I know you'll be in a hurry to beat the storm back to Augusta."

His sharp eyes cut to mine. "I've kept them busy with extended rehearsals and meetings after our performances, hoping to limit the amount of time anyone has to think about Tiffany's loss. But as a group, we need to take a minute to remember her. I'll say a few words over the charcuterie and offer the dancers time to remember her today, before they have to pull it together again for tomorrow's big show."

I deflated, feeling the pain and frustration in his low, gravelly voice, and I moved to stand beside him. "I know you think I'm a big pain. Maybe even a rude pain, but I'm not trying to be either of those things. I just want justice for Tiffany and everyone who cared about her." I locked him in my stare, willing him to say something I could use toward my cause. "I want the person responsible to be punished."

He shut his eyes for a long beat before reopening them.

"I assumed it was you at first," I said, watching closely for his reaction.

He frowned. "Why would you think that?"

I tented my brows and folded my arms. "A secret, illicit relationship is something some folks would go to great lengths to keep under wraps."

He screwed his features into a knot and turned to face me, bringing us only inches apart. His shoulders curved inward, and he loomed, outraged. "I would never have hurt Tiffany, and I wouldn't kill anyone."

I took a step back and craned my neck for a better look at his face, telling myself not to back down. "I don't know that," I reminded him. "I don't know you or anyone else who knew Tiffany. All I can do is collect the facts and try to assemble them like a puzzle. It's the only hope I have to make sense of what's going on in this town. Like it or not, you're the one in the middle of the picture. You were the center of Tiffany's world. You had a personal and professional relationship with her."

"I did not hurt her," he said, biting out each word.

I pressed my lips together and squared my shoulders. My instincts twitched at the sight of his pain. I wasn't so sure anymore that George could've hurt Tiffany, but there was one more thing I had to ask. "Are you Courtney?"

His angry expression fell. "What?" He relented his position, visibly confused. "How could I be . . . Courtney's a woman."

"How do you know?"

"Well, it isn't a guy's name."

I stared. "No one has ever seen her. So, it doesn't matter what name is being used. She could be anyone. Have you ever read her blog? Spent any time on her social media?"

George moved away, one hand rising to his forehead.

I released a shaky sigh, and he met my eyes, realization dawning in his expression.

"Sorry for—" He motioned to me, possibly indicating his attempt to intimidate me a moment before. "I have a temper, but I never act on it. I get snappy. I use my big voice, and it gets things done onstage. But that's where it ends." He set the mug aside. "Now, tell me what you're saying about the blogger."

I hoped that was true about his temper, but redirected my thoughts to take advantage of our limited time. I explained my perception of Courtney's online presence and her content. The way she knew so many things about ballet and seemed to be among the dancers and stage crew taking photos.

Stalking Around the Christmas Tree

He frowned and pulled a phone from his pocket, swiping his thumb across the screen. "What's her thing called?"

"Bun Heads."

He rolled his eyes, but tapped the screen a few times, then rested against the counter, perusing the feed.

"The blog is dense, but her social media feeds are mostly images and little bursts of thought. All have an enormous following," I said.

My phone rang, and I freed it from my pocket. Mom's number appeared. "Sorry," I told George. "I have to take this."

He nodded, eyes fixed on his device as he walked away, catching his hip on the counter as he left the room.

I hurried back to my private quarters. "Hello?"

"Morning, darling," Mom said, tone chipper and bright. "I'm just touching base about the reindeer games. Are you still able to set up for Bling That Gingerbread? I think I can take the afternoon events. We've had some tour buses cancel due to weather. That big storm has already hit a few towns northeast of us."

"Sure," I said. "I'll head over to the Hearth in a jiff. We can chat before the game gets started."

"Thank you, sweetie. See you soon."

I disconnected and returned the phone to my pocket.

I hoped my instincts were right about George, and he wasn't the killer after all. He'd had opportunities to dose Tiffany's shakes, but I couldn't fathom any motivation on his part.

Regardless, it was time to hit pause on my sleuthing efforts for now.

I had a reindeer game to coordinate.

Chapter Twenty-Four

I arrived at the Hearth a little earlier than Mom had requested, allowing myself more time than necessary for the walk. Mistletoe hadn't received any additional precipitation since the handful of inches the night before, and the farm roads had been thoroughly cleared. The temperature was in the upper twenties, and it seemed as if the local meteorologist had been wrong yet again. I almost rolled my eyes at the repeated failures to predict an actual storm in our town, but caught myself. I didn't want to jinx it.

I got busy on the setup for our next reindeer game. I loved Bling That Gingerbread and had the process down to a science. First, I put a sign outside the café, letting folks know the Hearth was open for takeout-only during this hour and that there would be a game in sixty minutes. Participation was first come, first served and limited to forty-five guests. Next, I set up wooden stanchions and rope, blocking access to the tables and booths, but allowing passage from the door to the counter, so guests could still pop in and grab something warm or sweet while they enjoyed the farm.

Mom handled guests, and I handled game prep.

I hustled to the kitchen and collected my supplies on the countertop, then stacked them on trays for ease of transport. Each player would receive a small, ready-built gingerbread house, a platter of assorted candies like gumdrops, mints, and licorice in red and black. Plus one blindfold. Once the trays were full, I ferried them to the tables and booths. Unloading was a cinch. One house, one platter, and one blindfold for every placemat.

My system was practiced and flawless. I finished in under thirty minutes, including time spent putting things away in the kitchen.

Mom lifted her hand in a silent high five on my way past her with the last empty tray.

Bling That Gingerbread was a classic reindeer game that everyone loved. Even those who didn't participate got a kick out of perusing the results and snapping pictures for fun. Players blindfolded themselves, then decorated the gingerbread house before them. First, they'd stick their fingers into the icing and smear it on the cookie surfaces to prepare for the décor. Then they'd apply the candies in the most attractive way possible, given they couldn't see what they were doing. As it turns out, relying on the sense of touch isn't as easy as most think.

Mom loved to take photos of the players in action while peppy holiday tunes rose from café speakers. A few guests inevitably tried to keep their hands clean by selecting a candy to dip into the icing bowl before placing the treat onto the house, but those folks usually gave up rather quickly. In the end everyone always had icing everywhere, and their houses looked like they'd fallen into a pile of spilled candies.

Mom and I would put the finished houses on display across the counter and on windowsills until closing, and the crowd would vote on the winner by placing mini candy canes into a small basket placed in front of each. Players received free hot drinks for participating, and others enjoyed the chance to vote. Mom's photos of the event were always hilarious, and at least one from this game usually made it into the Reindeer Games newsletter or onto the website.

When I returned to the dining area, Mom was strolling the perimeter, looking relieved to see things were ready.

"What do you think?" I asked.

Her eyes jerked to mine. "I think you're a magician. It would've taken me all night to get this many materials organized and distributed."

"I've had a little practice," I said, leaning a hip against her counter.

"You have," she agreed. "And there's no task you haven't mastered. Even at a young age. You were always such a motivated little thing. Moving mountains since nineteen—"

I raised a hand. "Don't say it."

Mom grinned.

"Young people today think anyone born in the nineteen hundreds is a relic," I said, not ready to be a relic.

Laughter burbled from Mom's lips as she wrapped me in a quick hug. "Speak for yourself."

"Is there anything else I can help with?" I asked, squeezing her back.

She released me, still obviously amused by my previous statement. "No. I think I'm all set. I finished the first round of pastries while you did this. I'd have burnt them for sure if I had to prepare the game between oven dings."

I inhaled deeply, attempting not to drool at the delectable scent of fresh-baked cinnamon rolls.

"They're still warm and gooey," she said. "Newly iced, and I was incredibly generous. Can I interest you in one or two?"

"I think you can twist my arm a little and convince me."

Mom patted the nearest stool, and I took a seat while she plated a sticky, sugary hunk of heaven, then poured me a cup of coffee. "Now tell me how you're holding up," she said. "Feeling good about tomorrow?"

"Definitely. I'm getting excited for the wedding, and I'm thrilled the snow hasn't come as predicted." I cut a chunk of cinnamon roll free with the side of my fork, then raised it to my lips. Long strings of melty icing stretched upward with the soft, cinnamon scent.

"Nervous?"

"Nope. Caroline has all the details sorted, so I know everything will be perfect. Far better than I could've planned it. Plus, you, Dad, and Evan will be there, and that's all I really need. Everyone and everything else is icing." I popped the bite into my mouth and let my eyelids flutter. "This never stops being the very best thing I've ever tasted."

Mom leaned her forearms on the counter, watching me enjoy her food. "I'm really proud of you, you know? It wasn't that long ago you came back to us with a broken heart and all your earthly belongings in a moving truck."

I smiled. "Best thing I've ever done."

"You changed the atmosphere here when you returned. It was one thing, you being here as a kid, but it's been different with you as an adult. I've gained a best friend."

My eyes misted and I set my fork down. "Mom."

"Really," she said. "I'll always worry about you, and you'll always be my little girl, but you're something altogether different now. You don't need me in the same way you used to, and I find myself looking to you for things now. Leaning on you when I struggle."

My throat tightened and tears welled, unbidden. She was my best friend too, and I wasn't sure when that had happened, precisely. But it had, even if we didn't pal around together the same way I did with Caroline and Cookie. Outside of our busy season, I spent loads of time with her and Dad, sharing meals, playing cards, watching shows, or just catching up after our long days.

"I'm glad things didn't work out with that other guy," she said, wiping her eyes and chuckling softly. "I got you back."

I got off my stool and went to hug her again.

We rocked there, foot to foot, holding tight to one another for long moments before she let me go.

"So what's on your agenda today?" she asked, pressing a handkerchief to her eyes and doing her best to rein in her emotions.

"Well." I sniffled, returning to my pastry, "first I need to wrap the rest of the toy drive donations," I said. "Then I have to schedule a pickup for them. After that I'm arranging a little post-ballet celebration for the dancers. George said I can set out a charcuterie and chocolates this afternoon. In between, I'm not sure."

"You're welcome to hang out here," she said.

"Then I will." I took another big bite and savored the unbelievably perfect flavors as they melted on my tongue. "I'll drop by when I finish my to-do list."

I polished off my coffee and dessert, then kissed Mom's cheek before heading back to the inn. The weather was perfect for skiing, ice skating, or sledding, three of my favorite outdoor winter activities. Unfortunately, I wouldn't have time for any of that until after the holidays, but I didn't mind waiting. The things I had to look forward to were far greater, and the next time I did any of those other things, I'd likely do them with Evan as my husband, which was definitely worth the wait.

I pulled my phone from my pocket and placed the call to arrange a pickup for the donated toys as I walked. The Build a Big Frosty competition was in full swing. Enormous snowmen had popped up in every direction since my walk to the café only an hour before. Some had elaborately carved and detailed features, and some were painted with food coloring and squirt guns. Others were simply large. All were acceptable. There weren't any hard or fast rules for this game. But when the time was up, Mom, Dad or I, would select a winner. The builder would get their picture in the local paper, a Mistletoe tradition. And my folks would be sure the winner also received something nice from the Hearth, along with bragging rights for a year.

I checked the time on my phone screen as I disconnected the call. I had three hours to complete the wrapping, which seemed like more than enough as long as I got started right away. I put the phone back into my pocket and grinned as Ray and Libby came into view.

They strode hand in hand across the field, heading toward the Hearth. Apparently they'd had a full reconciliation last night.

I waved them down.

"Hey!" Ray called.

We all adjusted our paths and met in the middle. He and Libby were bundled up to their chins, the faux fur lining of their hoods flapping around their faces.

"I have the morning shift," Libby said.

"I just set up for Bling That Gingerbread. I'm wrapping donated toys when I get back to the inn, and then I'm thinking of visiting the theater one more time. Any chance you two want to catch the final show?"

Libby nodded. "I missed half the performance last time."

"Sure," Ray said. "Meet you there?"

"It's a date." I hugged them each quickly, then set them free. I wasn't sure what I thought I might uncover at the ballet, if anything, but it felt like the right place to be.

Three hours later, the donations were wrapped and on their way to children across Mistletoe. I'd arranged fruits, chocolates, and cheeses for the dancers, as promised, and left a note on the fridge to let them know everything was inside, in case they beat me home. Then I dug up another dress to wear and slid my feet into pumps.

The simple black dress had a scoop neck and short sleeves. It was knee length and more casual than the blue velvet I'd worn to opening night, but this was a matinee. There would likely be a wide range of attire, and I wanted to be comfortable.

Ray and Libby followed me to the theater in his old green pickup. We parked in the lot across the street and walked to the ticket office, where we purchased the worst seats in the house.

"I guess we should've expected the last show to be a full house," I said.

Ray frowned at his stub as we crossed the empty lobby to the theater. "I think we could've seen just as well from the lot across the street."

Libby laughed. "They might not be that bad."

He checked his ticket again. "I didn't even know this place had a row double Z."

We entered through the large double doors at the back of the theater and stopped immediately, filing into the last row. The seats Libby and I had occupied during our trip with Caroline were barely visible in the distance. The space around us was still mostly empty. We'd arrived incredibly early, but that had been by design.

"Since we have a little time," I said, not bothering to sit, "who wants to sneak backstage and talk to the dancers with me?"

Ray's frown deepened. "Is that the real reason we're here? Because you could've said so and saved us from paying for these terrible seats."

"Come on," Libby said. "We all knew this would happen eventually. No use pretending we didn't. At least we aren't missing the show this time."

I smiled smugly at Ray as I followed his girlfriend around the theater toward a backstage entrance.

"What's the plan?" Libby asked. "Anyone in particular you want to talk to back there?"

"I'd like to speak with the dancer playing the Mouse King, if possible," I said. "We were interrupted the last time we spoke, and I have more to ask."

"So be it," she said. "Ray, we're going to arrange a tête-à-tête with Holly and the Mouse King."

My smile widened.

Ray sighed, resigned. "Alright. Let's do this, I guess."

I appreciated Libby's enthusiasm, a result of her repairing things with Ray, I presumed.

He kept pace at our sides. "I thought we'd already counted this guy out."

"I have, almost," I said. "I just have a feeling that when the truth comes out, it will have something to do with the blogger and her obsession with this conservatory. And Ian seemed to know Tiffany pretty well. If I'm right, he might be able to help me fit the final puzzle pieces into place."

"What if the Mouse King is Courtney?" Ray asked. He widened his eyes and performed an exaggerated gasp.

"You jest," I said, "but I'm willing to consider anything right now."

Libby opened the door to the backstage, and Zane looked up from his position as guard.

We piled against each other, Three Stooges style.

"Oh, hello," Libby said. "Nice to see you again."

Caroline strode in Zane's direction, steps faltering as she noticed us in the doorway. "Hey, what are you guys doing here? Come on in. Are you going to the show?"

Zane's eyes narrowed. "Please tell me that's why you're here."

"We absolutely are," I said.

Caroline clapped silently. "Excellent. I brought cupcakes. You should all grab one before they're gone. I set them on a table by the dressing rooms."

Libby's brows pulled together. "You brought cupcakes for ballerinas?"

"Yep, and they're a hit," she said. "I wasn't sure they'd eat them, but I had hope. And I figured in a worst-case scenario, the stage crew could take the extras home to their families."

I scanned the space behind Caroline and marveled at the number of dancers eating cupcakes. The empty space on her trays was growing fast. I wondered what George thought of the pre-performance sweets. I turned in a small circle, checking faces but not finding him. "Where's the ballet master?"

Caroline shrugged.

Zane shook his head. "I haven't seen him."

Ava appeared in the open doorway of her dressing room and set a box on the floor outside.

"Ava!" I waved as I hurried to catch her and ignored the resulting groan from Zane. "Hey. How are you?"

"Good," she said. "Just packing a little. I want to make it easy to leave after the show." She opened an arm to reveal the tidy room inside. "I've put everything away that I don't need for the performance. When we're ready to head out, I'll only have to grab a few items and go, which will make my life a lot easier. Especially since I will be exhausted."

"Smart," I said. "What's in the box?" I gave the open-topped container a look. A book. Hair clips. A pink wrap sweater. A scarf.

"That was Tiffany's," she said. "Little things I found as I packed my stuff. Someone took her bags and everything else, but there were odds and ends left behind. If I see George again, I'll let him know. He can probably get them to her family."

My eyes fixed on a small, red, rose-shaped pin attached to the sweater. "May I?"

"Go for it."

Stalking Around the Christmas Tree

I crouched to retrieve the wrap, intuition spiking, though I wasn't yet sure why.

* * *

"Holly?" Libby's voice turned me in a circle. She set a hand on her hip. "You okay?"

"Yeah. I think so. I—"

"Good, because look what I brought you." She motioned to the man leaning casually against a wall several feet away. "One Mouse King."

Ian stepped around her with a wink. "Thanks, Red. I can take it from here."

Her mouth opened, presumably to tell him what she thought of pet names, but Ray hooked an arm around her shoulders and offered her a cupcake.

Libby accepted the treat with narrowed eyes and allowed Ray to steer her away.

Ian wagged his brows. His sandy hair appear casually messy, but I was certain he'd placed every curl and wave where he wanted it before parting ways with his mirror. Big blue eyes dared me not to fall in love with him.

No problem.

I dropped the sweater into the box and focused on the dancer before me. "I had some questions I didn't get to ask when we spoke before," I said. "I'm hoping you'll lend some insight now."

He widened his stance and crossed his arms, appraising me with flirty eyes. "Try me."

"Great! Do you know if anyone was harassing or bothering Tiffany before her death? Was she fighting with anyone?"

"Cops already asked this," he said. "And the answer is still no. Everyone works hard and minds their own business around here."

"Okay, then what do you know about the blog Bun Heads, or the personality behind it?"

"Courtney?" he asked, sounding entertained, per his usual. "She's just some washed-up has-been who can't dance, so she found another way back into the ballet spotlight."

My jaw dropped. "You know her?"

He made a goofy face. "No. No one knows her, but also, yeah. Have you read her stuff?"

"I've read all her stuff."

He nodded. "Then you know. She's not just some super fan. She's obviously danced before. Probably professionally, because she knows things. Not just technical things, but stuff about the culture and dynamics in a group our size. I figure she's some middle-aged soccer mom reliving her glory days through the blog and getting the ballet-related attention online that she never could've gotten onstage."

I considered his words. Some of them felt incredibly likely. The rest seemed a little mean, and probably more reflective of his personality than whoever Courtney truly was. "She does seem to know a lot about ballet."

"More than a lot," he said. "She made Tiffany's career, and now we're all out here holding our breath to see who she advocates for next."

"But she's been silent since the murder."

He watched me. "So?"

We stared at one another.

"You think Courtney snapped and killed Tiffany?" he asked, eyes dancing with amusement.

"Maybe Tiffany figured out who she was," I said.

Something was definitely hinky. Courtney had been obsessed with Tiffany but hadn't bothered to post a single word of remembrance for the dancer following her death. George had been gutted by the loss. Why wasn't Courtney?

"Ian!" A pair of female dancers motioned to him from the stage, where they sat, open legged and stretching.

He turned his eyes back to me. "Look. I don't know what happened to Tiffany. And I don't know anything about Courtney, but I doubt she was homicidal. She's a blogger." He sniffed, obviously equating *blogger* with *pathetic*. "You need anything else?"

"No. I'm good. Thank you."

He hiked his chin in goodbye, then headed for the beckoning dancers.

I turned my attention back to the box of Tiffany's things. With talk of Courtney in my head and the rose pin in view, something slowly snapped into place. I pulled the sweater from the box once more and examined it closely. Then I freed my phone from my purse and navigated to Courtney's social media profile. I scrolled through the photos until I found the one I'd been looking for. An image with a red smear in the reflection of a nearby window.

Ava crossed the threshold and stopped short. "You're still there?"

I nodded, gaze bobbing between the phone screen and the enamel pin.

"That rose belonged to her grandma," Ava said. "Tiffany wore it on her wrap for good luck. Her Mom will want it back." She stepped around me and headed for the group of stretching ballerinas.

I couldn't speak for long moments as I toggled my eyes and brain between the pin in my hand and the pin reflected in the glass beside a stage with ballerinas on pointe.

The person taking the photo was nothing but wavy shadows, yet the tiny, long-stemmed rose was visible in a stream of light from the flash. It was easy to understand what it was, now that I knew.

Courtney had been silent since Tiffany's death for good reason.

Tiffany had been her own super fan.

Chapter
Twenty-Five

I dialed Evan and filled him in on what I saw, then sent him a photo of the pin and a screenshot of the image in question via texts.

"Excellent eye, White," he said, speaking to me as if he was addressing one of his deputies.

"Thank you, Sheriff," I said, appreciating the pride in his tone.

"At least that's one mystery solved."

"And we can rule out the blogger as Tiffany's killer," I added.

"Exactly."

"Tiffany probably set up all those Bun Heads accounts as Courtney for the explicit purpose of driving her career," I said. "She used every photo and word she shared to raise awareness and bring attention to her and her work. She was incredible with social media and marketing. Not to mention public relations. She knew how to connect with people and make them take notice. She brought fans to her cause. If she'd ever decided to leave ballet, she would've had a successful career doing this for other people."

I turned slowly in a small circle, checking to see if anyone was nearby and listening. No one seemed to notice me, so I continued. "She compelled patrons to attend events, increased ticket sales where she was the lead, and cemented her position as Clara in the process, even when other dancers were equally or arguably more qualified."

"The ticket sales secured her spot," Evan said. "I spoke to the conservatory, and they admitted money talks. Once it was proven that placing her in the lead role brought more cash to the ticket booths, that was what they planned to do. They described it as satisfying patrons of the art, but the two were one and the same this time."

"She had a brilliant plan," I said. "And it worked."

"Agreed. Anything else I should know before I turn this information over to the team?"

I thought for a long moment. "I spoke with Ian again today. I don't think he's our killer."

Evan made a sound like a puff of air leaving his nostrils. "No?"

"No. You were right. I think he gets plenty of attention from women, and he might've even had a tryst with Tiffany, but I don't think it had anything to do with her death."

"We agree on so many things tonight," Evan said.

"So true." I smiled. "Maybe we should get married."

"How's your schedule looking for tomorrow?"

"Like a wedding," I said.

"Perfect. Anything else?" Evan asked, a lightness in his tone.

"Yeah. George isn't here again. I don't know if that means anything, but I wish I knew where he keeps going. It's the group's final performance in Mistletoe. Seems like he should be here." I couldn't help wondering if George had known the truth about Courtney's identity too. Or what it would mean if he did.

"Are you sure he's not there?" Evan asked, not sounding overly concerned.

I gave the space around me a more careful look. "No, but the dancers were eating cupcakes thirty minutes before showtime. So they had to be confident he wasn't nearby."

Evan grunted.

"Hey," I said, something else crossing my mind. "Why aren't you complaining that I'm here?"

The question earned me a long beat of silence.

"Would you have gone home if I'd asked?" he asked.

"No, but something's off," I said, mentally replaying our conversation. Then it hit me. "Did you already know Tiffany was the blogger?"

Evan released a breath.

"You did!"

"After you turned me onto the importance of the blog, I had tech support look into it."

"How did they know it was her?"

"The IP address was traced back to Tiffany's phone and personal laptop. We have both in custody, to be released to her family at the close of the investigation."

I blew air over my lips, causing them to vibrate. "You didn't tell me."

I was glad to have figured it out on my own, but a little offended that he'd kept me in the dark. Also, irrationally, I was bummed that he'd known first.

"It was only recently confirmed, and we're still not sure it's relevant in regards to her murder."

I rolled my eyes.

"Are you rolling your eyes?" he asked, knowing me far too well.

"Maybe."

"Are you going home after the show? Because I'd love to come by and check on you," he said, a titter of mischief in his voice. "Maybe bring you something sweet."

I briefly considered asking if his words were a euphemism, but decided it didn't matter either way. "I am and I'd love that," I said.

"The dancers are checking out, so we'll have the inn to ourselves. I'll pick up a bottle of champagne, in case you want to celebrate."

"I might," he said.

"Me too. And I have the perfect snack, courtesy of Jean and Millie."

"Can't wait. See you soon."

I laughed and said my goodbyes.

We might not solve a murder today, as I'd hoped, but it was shaping up to be my kind of night.

* * *

The ballet was phenomenal, as expected, and afterward I stopped backstage to tell the dancers I loved every moment. I walked to my truck with Libby and Ray, then headed home, feeling hopeful and filled with holiday cheer.

The roads were clear, and the moon was bright. It was barely six o'clock in Mistletoe, but thanks to daylight saving's time, a multitude of twinkling stars already glittered overhead. Even the gentle flurries caught in the beams of my headlights were graceful and enchanting.

I'd solved a mystery today—not the big one I'd been working on, but I had discovered Tiffany was Courtney. And I hadn't needed the help of tech support to do it.

I turned toward downtown, thinking about the champagne I'd promised Evan. At this time tomorrow night, we'd be eating dinner as husband and wife. Feeding one another cake and dancing our first dance as a married couple.

I slid the pickup into an open spot outside Wine Around. The streets were as packed as usual, the sidewalks heavy with foot traffic.

I hopped out, thankful for amazing parking, and headed for the shop.

The door opened easily under my command, and a burst of warm, apple-cinnamon-scented air rushed over me as I stepped inside.

Samantha looked up from her place behind the counter. She'd twisted her hair into an elegant bun and stabbed two silver stakes through it in a crisscross. Her cheeks were rosy, her lipstick crimson, and her dark lashes were dramatically long. She'd chosen a red velvet wrap dress that accentuated her lean figure, and paired it with knee-high black leather boots.

I whistled, and she shot me a catlike grin. "Big plans after work?"

"Maybe," she hedged.

"Do tell," I encouraged, taking a quick look around the place for listening ears.

No one took notice.

"Hot date," she said, looking a little proud of herself. "How can I help you? You've already come for your mom's gift, so you must be back for wine. I knew the day would come that you'd give in to these temptations. I just didn't think it would be so soon."

I smiled as I made my way to the counter. "I would love a bottle of your best medium-priced, low-alcohol-content champagne. The ballerinas are leaving today, and I want something I can share with Evan without getting goofy the night before our wedding. Can you help?"

She snorted and gave me a bored, heavy-lidded look, then pulled a bottle of sparking grape juice from a display on the countertop. "I'm selling this through the new year. Adults are always looking for something to serve children at their holiday functions. Get it while you can."

The bottle was pretty, deep royal blue with a silver label. My artist's mind was already imagining the jewelry I could make with the glass when it was empty. "Perfect."

Stalking Around the Christmas Tree

Samantha wrapped the juice in paper, then placed it in a handled bag. She didn't ring up the sale. "This one's on the house. I hope you and Evan enjoy your last night as single people."

"Thanks." I hustled around to her side of the counter and hugged her

She patted my back awkwardly. "Don't mention it, and please drive safely. It's starting to snow."

I headed back to the truck, eyes watching the sky. The temperature seemed to have dropped in the few minutes I'd been inside Wine Around, and the snowfall had significantly increased. I slid a little on the sidewalk when a gust of wind sent a full body shiver down my spine.

The sight of a long-stemmed red rose on my windshield hurried my steps. A small white envelope was tucked beneath its petals and my wiper. The rose worried me, bringing the small enamel pin into mind, but the neatly typed words on the pretty white stationery melted my heart.

Meet me at the covered bridge.
—Evan

Chapter
Twenty-Six

I reversed out of the parking spot and headed toward the covered bridge, where Evan had proposed to me last Christmas. My heart soared, and I wondered if this was the reason I'd sensed mischief in his voice over the phone. Was it also the reason Samantha was so dressed up and a little coy about her evening plans? Was Evan planning a second surprise? This time on the eve of our wedding?

Last year, it'd felt as if the entire town had shown up. The proposal had been a massive, coordinated event. Everyone seemed to have known ahead of time except me. Cookie was part of a choir who sang for us. Caroline and Mom made desserts. The bridge was covered in twinkle lights, and a small table had been set for two.

My heart softened and soared at the memories. The nervous look in Evan's eye as he'd gotten onto his knee, as if he wasn't certain I'd accept. The joy and surprise when I'd agreed.

I pressed the gas pedal underfoot with more purpose, imagining all the things that might be waiting for me this year. And Evan's bright smile when he saw me approach.

McDougal's lights came into view a few minutes later, and I slowed at the back of a line of slow-moving vehicles, out to admire the show. Mr. McDougal spent the better part of his days between

Stalking Around the Christmas Tree

Halloween and Thanksgiving setting up the display along the county route leading to the covered bridge. He rented the land to farmers from spring until fall, but after the harvest, he was back to work, hauling and erecting his famous mile or two of holiday light displays. He'd been at it all my life, but in the early years, there were far fewer things to see. Locals loved it so much they'd held fundraisers to support and raise money for his cause. Not only did the work take months of his time for a few minutes of viewers' enjoyment, but the electric bills must've been astronomical.

I adjusted my radio to the AM station associated with the lights and turned up the volume for optimal enjoyment. Outside my window, carefully organized strands of twinkle lights beat in time to a playlist coordinated by Mr. McDougal. Motorized reindeer with red noses grazed the snowy fields before looking to the sky. Piles of presents blinked brightly in the inky night. Lighted children on sleds cruised over the hills, and Santas on rooftops climbed into chimneys on repeat.

I followed the traffic as far as the covered bridge, then broke away and took the gravel lane to an empty parking lot where Evan had driven us last year. Ours had been the only visible vehicle then as well.

I checked my face in the visor mirror, thankful I'd taken the time to look nice for the ballet, then sent a text to Evan, letting him know I was there.

I climbed out and headed for our rendezvous destination, carrying the sweet rose and his note. The bridge was visible in the distance, fully outlined in twinkle lights, just as it had been a year ago. The moon and stars reflected enchantingly in the water below. Sheets of heavy plastic had been hung over the cutouts in the bridge's sides, likely retaining the heat from a set of outdoor space heaters like before.

My phone buzzed in my palm as I crunched over icy rocks along the path. Evan's number appeared on the screen, and I swiped to read the message.

Evan: *Where?*

I took a photo of the rose and note, then sent it to him in a new message bookended with hearts. I wasn't typically one for sending emoticons with my texts, so I hoped he would see the pure delight in these.

The bouncing dots appeared again, indicating he was typing.

Instead of receiving a message, the dots disappeared abruptly.

I checked the signal strength, wondering if service was weak in my current location, though I didn't recall that being true. I had all my bars, so I hurried through the blowing snow, looking for his message to appear.

My phone began to ring instead. Evan's number graced the screen, and I grinned.

"Hey," I said, reaching the end of the bridge and ducking through the plastic sheeting, eager for the warmth of the heaters.

"Holly," Evan said. "I don't know what's going on or who left you that note, but it wasn't me, and you need to get out of there. Turn your truck around and head back to town. Meet me at the sheriff's department."

I stared at the empty bridge. No heaters. No Evan. No waiting surprise.

Then I looked at the rose and message in my hand.

"I don't understand," I said, but that wasn't true. Evan had said all I needed to put the ugly truth together. The facts just hadn't registered yet.

Evan hadn't left me a romantic message. I'd be tricked into isolation by a killer.

I tucked the note and rose into the pocket of my thin wool dress coat. And I froze at the sound of plastic sheeting shifting nearby.

Stalking Around the Christmas Tree

"I know who killed Tiffany and left those threats," Evan said. "I've got what I need to make the arrest, and we're looking for her now, but she's already left the theater, and she isn't with the group at the inn."

A small blonde stepped away from the shadows, and my heart gave a quick, panicked jolt.

"Ava," I said, greeting her and answering my own unspoken question.

"That's right. How did you—" Evan cursed. "Is she there?"

"Yes." I swallowed, attempting to appear casual. "What brings you to the covered bridge? I thought you were heading out of town after the show?"

"I'm on my way," Evan said, "but it's going to take me a few minutes to cross town. I'll call for backup. Someone should be in your area. Do not go anywhere with her, and don't let her get her hands on you."

"That's the plan." I forced a smile. "I should go. I'm meeting Evan," I said, hoping to make Ava believe I wasn't on the phone with him. And maybe that I hadn't put together what was happening yet. I needed to buy local law enforcement time to arrive.

Ava moved slowly, silently, in my direction, one hand outstretched, fingers curling on repeat.

I frowned. "I'll talk to you later," I said pertly, then dropped the phone into my pocket without disconnecting.

She shook her head. "Hello, Holly."

I wrinkled my nose. "What are you doing here?" I croaked, traitorous voice trembling against my will.

"Don't play dumb," she said. "It's not very becoming. Now hand me the phone."

"I don't understand." I chuckled, as if I thought she was joking.

"Yes, you do," she said. "And I believe you were just on the line with the sheriff, which means I don't have much time. So, hand over the phone. Now."

I stepped back, scanning her empty palms for a weapon and wondering if I could take her in a fist fight. She was at least five inches shorter than me and thirty pounds lighter. Did size really matter? For once I wished I knew.

Ava matched her advancing steps to my retreating ones. "I've watched you put it all together. I'd hoped you'd miss something, or we'd be gone before you made sense of it, so I could move on in peace. But it's like George keeps saying: you just won't stop asking questions. You won't leave things alone. Then I saw your expression at the theater today. Heard you rush away to call your sheriff boyfriend, and I knew you'd figured it out."

"I don't know anything," I said. "I saw the enamel rose pin on Tiffany's sweater and remembered seeing it in a reflection on Courtney's blog. I called Evan to say Courtney was really just Tiffany advocating for herself under a pseudonym and false persona. She'd driven her own career to the top, not some mysterious, unknown superfan."

Ava frowned. "Really?"

I nodded.

"Well, that explains a lot." She scoffed. "Totally Tiffany too. She knew she wasn't the best dancer—not even close. And anyone who knew anything about ballet also knew that." She gave a humorless laugh. "She boosted herself to the top. How utterly ridiculous."

"Right?" I said, trying to laugh along.

Ava narrowed her eyes on me, and I zipped my lips. "I didn't want to kill her. I tried to make her sick so she'd have to step down, maybe see a specialist or something. But it didn't stop her. She was seeing George, so instead of kicking her off the stage until she got her stuff together, he coddled her, let her rest or take breaks. Whatever she needed. Anyone else would've been cut. So I gave her more. I needed her to be too sick to perform by Christmas Eve."

"Apple seeds in her shakes," I guessed.

She tapped a finger against her temple. "It's genius, because she lived on those shakes. It took a long time for me to get enough seeds to make an impact, but eventually she started complaining. I knew I was on the right track, so I added more. She thought I offered to make her shakes because I was her understudy and we were bonding. She was really too naive for this job."

"It sounds like a complete misunderstanding," I said. "You didn't mean to kill her. You aren't a murderer." My back hit the plastic sheeting on the opposite side of the bridge, and I bumbled out, onto the gravel road.

Gusts of icy, snow-filled air raked my skin and flung my hair. My eyes burned and cheeks stung. I cursed the ridiculous coat and its utter inability to handle the plummeting temperatures and devolving weather.

Ava pulled the hood of her thick parka up and tied the strings beneath her chin. "Of course I didn't want to kill her! I just wanted her to step down. I wanted to see a dancer who deserved the spotlight fill her role. The internet said it could take thousands of apple seeds to kill an adult! I did not feed her thousands. This isn't my fault. And I overheard you, your friend, and the sheriff at the inn, adding up what you knew."

I recalled the eavesdropper from the other day. The opening and closing of the front door, and the pile of snow on the mat, suggesting someone had just rushed out. The snoop had been Ava.

"I can't go to jail," she said flatly. "Do you know what will happen to me in prison?"

I had a good idea but didn't think sharing would help matters. What I needed to do was keep her talking. "You were the one who left the Mouse King mask on her float and rubber rats on my windshield?" I asked. "Those were decoys to misdirect local law enforcement?" I thought of the way she'd spoken of Ian and took another guess. "You wanted to frame Ian because the two of you had a falling out."

She sniffed, expression hard. "He'll tell a girl anything to get her to do what he wants."

I cringed. "I'm sorry."

"So am I," she said. "But live and learn, right? Believe me. I've learned."

Then something else came to mind. "You put a pile of rats in your own dressing room for the same reason." And it'd worked. The presumed threat had all but knocked her off my suspect list.

Ava puckered her brows. "I didn't know about the tunnel, but that worked out nicely for putting suspicions on George. It helped that everyone thought she might be seeing him, and he's been sneaking off to cry in peace all the time since her death."

"Really?" I asked, stunned. "That's where he's been going?"

My heart went out to George's, realizing how devastated I'd be in his shoes, and knowing he had to hold it together for the sake of the show and all the other dancers' careers and futures.

Ava nodded. "Everyone's talking about it. I figured the police would put all those things together by now and build a case against him if they didn't go for Ian."

"They might've if he'd had any kind of motive," I said. "But he loved her. He had no reason to want her hurt or out of the picture. Not like you."

Ava took a sudden step forward and whipped out a hand to catch my sleeve. "I'm sorry to do this to you, but I'm in a predicament now. Everyone's expecting me at the inn, and I can't exactly poison you, so you're going to fall in the water."

"What?" I squeaked, eyes darting to the icy stream over the hill to our right.

"Give me your keys."

I jerked my arm free. "No."

"Come on—hurry up!" She opened and closed her fingers in the universal sign for *gimme*.

When I didn't comply, she reached into her pocket and retrieved a taser. "Keys," she repeated.

Anger seeped through my fear, curling my fingers around the keys in my pocket. "The water's a dead end," I said, cringing inwardly at my word choice. "I know how to swim, and the stream's not very deep, so I won't have to bother."

Ava smiled. "You don't have to drown. You only have to get all wet and walk home from here. You'll die of hypothermia before you get anywhere near civilization. It'll look like an accident, given the temperature."

I glanced at the stream once more, then to the dark road leading to the bridge. Not a car or headlight in sight. "You've really given this some thought."

Her expression darkened. "Well, it's kind of a big deal. Isn't it? I've accidentally killed someone I mostly liked, then the sheriff's fiancé spends all week trying to figure me out. I can't let you talk, and I don't have time to spare concocting anything elaborate. We're leaving this ridiculous little town any minute now, and all I have to work with is snow."

I guffawed, struggling against the urge to defend my town. "Do you even know how to use that thing?" I asked, nodding to the weapon in her hand. "I've only seen them used on television."

"Sure," she said. "My dad gave it to me for protection."

"Ironic."

She shrugged. "Keys."

I steeled my resolve as I freed my hand from my pocket, inhaling deeply and preparing my body to comply. "Fine."

I slapped the keys into her open palm, and when her gaze dropped to our hands, I ran.

"Hey!" Ava gave chase and we slid over snow and ice. The world on this side of the covered bridge had been wholly untouched by road crews.

Wind sliced through my too-thin coat and dress, biting my skin and burning my throat with each gulped breath. My heels tugged away from my feet with each plunge into knee-deep snow.

Images of the taser stopping me in place raced through my mind. I imagined Ava catching me while I was weak and rolling me into the water, then leaving me to walk home, as promised, in the gusting winds.

Something hard hit my back and my knees bent, pitching me forward on a scream. Pain radiated up my spine, and my legs tingled. From the cold or the hit, I wasn't sure.

Ava grunted behind me, and something pegged my shoulder, then hit the ground at my side. Rocks. Big ones.

I heaved myself upright, daring a look behind me.

Ava raised her taser from only a few feet away. She jerked her head toward the stream. "Get in the water."

I considered my options. The road was still dark. No rescue team on the way. My limbs were on fire from the cold. The wind whipped my hair into my eyes and attempted to freeze them solid. I wouldn't last long out here like this, even if I wasn't wet. But my back ached, and my chest burned. She was in better shape than me, could likely run faster and farther, even if I wasn't slightly injured.

Her footfalls slowed, then halted an arm's length away.

A shadow loomed beside me, cast in the light of the moon and twinkle lights. I recognized the shape of Ava's outstretched hand with the taser.

Then distant sounds of sirens rent the night, and Ava's soft gasp rose on the wind.

I pushed off like a track star, sprinting forward and losing my shoes.

The sound of a taser registered seconds before electricity coursed through my limbs seizing them and sending me into the snow with an *oof*.

Ava threw herself at me as I rolled onto my back in the snow.

I raised weakened arms to shove her away, but she was strong, and I couldn't gather my wits. Thankfully, adrenaline and a very strong sense of fight or flight—or both—worked my limbs and torso as I bucked against the tiny attacker.

Her thighs gripped my hips, and her hands came into view, holding a rock.

My own hands rose on instinct to catch her wrists. Our fingers were red as we battled in the moonlight, my hair and neck wet from the snow. The striking pain of cold on my legs and feet had become an uncomfortable numbness, and I realized Ava didn't have to plunge me into the water to kill me. In this condition, at these temperatures, I was as good as dead if I stayed out here much longer.

I thought of my wedding, of my parents' broken hearts, of a town in mourning if I gave up. And I thrust myself sideways, chucking Ava off in a burst of determination. The rock she'd been holding fell and crunched the space between my eyes. Pain blinded me a moment before something hot burned my skin.

Ava stumbled as she stood, rolling her ankle on the uneven ground. Her arms pinwheeled and eyes stretched as she tumbled backward over the bank toward the stream.

I wiped blood from my throbbing head, then shifted to work the metal Taser's prongs from my skin with numb fingertips. I staggered upright, eyes blurry and went to search for Ava on ghost limbs.

Flashing emergency lights appeared above headlights racing toward the bridge in the darkness. The sounds of tires on gravel came loud and fast, bringing tears of relief to my eyes and returning hope to my frozen heart.

"Holly!" My name was in the air, followed by the sound of slamming car doors. "Holly!"

"Here!" I said, far too quietly to be heard as I dragged myself in his direction.

On the bank near the water's edge, Ava rose with a moan, one knee bent, a foot lifted from the ground.

A spotlight found her, and the heartbroken expression on her face was nearly enough to make me feel remorse.

"My ankle," she said. "I think it's broken."

I supposed, that for her, the injury was far worse than going to jail. She'd done a rotten thing, trying to make Tiffany sick, then made it worse by attempting to cover her tracks when she'd accidentally killed her. Ava might not have started out as a killer, but she'd been more than willing to murder again today. Whatever other punishment she got, her dancing career would be over, and that was what she'd truly cared about. If her injured ankle didn't do it, then her irrefutably ruined reputation would.

My teeth chattered hard enough to break, but it was beyond my power to stop them. Fatigue racked me suddenly, and my knees gave out once more, folding me into a heap on the ground. Thankfully the snow no longer burned my skin. I let my eyes close as my vision darkened, and I laid back for a minute to catch my shallow breath.

Footfalls banged across the bridge, and Evan slid into place at my side. I smelled his cologne and heard the echoes of his voice in the night.

"I'm here," he said. "Deputy Mars has Ava, and I've got you." He stroked my cheek with hot fingers and hollered for a medic.

Stalking Around the Christmas Tree

"I know who killed Tiffany," I whispered.

Evan kissed my wet hair and gathered me into his arms, rising to his feet as if I weighed no more than a child. "Good work," he said, voice strangled as we began to move. "I need you to do something very important for me now, okay? Hey." He jostled me. "Holly, I need you to stay awake."

I tried to nod, but the unyielding pull of fatigue was too much.

Something warm hit my cheek a moment before the world went silent, and I had the strangest feeling it was a tear.

Chapter
Twenty-Seven

I woke in an ambulance, cocooned in warmth.

Evan's face swam into view, clearing immediately.

"Hey," I said, squirming slightly, wanting to sit up and get my arms around him.

A firm hand pressed me down. A woman in an EMT uniform smiled. "Be still until we get to the hospital. Then we'll see what the doctor has to say."

I frowned, then winced.

"Yep," she said. "You've sustained a head injury, and you're going to need a couple of stitches."

I looked to Evan, whose expression was grim. He appeared pained, and for a fleeting moment, I wondered if he was the one who needed help, and the woman had gotten confused.

Then images of Ava returned to mind. "Oh no."

Evan folded his fingers over my free hand. An IV line led from the other one to an elevated bag of fluid. "She's in custody and going to jail for all the awful things she's done."

"She wanted me to get in the water so I'd die of hypothermia," I said.

"You nearly did," the woman said, drawing my eyes to hers. "It's a nasty night to be out, and you're not dressed for it. You were lucky Sheriff Gray got to you when he did. Your body temperature was low enough to have caused serious permanent damage if it'd stayed that way any longer."

"I was at the ballet." My memories returned with a smack. "Ava had a taser." I turned back to Evan. "She jumped on me. She tried to hit me with a rock."

His brows rose and his eyes flicked to the wound on my head.

"Looks like she did that too," the EMT said. She stopped cleaning scrapes on my wrists and palms, then shined a light in my eyes.

I blinked. "Ow. Jeez." I released Evan and tried to swat her away, but my limbs were heavy and slow.

The woman looked to Evan. "They're going to need to run some tests on her to be sure she doesn't have a concussion."

He nodded, eyes red and jaw tight.

I recalled the sensation of a tear on my face and realized it had been his. "Hey," I said, reaching for his hand once more, "I'm okay."

He batted his eyes, then pressed his opposite hand against closed lids.

"Look," I said, tugging on him. "Hey."

He took a deep breath and dropped his hand to his lap, fixing his gaze to mine. "You don't look okay," he said, voice quiet and gravelly. "You were covered in snow, bleeding from your head, unconscious."

"I was just resting until you got there," I said, attempting a joke to lighten his burden.

His lips ticked at one corner, trying and failing to smile. "I thought I was too late."

"You were right on time. Now let's finish up this medical stuff and go home. I have sparkling grape juice and gold-dusted pretzel rings." I frowned, then winced at the ache in my forehead. "Actually the juice is in my truck."

"Your parents are on the way to bring it home," he said. "They have the spare keys for the fleet. I'll let them know about the juice."

I smiled and puckered my lips.

Evan kissed me gently, and I knew everything would be just fine.

* * *

We left the hospital several hours later. The roads were in terrible condition, but we seemed to be the only vehicle on them, so Evan took it slow, and we managed okay.

"I guess the meteorologist was right this time," I said, slightly loopy from the pain meds administered via IV. Thankfully, I didn't have a concussion, and all my fingers and toes survived the time spent in the storm. The EMT had brought my body temperature back to normal pretty quickly, and aside from a single stitch in my forehead, I would be in perfect shape for my wedding. The freezing temperatures had probably even helped prevent swelling.

Evan adjusted his white-knuckled grip on the wheel as we made the final turn toward home. "Let's just hope the road crews get this all cleared up by tomorrow afternoon."

Our wedding was scheduled for five, with dinner and reception to follow, so the sooner the roads were clear, the better.

My parents had reluctantly agreed to return to the farm after picking up my truck. The Grays had been halfway between Boston and Mistletoe when the storm kicked up, but they too had persevered. Now, they were with my folks, waiting for our safe arrival.

Stalking Around the Christmas Tree

The ballerinas had left for Augusta, as planned, except for Ava, who was being held at the Mistletoe jail.

I wondered which dancer was the understudy's understudy.

"You should stay in a guest room tonight," I told Evan. "You can't go home in this. It's not worth the risk."

He stole a glance in my direction. "I had no intention of leaving you alone. What if the doctors missed something at the hospital, and you got sick during the night?"

"Silly," I said, setting my hand on his shoulder. "I feel fine."

"Well, that's the drugs talking," he assured me. "You told the ER nurse this was the spring of our love while she was preparing your head for that stitch."

I laughed.

Evan piloted his cruiser up the Reindeer Games driveway and parked outside the inn. "Your dad has these roads in great shape. We should let everyone know we made it safely after we get inside."

"We can invite them over," I said. "We have shark cutey. Char shooty."

Evan chuckled. "We have charcuterie, and you have a head wound. My family is fine at your parents' home for the night. Cookie's there too, and I think Ray's with Libby."

He parked and climbed out, then circled the hood to open my door. "I think we need to get you into bed and see what happens tomorrow. If you're not up to a wedding, it can wait."

I frowned. "Are you saying you'd call it off?" My warm and fuzzy feelings burned away. If Evan would abandon our wedding over a single stitch in my forehead, what did that say about his desire to marry me? Had he been waiting for something to go wrong so he could run?

Cold wind whipped over him and into the car. I shivered.

"Of course not," he said. "I meant we can push the ceremony back if you need to sleep in tomorrow and recuperate. Unless you've changed your mind, I'm marrying you as soon as possible. I just don't want you to look back and remember how exhausted and sore you were from a fight with a homicidal ballerina. She shouldn't be any part of our day."

I hugged him, and he dragged me out of the cab.

Evan swung me into his arms and cradled me to his chest.

I nuzzled my nose against his neck, and somewhere in the distance, a woman screamed.

Evan tensed, and I raised my head, temporarily frozen in wind and flying snow. The distant sound of voices snapped him into action.

He put me back in the cruiser and closed the door, then jumped behind the wheel. "I think that came from Libby's place." He shifted into gear and tore over the road toward the guesthouse.

My phone rang as we rocked wildly across mounds of drifted snow. I dragged the device from my pocket with awkward fingers. Cookie's number appeared on the screen. "Hello?"

"We caught her!" Cookie yelped, voice echoing through the phone.

I slid my gaze to Evan, who seemed to have heard her.

"Who?" he asked, projecting his voice.

For the briefest of moments, I wondered if Cookie had wrongly captured someone she thought was Tiffany's killer.

"The Boston criminal's baby mama," Cookie said.

Evan took my phone, eyes fixed on the guesthouse, growing closer by the second. He pressed "Speaker" and raised the device closer to his mouth. "Say that again?"

"Hello, Sheriff," she said. "The Swingers and I were going to check on Ray and Libby because they weren't answering their phones, and we wanted them to play gin rummy at the house with your mom, your aunts and the Whites. And we saw someone sneaking around near the back window."

Evan slowed, then parked outside Libby's home.

A mass of silhouettes came into view around the side.

I climbed out on my own this time. The fuzzy feelings I'd leaned into before were long gone, replaced by a sobering reality. Libby's stalker had been at her home, unbeknownst to her and Ray. Anything could've happened. Probably something very bad.

Snow fell in sheets, creating a near whiteout around us as Evan met me at my door.

"Over here!" Cookie hollered. "Bring your handcuffs!"

We trudged in her direction until we reached the lot of them, shivering and wearing a variety of expressions. Ray, proud. Cookie, elated. The Swingers, collectively concerned. Libby wore the expression of a warrior who'd dispatched her enemy and held victory in her grasp. She also fastened the arms of a familiar blond woman behind her back. I recognized the woman from social media as Gina Dupree. Libby's stalker. Gina had blood smeared over her face and fire in her eyes until she noticed Evan. His sheriff's uniform had that effect on criminals.

"We saw her trying to get in through the window," Cookie said. "So we attacked."

"Attacked how?" Evan asked, sliding the handcuffs from his utility belt and scanning Gina from head to toe.

"Snowballs," Cookie said. "Marianne has a great arm, and we had the element of surprise. Libby and Ray heard the commotion and came outside. Then Libby popped her in the nose, and she fell down." She motioned to a spray of blood on the snow and an imprint of a human with arms splayed.

A bark of laughter burst from my lips, and Evan gave me a small shake of his head.

I pressed my lips into a line and mimed turning a lock.

Gina struggled to break from Libby's hold. "I hate you!" she screamed, and for the first time, I noticed the tears streaming over her cheeks and into the smears of blood. "You took him away from us! You should've minded your own business. You should've stayed out of it!"

Libby tightened her hold as Evan closed the distance to their sides. "Kellen Lance is a bad man," she said, voice calm but firm. "He does terrible things, and he hurts people. I think he's hurt you."

Gina stilled, eyes darting to the group of watching faces. "He loves me. I found out I was pregnant during the trial, and he said he'd be there for me, but you testified against him. Now he's stuck in that jail, and I'm out here alone!"

Libby released her, a look of deep sadness on her brow. "What he does isn't love."

Evan raised his cuffs in one hand and motioned for Gina to bring her wrists forward.

She obeyed, apparently still stunned by Libby's words. "Kellen has a temper, but he only uses it when things go wrong."

"Is that why you're doing this?" I asked, drawing her eyes to mine. "Trying to gain his favor? Make sure he knows you're dedicated? So you don't get blamed for his jail time somehow?"

Gina's gaze dropped. "I was miserable after Antonia was born, exhausted and alone. I started thinking of how this was all her fault." She shot a pointed look in Libby's direction. "I found your town's name in a news article, and I sent a card. When I wished I could be with Kellan on his birthday, or when I was missing him so much it hurt, I sent another card." She sniffled and huffed. "The cards didn't come back. So I knew they'd made it to you, or to someone who'd accepted them. Then I got a sitter and drove down here. I couldn't believe you lived in this fairytale Christmas town, moving happily forward after crushing my world. It made everything worse. So I kept coming back. Wanting to find you so you would know what you've done. All the pain you've caused. All the memories you've stolen from me. The father you stole from my little girl."

* * *

Evan fastened the cuffs, searching Gina's broken expression with caring eyes. "I don't know you or him," he said gently. "But love shelters and protects. It doesn't punish or ask for revenge. What you've been doing here in Mistletoe—following Libby, leaving notes, and trying to break into her home—is illegal. It will be up to Libby if she presses charges, but I know someone in Boston who can help you get clean, and I can put you in contact with people who will relocate you and Antonia somewhere safe, if you want. But the rest will be up to you."

Her eyes widened and snapped to Evan at the sound of her daughter's name.

"You've got some tough decisions to make," he said, "but I know you can make them."

With that, they moved toward his cruiser.

"I'll be back after I get her to the sheriff's department," Evan called.

Ray lifted a hand. "I'll get everyone else inside."

We watched in silence as Evan opened the back door for Gina and waited for her to take a seat. He passed her a handkerchief, and she accepted with a nod.

"I won't press charges," Libby told us. "I hope she takes the olive branch he's offering."

"What he's offering sounds more like a life raft," Ray said, pressing a kiss to Libby's temple. "I think she's lucky tonight turned out the way it did."

Cookie and the Swingers closed in on us, forming a circle against the driving snow and beating wind.

"Thank you all for saving me," Libby said. "I don't know what she planned to do once she got inside, but it probably wasn't good."

"No problem," Cookie said. "That's what friends are for. And I haven't had a snowball fight in decades!"

"Wasn't much of a fight," Marianne said.

Cookie grinned at her friend. "Not with the dance league's star softball pitcher on my team."

I wrapped my arms around myself as we moved toward Libby's front door and Ray's truck. "I hear Libby has a mean right hook."

Libby frowned. "I'm feeling guilty for that now, but I wasn't sure if she was dangerous. I employed the tactics my big brother taught me before I started dating in high school. Disarm the threat. Act first. Apologize later if needed."

"She only hit her once," Cookie said. "She went tail over tea-kettles. You wouldn't think one nose could make that big of a mess."

"I patted Gina down," Libby said. "She wasn't carrying any weapons."

I turned to the group, feeling the pull of fatigue on my limbs. "You were all great tonight. I think the reporters have it all wrong. The real news story isn't that Mistletoe has a murder every Christmas. It's that this town does not welcome crime. And we always get our man. Or woman."

Libby looped an arm around my shoulders. "Speaking of crimes, I believe you have a story we're all waiting to hear too."

"I do," I said. "Why don't I tell you about it over shark cutie."

She frowned, and Ray laughed.

Cookie clapped her gloved hands. "I love shark cutie. The Swingers and I will help set it up, and I'll give your families a call at the farmhouse. They can meet us at the inn."

Stalking Around the Christmas Tree

Libby moved to her porch and unlocked the door. "Wait inside, where it's warm, until Ray comes back for you."

"Let's go before we're buried alive out here," Ray said, unlocking the passenger door of his pickup.

Libby and I climbed aboard, and I rested my head on her shoulder. "You caught a bad guy. I think this makes you an official Mistletoean. Now you have to stay here forever."

I sensed a beat of charged silence as she looked across the cab to our driver. "I think I might."

Chapter
Twenty-Eight

I woke to the sounds of soft voices in the kitchen and dust motes illuminated like silver confetti in the sunlight overhead. A wide smile split my face, and I jolted upright, regretting it immediately. My head ached, and I touched the bandage gently. With a little makeup and know-how, I was sure Mom's friends could cover the bruising and single stitch. And if they couldn't, I didn't care. The photographer could edit it out or leave it, as long as I got to marry Evan today.

The door to my room opened as I swung my feet off the bed. Mom stepped inside with a tray. "Oh." She paused. "You're up." She was dressed in jeans and a heavy sweater, her hair pulled back in a low ponytail. The lack of joy in her tone sent a sharp pang of worry through my core.

"What's wrong?" I asked, suddenly recalling the storm that had come through the night before. "Is someone hurt? Was there a car accident?" My mind raced through all the most common problems that occurred when the weather got rough. Then I remembered Evan leaving with Gina in his cruiser. "Evan."

"He's okay," she said. "He came back last night, but you'd already gone to sleep."

Stalking Around the Christmas Tree

A vague memory of him whispering goodnight surfaced in my mind like a dream. And my heart relaxed by a small measure. All in all, it'd been a good night. Ava and Gina were in custody for their crimes, and I'd fallen asleep to the sounds of our families' laughter in the next room. Evan's mother's voice weaved into conversations with my parents. His cousins' and aunts' voices mixed with Libby's, Cookie's, and the Swingers'.

My long and blissful sleep was partially a result of whatever the hospital had put in my IV bag, but the fact everyone I loved was finally safe, and many of them were right here with me, had been the real reason behind my incredible peace.

Mom set the tray on the nightstand and offered me a couple of over-the-counter pain meds, then poured a cup of tea.

"Something's bothering you," I said, tossing the pills into my mouth and swallowing them with a sip of tea. The clock on my nightstand caught my eye, and I nearly choked. "It's ten o'clock."

Mom nodded.

"I set my alarm for six."

"I shut it off," she said.

I blinked at her, torn between sheer confusion and anger. "Why would you do that? I have a hair appointment in an hour. I still have to eat and get ready, then drive into town, and the roads are probably a mess. I should've left by now."

Mom and I also had a late lunch planned after the salon. The photographer was meeting Caroline here while we were out. She said he needed to set up for the pre-wedding shots. The entire day was planned to the minute. And I'd already lost four hours.

My stomach clenched, and my heart launched into a sprint. I'd spent weeks worrying I'd ruin the wedding by tripping on my heels or damaging my dress, but missing half the day's events, then arriving at the ceremony with my hair in a messy bun suddenly seemed just as bad.

Mom watched me with sad eyes. "You didn't miss the appointment. Theresa from the salon called to cancel your appointment. She couldn't open this morning because the roads haven't been cleared."

I frowned, processing the information. "Oh. That's too bad." I glanced toward the window. Uncleared roads would ruin the rest of our afternoon plans. Thankfully, the ceremony wasn't until five. I pushed my feet into waiting slippers and moved around my bed to the window. "I guess doing my own hair for the wedding isn't the worst thing that could happen."

"No," Mom agreed, accompanying me to the sill.

We each pulled a curtain back, and I raised my brows.

"Holy holiday snowstorm," I gasped.

I had to stand on my tiptoes to peer over the snow piled against the pane. The sun was bright and warm, but the world was a blanket of white for as far as I could see.

"The nor'easter hit us pretty hard," Mom said. "We got nearly four feet of snow on top of the three or so that was already there. Your dad's been out for hours, just trying to get to the horses."

I scanned the scene until I found the mini bulldozer in the distance, still a ways from the barns. None of the farm roads were clear. They weren't even visible. "But I heard voices," I said. "Who's here? And how?"

Mom pushed a pile of sleep-tangled hair behind my ear, eyes soft. "Honey, no one left."

I glanced to the door. "No one?"

"No. We played cards and talked until after midnight. When we tried to leave, we couldn't. Your dad and I made up all the empty guest rooms and the couch. We all just stayed here. Evan's family. Libby and Ray. Cookie and her dance friends."

"Evan?" I asked again, turning my eyes back to the endless snow.

"He barely made it back from taking Gina to the sheriff's department last night. It took him more than an hour to make the ten-minute trip. He checked on you, then visited with his family before sleeping on the couch. He and your dad rose with the sun today and started trying to clear paths," she said, a faint note of hope in her tone. "He's determined to marry you today."

I laughed, my heart instantly refilled with joy. "At least we have all day. A lot can happen in seven hours. Especially in Mistletoe."

"True." She returned to the nightstand and poured a second cup of tea. "So, I'm going to see that you rest, eat, and are pampered to the extreme. Thanks to fate, I have a whole host of women on hand to help."

The door cracked open, and Cookie's head poked into view. "Can we come in?"

Mom motioned her inside, and a line of others trailed behind. Evan's mom, aunts, and cousins. Libby, Cookie, and the Swingers. All wore bright, cheerful smiles.

Libby took a seat at my side. "Caroline called to say she's got this covered."

I laughed, because of course she did.

"She's calling Christopher!" Cookie beamed. "The two of them can accomplish anything."

"Caroline thinks he's Santa," Libby explained to her family, who promptly frowned, drawing another laugh from me.

I loved my ever-hopeful friends and our little town filled with holiday magic.

"I'm glad you're here," I said, to the smiling group before me. "All of you."

And the women moved in closer for a massive group hug.

*   *   *

Eight hours later, I'd had the day I didn't know I needed. I'd been surrounded by love and laughter, along with plenty of good food, great friends, and warm drinks. Dad had stopped by several times to provide updates from the outside world. Sadly, the weight of ice and snow on power lines had caused a blackout for most of the town, which meant plenty of people were without heat or running water. Dad had done what he could to let others know we had plenty of whatever anyone needed, but we were waiting to hear back.

I hadn't seen Evan, both because it was bad luck for the bride to see the groom before the wedding and because he hadn't returned from his mission to retrieve our pastor. But I hadn't given up the hope of exchanging our vows. I knew he'd move heaven and earth to marry me today, and I had faith anything was possible.

So, when the time came, and I'd been zipped into my family's heirloom wedding gown, with hair, makeup, and nails done by the women I loved instead of at a salon, I considered it a perfect gift.

"Ready?" Mom asked, ushering me into the foyer, where the others had bundled into warm coats over their coordinating emerald green, gold, and scarlet gowns.

I nodded, and Libby opened the door.

I marveled at the beautiful sunset over the world beyond.

Dad waved from the side of a horse-drawn sleigh, suit pants visible beneath his coat. He'd made incredible progress on the farm roads. He'd even shoveled the inn's porch and steps. Not everyone on our guest list would make it today, but everyone I needed was already here.

I sent up a prayer that Evan had made it back with the minister and that Caroline had spoken to Christopher, because today I wanted to believe in Santa Claus too.

I stilled as the line of horses and sleighs behind my dad came into view. His farmhands sat at the reins.

Stalking Around the Christmas Tree

The others in my party hurried to meet the horses while I stood, in awe, on the porch.

"Come on," Mom said, walking me to the waiting sleigh. "It's cold out here."

My eyes stung with tears and wonder as I began to notice all the details I'd missed before.

Twinkle lights and pine greenery wrapped the fence from the inn to the big barn.

Hundreds of glass canning jars were arranged in the snow. Each with a spring of evergreen, a pine cone, and a single white taper candle to light our way to the ceremony.

I climbed aboard the sleigh with Mom and held her hands as Dad took his seat and gathered the reigns.

Before I could tell her how perfect everything looked, the horse began to move, and the beauty of our world stole my breath. Ice crystals winked and glistened in every shade of orange and gold in the fast-fading sun. And the flickering candles beckoned us onward.

When the barn came into view around the bend, so did dozens of familiar faces outside the massive doors. Each person held a jar and candle. Behind them a makeshift parking lot of snowmobiles and four-by-fours lined the barn. Snowshoes and skis were leaned and stacked against the exterior wall.

I blinked through tears, stunned and mildly confused, as I looked to Mom. "I thought no one could get here."

"The roads haven't been cleared," Mom said. "But you know this community. Always ready to party."

I laughed, warmed impossibly further by the faces of folks who'd been present at every major event in my life, from kindergarten graduation to seeing me off to college. Teachers and neighbors, old classmates and new friends.

Dad glanced over his shoulder as he coaxed the horse to a stop. "Folks started arriving hours ago, asking how they could help. They came on foot. They came by sleigh. They came. And they came. Then they made trips back and forth, delivering others."

The instrumental music I'd chosen for my wedding began to play inside the barn, and the massive doors parted by a fraction.

Evan stepped into view. He was dazzling in his black suit, dress coat, and gloves.

I laughed, beyond delighted to see him. "You made it!"

"Nothing would've stopped me," he said, approaching the sleigh and reaching for my hand. "Let's get married."

The other women piled out of the sleighs and met us on the patch of clear ground near the barn.

"You look beautiful," Evan said, lifting my gloved hands to his lips.

I blinked through a fresh round of tears. "I can't believe you're here. And all these guests. How is any of this happening?"

"Haven't you heard?" he asked, a small smile on his lips. "You are beloved. There wasn't any stopping these folks from being here. Caroline arranged transportation of every variety and sent out the word."

We moved toward the open doors, and Dad took my arm.

"I'll meet you down there," Evan said. Then he set me free.

I watched as he jogged to the end of the aisle and waited at the alter with Ray and one of the town's deputies.

Caroline stood with my bouquet in her hands, a small cat-that-ate-the-canary smile on her lips.

I caught her eye and mouthed the words *thank you*.

She responded with *Thank Christopher*, and a cascade of goose bumps trickled over my skin.

I glanced skyward and vowed to thank Christopher the next time I saw him for whatever part he'd played in today's perfection. And for the first time, I wondered if he was actually Santa. It would make sense, given the miraculous set of others in my world. Why not Santa Claus too?

My circle had grown so much in three short years. When I'd returned to Mistletoe, I'd only had a broken heart and my parents. But I'd found best friends in Caroline and Ray, true love with Evan, and a sister in Libby. All while making a place for myself in this town as an adult. And I knew, in that moment, it was the only place I ever wanted to be.

It was where I would raise my children with Evan. On this farm. Surrounded by love, laughter, and trees.

My stomach squeezed, and I stood a little straighter, pulling in a deep and steadying breath.

The inside of the cavernous barn was breathtaking. Draped in tulle and twinkle lights, with silver cutout stars hanging from exposed rafters. Lighted evergreen lined the perimeter and formed a makeshift wall between the ceremony and larger reception area beyond.

Guests filed inside, filling the rows of folding chairs tied with broad red bows.

The crowd remained on their feet as the first notes to "Bridal Chorus" began to play.

"That's our cue," Dad said, taking a step forward.

"Wait." I gripped his arm and stared at the empty podium. "Where's the minister?"

Dad's mischievous eyes twinkled. "We weren't able to reach him. Evan tried, but his whole neighborhood is snowed under."

"Then what are we doing?" I whispered.

"Evan found a work-around."

I looked to my fiancé as a cloud of white hair hustled past me.

"Coming!" a spry voice announced. Cookie beetled up the aisle and sloughed her overcoat to reveal a plain black dress and tights. She stepped up to the podium and grinned. "Ready!"

The song started over, and I moved on air to Evan's side, a painfully wide smile on my unprecedentedly joyful face.

Dad sniffed and cleared his throat as he kissed my cheek and stepped away.

I tried not to cry when I saw the look of promise and trust that passed between him and my groom.

"Dearly beloved," Cookie announced in a terrible British accent, "I was recently ordained to marry my goat. Not to myself, but to another goat," she clarified. "And after checking online this morning, I learned I can marry people as well."

The crowd laughed, but I was already lost in Evan's eyes.

"I love you," he whispered.

"I love you too."

Together, we exchanged our vows.

Sunset fell into twilight, then darkened to the inky velvet sky of Mistletoe at night, and we danced beneath twinkle-light-strewn rafters. Our massive, historic barn brimmed with wide wooden tables, their runners made of pine greenery, the place markers made of pine cones, and each lined with the smiling faces of our family, friends, and neighbors. Our first dance as husband and wife was everything I'd dreamed it would be.

Soon others joined in. My parents. Libby and Ray. Zane and Caroline. Until the floor was filled with couples, the barn overflowing with music and laughter.

When it was time to cut the cake, the barn fell silent in anticipation.

Zane helped Caroline roll the table into view, and gasps of delight rushed through the crowd.

Set on a wide slice of faux tree trunk, the three-tier work of art was iced in white, sprinkled in glittering sugar crystals and airbrushed with stenciled evergreens. A pair of little trees stood on top, one with a tiny Boston Red Sox ornament, the other a miniature framed Van Gogh.

Evan and I joined hands to cut the first slice and locked eyes as the distinct, but distant, sounds of sleigh bells echoed outside. "I guess there really is magic in the air," he whispered.

Indeed there was.

Acknowledgments

Thank you, lovely reader, for joining Holly on another Christmas adventure. Your dedication to this series makes every book possible, and I truly, sincerely appreciate you. I'd also like to thank my critique partners, family, agent, and friends for their unending support and encouragement as I chase my dream. And to the power house team at Crooked Lane Books, thank you so very much for bringing these pages to life.